The White Flower

GRACE LIVINGSTON HILL

The White Flower

Fleming H. Revell Company
Old Tappan, New Jersey

Library of Congress Cataloging in Publication Data

Hill, Grace Livingston, 1865-1947.
The white flower.

I. Title.
PS3515.I486W46   1985   813'.52   84-16010
ISBN 0-8007-1238-2

Introduction

Once long ago, when an aspiring writer asked my mother how she went about planning a story, she answered, "Oh, I don't plan. I just start with a few people in a difficult situation and let them work it out."

Of course, that might not be practical for every writer, but it was for her. As a little girl she had always loved to "make up stories," and judging by this one, sometimes she outdid herself! But one thing always overruled any temptation to let the plot run away with her: She never eased her standards of true love, unself-centered and pure. And she never forgot her goal of presenting the Lord Jesus Christ as the one sure answer to any problem of the human heart.

Her love of beauty and familiarity with the classics and art are obvious, and her constant references to well-known characters in literature show the influence they had on her own character. But never did she desire to lower the stature of the Lord Jesus Christ by considering other literature on a level with His Book!

RUTH LIVINGSTON HILL

The White Flower

Chapter I

The girl had red hair, the old-fashioned, deep-toned kind with glints of gold in it that can never quite be imitated. Chan Prescott noticed that at once as he entered the train.

She wore it, too, in an old-fashioned way that suited her delicate features perfectly. It was coiled low, showing richly below the plain little brown hat that was conventional enough, yet, somehow, was oddly out of harmony with the world of the present day. Or perhaps it was her face beneath it, the young man thought, as he tried in passing to get a fuller glimpse beyond that pale, clear oval of cheek and line of exquisite brow. But his suitcase came into sudden collision with the big sole leather bag of a passenger coming down the aisle in the opposite direction, and he was obliged to give momentary attention to his progress past this obstacle.

She had glanced up for an instant as the two men swayed in the aisle with the lurch of the starting train, and he caught a glimpse of wine-brown eyes with topaz lights that went with the hair, eyes full of perplexity—trouble perhaps—sad, wistful eyes, with depths to them. Where had he seen them before? There was something familiar about the girl, yet she was utterly different, almost startlingly different from anyone he knew.

He had to pass on of course. One cannot pause on the way to one's seat in a railroad train and analyze the face of a fellow traveler just because she happens to be beautiful and unusual.

There was no seat left in the car save the place beside the girl. Chan Prescott would have liked to have taken that but there was something about the girl that forbade it, he could not quite tell why. She seemed to be a girl who had a right to the privacy of her seat without intrusion from strange young men. Now if she had used a lipstick, and worn bobbed hair and one of those saucy, slick, caplike hats it would have been different. Somehow this girl seemed to be surrounded by a seriousness in which he, Chan Prescott, did not belong.

He found a seat eventually in the parlor car which had been his original destination when he boarded the train, and he settled down half dissatisfied and looked around with a bored air for some human interest wherewith to while away his idle thoughts.

There were magazines in his suitcase, and a new book that was the talk of the world, but he did not feel like reading. Something in the profile of that girl he had passed in the common car held his thoughts. What was there about her that had been like a delicate fragrance as he passed—something forgotten long ago? As one remembers the crab apple blossoms one climbed a tree ages ago to get for a girl with pigtails and a pinafore, who waited beneath with bated breath.

There was nothing in Chan Prescott's life like that, but where had he seen that girl? *Had* he ever seen her? If he had, why should the sight of her delicate profile beneath that somber little hat, the burnish of her copper hair, the sadness in her wine-brown eyes cling and haunt him here in a world that all too evidently was not hers, and did belong to him?

Eventually he got out the new book and plunged into its mysteries, bringing a sated taste and a critical, impatient mind to its reading. But the book had not been a best-seller without reason, and the plot presently began to take hold of his interest to the exclusion of all else. He was in a fair way to be lost to the world until it was finished, if it had not been for a conversation that by some strange freak of acoustics came straight into Chan Prescott's car.

It was most annoying. He swung his chair around trying to escape it, but only succeeded in making the voices more distinct:

"She's some little beaut!" the voice was saying meaningfully, "real titian red hair. You'd think she fell out of the frame of an old master, and a face to match! But she's green as they make 'em, and twice as trustful! You can lead her like a lamb. She thinks she's going out west to be the companion of a dear old lady on a salary of twenty bucks a week and her keep. She thinks the position dropped down out of the kind hand of Providence. She's even grateful that I was willing she should take the journey on the same train with me, for she is not used to traveling alone——"

The conversation dropped lower for a moment as the man next to Prescott asked a question in a rumbling voice. Then the other replied:

"What's that? Marriage? Oh, no. That wouldn't be necessary. You can make all the promises you want to of course. She hasn't a living relative in the world. Her father died not long ago, the last of her family. You see, it would be like this. I take you back and introduce you. I've received a telegram and have to get off at Chicago and take the train back. Urgent business, see? And I'm putting her in your charge. The rest is absolutely up to you. And you won't have any trouble. She's got a face like an angel. She'll never suspect anything. Wait till you see her. Man, she's a peach! Come on back and have a look. We can stand at the door and she'll never notice us."

Up to this point Prescott had noticed the conversation only to be annoyed at its interruption of his reading.

As the two men arose he glanced up idly at their faces. Something in the heavy, self-indulgent underlip of the elder man who had sat in the chair next him, the baggy pouches under the sensuous eyes, recalled certain words and phrases dropped into his disinterested ears, and brought a wave of disgust and distrust. But it passed with his relief that the interrupting voices were gone and he was almost back into his book again. When suddenly, some hidden mysterious radio within his being began to tell over the words they had spoken. "Red hair!" They had said red hair! Titian red! That was—that must be the little girl back there in the common car!

The girl with the topaz lights in her eyes; the glint of gold in the red of her hair! The delicate sensitive lips that were not painted! He could see her face again as in that instant's glance, as if some power were reproducing it. Again he felt that fleeting memory of a face he had known. Where had he seen that girl before? Who was she? Had he known her in some former incarnation? Was it a trick of the brain, a passing fancy? How had it taken such hold upon him? And those hounds! Had they formed some evil intention against a girl like that?

He started upright in his car and looked wildly toward the end of the car where the two men had disappeared. He half rose with a hesitating thought of following them, and then reconsidered. What could he do? What was it all about, anyway? Was he developing a case of nerves to be upset by the casual remarks of his fellow travelers and a pretty, unknown face?

He sat back and tried to think, to collect his scattered senses and bring back his habitual calm indifference to those about him, but the words of the two men, their cold proposals, would keep surging through his mind. Suppose it were true, what was the obvious deduction of the conversation to which he had been listening? Suppose they were setting a trap for that beautiful girl back there in the common car—or for some other girl if not that one—some girl who was not beautiful—did not common decency demand that he do something about it, something to help the girl?

Of course there were girls and girls. There were a lot of bold flappers running around these days who could take care of themselves if they wanted to be cared for. Most of them did not. He would not lift his hand for one of those. They deserved what they got. It was what they seemed to want. But this girl with the glorious hair and the sad brown eyes was different. There was something about her that was clean and good and made him think of his mother—as much as he could remember of his mother. She had died when he was seven. His impression of her had been like a faint sweet breath of lavender flowers as it is wafted from fresh linen, clean and white. Her eyes had been deep and true and beautiful. If there were any more clean eyes like that in the world he would like to help keep them so. Not that he felt that he was mightily worthy to champion the cause of righteousness in any form, simply that it appealed to the finest and truest things of his soul. Besides, had he not known or at least seen that girl before?

The two men were returning now, swaying through the aisle with every lurch of the train, the younger, more cunning-faced of the two, with quick alert movements, the elder man with flabby lumbering gait, as if his muscles were too inert to respond to the necessity. Chan watched him from under his hat brim, a heavy sensuous mouth, eyes that lost no detail about the women in the chairs he passed, a massive diamond in his shirt front, a cluster of them on his fat, white finger. A man who had lived for himself all his life, and who would as soon sacrifice a young sweet life to his pleasure as a crocodile would champ down the tiny living sacrifice of the deluded mother of the Nile, and with no more compunction. Chan's fingers suddenly gripped the velvet arms of his chair, itching to fling out and grip that flabby throat above its blazing diamonds and throttle the creature. Such men were beasts!

But he held himself rigidly with outward calm, alert to catch every word that might be spoken.

"Well? What do you think of her? Isn't she a humdinger? Isn't she a little gem of the first water?"

"She's a little stunner, all righty!" said the older, heavier voice, with a touch of the wily bargainer in the reserved inflection. "Of course, you can't be sure just how she'll take to the right kind of rags. Some of those innocent baby-eyed ones don't have a particle of style to them when you get them dressed. Have to be in their native environment to shine, you know, and that sort of thing."

"S'all right! I know two men out in California will either of 'em give me a thousand more than I've offered the chance to you for. The only reason I made you the offer was you seemed interested, and besides I wouldn't mind saving the rest of the trip for I've got a business deal on at home that needs me. But she's the type they want. In fact they wired me a couple of days back to hunt up someone for 'em. No, I couldn't think of taking a cent less. And really I ought to run out to Frisco anyway. There are several matters out there needing my attention. I can get most anything I like in the way of a commission out in Hollywood if I just show my little Rachel's wide eyes to some of my friends out there. They would jump at the chance."

There was a rustle of paper and Chan could see by the tail of his eye that the older man had got out his checkbook and was rumpling over the leaves. He had a fountain pen in his hand.

"By the way, what's her name?" he asked. "I'll need to know if I'm to be left in charge."

Chan listened intently.

"Rachel Rainsford." The other man cast a furtive glance about and lowered his voice as if he feared to be overheard.

"Rachel Rainsford? Not related to that shady character I've heard of, is she?" the older man said, puffing his lower lip out speculatively.

"Oh, not at all! Her father was a plain American schoolteacher, respectable and all that. By the way, I've been thinking. You'll probably be able to put the thing through with less trouble if you go through a ceremony. Of course it needn't be legal if you don't want to get yourself tied. But she's been brought up to feel that's the right thing, and she might make a stir if she thought there was anything else. . . ."

The voices trailed off into the din of a passing express and Chan sat with his heart pounding hard at his chest.

Rainsford! Professor Rainsford! And Rachel was the little girl with the halo of bronze-copper hair that used to stand waiting for her father at the corner nights when he went home!

The girls one met nowadays did not give an impression of kindly scholarly fathers in the background. They seemed to be more as if they had sprung up themselves to some little jazzy tune, a kind of product of the times. But—a daughter of Professor Rainsford in a strait like this! It was incredible!

The voices grew audible again with the passing of the express and he listened painfully lest some minute detail of the fiendish scheme should escape his ear, his fingers fairly twitching in their impatience for action while he tried to hold his book before his unseeing eyes and keep an outward calm.

But presently the two seemed to have completed their conversation and betook themselves in a friendly companionship to the smoking compartment.

Chan seized his fountain pen at once and began to write in his memorandum book. He tore out the written leaves, folded them carefully, and wrote a name on the outside. Then he rose with a studied air of casualness and sauntered down the aisle to the end of the car.

Rachel Rainsford was sitting quietly by her window in the common car staring out at a landscape that could not interest her. Her thoughts were perplexed and sad. She was struggling with a sense of uneasiness. Somehow she could not shake off a feeling that perhaps she had been too hasty in acceping this first position which had offered itself to her in her time of need. It seemed so final to be going so far away from the people she knew, in answer to an advertisement! Perhaps it had been mistaken independence to draw away from all their kindly hands and want to make her own way without their pity and help. Still, she knew she had been right in that. There was not one of her father's friends and colleagues who could really afford to take her in until she found some lucrative position. And there had been more than one who had offered. They all loved him and were ready to go as far as sacrifice to stand by her father's daughter.

But it seemed so wonderful that the very day after the funeral she had found this advertisement about the dear old lady who needed a companion and was willing to pay a good salary and her expenses to get someone. Twenty dollars a week seemed a fortune to her now, with her slender purse, and bank account that was wiped entirely out when her father's funeral expenses were paid! Why was it that she was so filled with misgivings now that she was actually on her way? It was against all good sense, and most decidedly against her principles that she should be so downhearted, with fortune thus smiling upon her. A dear old lady they said she was, not at all exacting. Not really an invalid, only not very strong, but lonely. Well, it was fitting that she who was so sad herself in the loss of her dear father should devote her life to trying to bring sunshine into another's life. Only so could she hope to get any joy herself now, since the tragedy that had entered her life so suddenly.

It had seemed good, too, when she first started, that she did not have to take this journey alone, she who had never gone about much without either her father or mother. Such a desolate journey into the unknown it seemed to her. But now, after eight hours' experience with the man who had hired her and promised to look after her to her journey's end, she began to have a great longing to be alone. She was glad that he had found a friend in the car ahead, and had left her for a little while. She was tired of his perpetual kindness, for that was what she supposed he meant it to be. She somehow could not like him. She hated the oily smoothness of his voice, and the way he looked at her with his fishy eyes. She shrank from his close contact as he leaned over her to point out something of interest in the landscape they were passing. She wished she had declined his offer when he had told her he was taking a trip across the continent and would be glad to see that she reached her destination safely and look after her baggage for her. His company had ceased to seem the gracious providence that it had been at the start. He was old enough to be her father, but he was not in the least like her father. There was even growing to be a quality of fear about her feeling for him. She dreaded the approach of evening. She wished inexpressibly that she might disappear, now while he was gone, and find her way back home—only there was no home anymore to go to. She wished she might never see this man again. She was even ready to give up the good salary he had promised her. Surely there would be something nearer to the only friends she had left!

But of course that was foolish! She had no money to pay her way back, at least not enough, even if there were any honorable way to break her contract, now that the man had taken all the trouble for her, and telegraphed the woman who was going to employ her. She must just put down her feelings and be a woman. This was something she must go through with bravely.

She felt the tears coming suddenly to her eyes, and shut her lips firmly. She must not be weak and silly. This world was a college to which she had come to be tested. So she had been taught. She must not fail at the outset when the first hard thing appeared.

Then something touched her hand lightly, and turning quickly she saw that a young man was standing in the aisle lifting his hat, and that something lay in her hand—a bit of folded paper. The young man had just picked it up from the floor, apparently, and handed it to her, passing on immediately to the back of the car. Her first thought was that it must be her ticket or possibly something from her handbag she had dropped when the conductor came for her ticket.

But when she looked the paper bore her name, and in handwriting which she did not know.

Puzzled she unfolded it and began to read:

Don't look startled! Sit quietly and read this. I used to go to high school under your father, so you needn't be afraid. I'm Chan Prescott. Perhaps you've heard him speak of me. Has that tall, thin man with glasses, that seems to be with you, any right over you? Because I've been hearing him

talk to a man in the parlor car and I'm sure he's framing up
something against you. He's going to beat it at Chicago and
leave you in the hands of an old crook with money who has
taken a fancy to you and will maybe pretend he wants to
marry you. But don't you believe him. He's a rotten liar.
I've been hearing him talk and he means you no good!
Sorry I had to frighten you, but you need protection.
They've told the conductor that you are mildly insane and
they are taking you to an asylum. I heard them. Now don't
get worried and try to turn your head around to see me.
We've got to keep cool and not let people see us or they will
get onto it. If you've got any friends on this train you can
trust go tell them this. If you haven't and would like me to
help you, take your hat off and lay it on the seat beside you.
I'll be where I can see you and I'll know you understand.
I'll find some way to take care of you, so don't be afraid.
But when I come back down the aisle don't look at me. Just
keep your hat on the seat beside you till I go by. If that is
your suitcase in the rack over your head just pull down
your window curtain a few inches. I'll be back again and
tell you what to do next. We ought to get off this train if I
can manage it. If you want to say anything, write a note
and drop it on the floor just inside your seat. Don't address
it. Don't get nervous. It's three hours yet to Chicago, and
your man has just gone to the smoker with his friend. I'll do
anything to help the daughter of my old prof.

C. P.

Rachel felt all the blood in her body gradually receding
from the surface, and gathering in a great choking flood
around her heart as she read this, and her thoughts were like
flocks of frightened birds quivering in one throbbing spot in
her brain. She did not know what to think or where to look,
or whether she could hold herself still and get calm. It
seemed to her that her body was shrinking and shriveling
down into the upholstery of the seat and that everybody
must be looking at her. But she sat quite still and read the
letter, steadily, over again, trying to know what to do and
whom to trust. Should she take her hat off or not?

Chapter II

Chan Prescott was standing on the rear platform of the car, a little to one side, where he would not be observed by anyone inside. He had an alert eye out for any chance brakeman or conductor who might meander that way, though he had assured himself of their presence in another part of the train before he started on his quest.

He was watching the little brown hat in the fifth seat from the back of the car with an interest and eagerness that amazed himself. Why did he care, he asked himself, whether that girl accepted his offer of help or not? If she wanted to be fool enough to trust herself to two sharpers, who were trading in human lives, it was nothing to him. It was years since he had been in high school and he had never known Professor Rainsford very well anyway. Why on earth did it suddenly seem so absolutely necessary for him to abandon any interests of his own and take care of that plain little brown mouse with the wistful eyes and the glorious hair? There was perhaps some other explanation of her situation and maybe he had read it all wrong from the lips of those foul-mouthed plotters in the parlor car. Or the girl might have resources of her own that made her independent. Or, it was barely possible of course that she was here of her own choice and was the kind of girl who could take care of herself. In these days most girls could. And she looked as if she had character. Still, there was something about this clear-eyed girl, a high-minded lack of sophistication that made him at once reject any such idea as that she was one of the modern brazen young women who are in for any sort of an experience, so long as it is an experience. He was perfectly certain she was a good girl, and a true girl, who loved right things and was not just wanting a good time in life without a thought of the

consequences. She seemed a girl who would scorn to do anything just for daring, as so many little ignorant flappers of
the day were doing.

Whatever it was that appealed to him in her, he realized
that he was all for her, and that if she would not accept his
help of her own accord then he was going to find some way
to force it upon her.

Of course it was quite possible that she might never have
even heard his name, or had forgotten it, and that she would
be as much afraid of him as of the other men.

So he waited with almost bated breath, anxiously watching the bent head, the curve of delicate chin, which was all
he could see of her face under the drooping brim of the plain
little hat.

Did he fancy it or had he really seen a quiver run through
the slender shoulders as she read his note? She was reading
it, at least, that was encouraging. She had not thrown it
aside without noticing what was in it, and she had not
turned her head to look after him. At least she showed self-
control. Perhaps she had more poise than he realized. Perhaps she was able not only to protect herself against the two
men who were her enemies, but could also protect herself
from him. For how did she know but that he was an enemy
also?

It seemed a long time that she sat there immovable, reading that letter. He felt sure that he could have read it over
three times long before this. He repeated over to himself
what he had written and with a sinking heart began to wonder what he should do next in case she did not mean to give
him any sign that he might go on with his plan to help her. It
really looked as if she were not going to pay any attention to
him!

And then he saw her hand go slowly up to her head and
quietly remove the little brown hat, laying it on the seat beside her, the other hand reaching up to pull down the window shade. He could not see her face for it was turned
toward the window as she worked with the shade to make it

lie straight in its groove. But after she had adjusted it, she took out her handkerchief from her handbag and pressed it to her lips as if she might be trying to still their trembling and hide her emotion.

He watched her for a moment and then went quickly on to the end car where he hoped to find a brakeman.

Rachel, as she waited through a long hour for developments, was passing in review various experiences of her little girlhood in her beloved home, where her exquisite invalid mother and her tender, scholarly father had been her constant companions through childhood. She recalled the stories her father used to tell of his school, his favorite pupils, which ones were scholars among them, which were talented, which the bad boys. Many an hour of pain had been whiled away for the dear little suffering mother by the father's droll caricatures and impersonations of happenings in school. And Chan Prescott had often figured in these recitals. Chan had been one of the bad boys, yet her father loved him. Clever, always clever, and brave, irresponsible sometimes, brilliant when he wanted to be, loyal to a fault, impudent to those he disliked, ready to visit vengeance where it was due, and often where it was not his right. Memory brought incidents. The time he disconnected the school bell so that it could not ring till Willy Watts, the lame boy who had a perfect record so far for being on time, could get inside the door in spite of his rival who had tied a string across the path and made him fall. The time he saved the janitor's little girl when the high school was on fire and nobody knew where the child was. He had dashed up to the third floor in spite of the firemen, who tried to stop him, and brought her down. The time he stood up against the high school principal and told him in no chaste language what he thought of him for letting the true criminal go scot-free and expelling Joe Blaisdell for putting the cow on the chapel platform, when it had really been Allister Allison, the son of the richest man in town, who had instigated it, and paid Joe Blaisdell to do it—and everybody knew it. The time her fa-

ther had told Chan that he had a good mind and could easily be an honor man if he would work, and had let him see
that he cared, and Chan had sat up all night and written his
essay for commencement which won the prize over everybody! The time—but there were so many times. She knew
her father had considered Chan undisciplined, but she knew
he felt that there was great depth of character and wealth of
possibility in him. She somehow knew that under the present circumstances her father would have trusted Chan Prescott.

And yet, she also knew—and the thought was not without
some weight in her quick decision—that this world held
many possibilities of evil. She knew that Chan might not be
the same boy that he had been in the days of his school life.
In fact her father might have been deceived in him even
then. Chan himself might have some evil intention toward
her! How could she be sure to trust even him? Had she been
wrong to take off her hat? Ought she not perhaps to have
trusted only in God to help her and ignore Chan's offer of
help? Yet what could she have done by herself? And might
not God have sent Chan? If it was true that that awful Mr.
Trevor, who was supposed to be protecting her, had actually
told the conductor she was insane there really was no one on
that whole train full of strangers to whom she could turn.
Even if she dared approach someone with her story, no
stranger would dare do anything against the word of the
conductor that she was insane! Everybody would be afraid
of her! And what better chance would she have in the Chicago station?

As these thoughts multiplied in detail, horror seemed to
freeze her veins, and she felt a choking sensation in her
throat. It began to seem as if the heat of the day and the
noise and smoke of the train were a great smothering blanket that was being let down about her and that presently she
would be beyond help.

She roused herself and tried to think. What could she do

but wait? At least she must be ready for whatever rescue the young man might be preparing.

She smoothed back her hair and put her hat on again, pulling it down closer over her head to hide her face as much as possible, tucking her gorgeous hair in out of sight and trying to make herself trig and neat for a disappearance, hoping it would come soon. She held her little handbag in a tense grip, and without knowing it held all her muscles tense, alert, awaiting a signal, wondering how he would manage it, wondering if he *could* manage it. How was a single young man to stop a train and get her off if those two other men wanted to keep her? Why did they want to trouble her? Then came back the words of an old friend of her mother's at home. "My dear, you are too beautiful to travel alone. I am glad you are to have someone to look after you." And Rachel had laughed and kissed her and thought the compliment a foolish fondness of one who had loved her mother, and thought nothing more of it. Now the words suddenly took on new meaning, vague menace of unnamed peril, till she caught her breath as if she had been running, and realized that she must be calmer if she would not rouse the suspicions of her fellow travelers.

But another half hour passed by and nothing happened and Rachel, consulting her old-fashioned watch that had been her mother's, and studying her timetable, realized with sinking of heart that they were drawing nearer and nearer to Chicago, and that there was no scheduled stop before they reached there. Ought she not to begin to try to do something else for herself? She could write a note at least, asking someone to send a telegram for her to Mr. Becker, the president of the home bank and the president of the board of trustees of her father's school. If she handed it with plenty of money to pay for it to someone in the car, now, quickly, before anything else had been done or the conductor had appeared, perhaps she could outwit them all.

In feverish haste she got out her pencil and paper and began to write:

"Am in great danger. Please have police meet me at Chicago station, and give me protection."

She began to study the faces of her fellow passengers eagerly. To which one should she entrust her telegram? They did send telegrams from trains en route, she was sure. She had heard her father tell about it. There was a nice old lady across the aisle that looked kind and wise. Would she dare ask her to send the telegram for her? But no, it must be a man. The conductor would think it strange if a woman came hunting him the length of the train. A man would know how to go about it. But which man should she approach? And wouldn't almost any man want to know more about it before he troubled the conductor to send such a telegram? And wouldn't he go and tell the conductor who had asked him to send it? Especially if he did not know the circumstances. And *the conductor thought she was insane!* Oh, what a net she was in! What should she do? If Chan Prescott did not do something for her how ever could she hope to escape? Was it possible that such terrible things could happen in this free Christian land? And then suddenly she remembered that there was one refuge she had forgotten, one helper who was always near, and frantically she began to pray.

And while she waited, and prayed in her heart, asking to be guided, in a frenzy of fear and anxiety, Chan Prescott was busily talking to the brakeman out in the last car.

He had managed somehow to establish deftly a mutual reminiscence of France and the great war, with a sentence or two, and then dropped down in the vacant seat beside the man and began to ask a few questions.

"This train ever make any stops between here and Chicago?" He asked it quite casually as if it were nothing to him.

"Not usually," said the brakeman, flattered that this young man with a fraternity pin on his vest and a great diamond flashing from his little finger, should care to stop and talk with him. He was from the parlor car, too, he was pretty sure of that. "We are today, though. There's been a bad wreck up a few miles ahead, just above Cranberry Crossing, and they had to lay a temporary sidetrack, and switch us off while the down express passes. But they don't havta wait long. The down train usually passes us on time every day. It'll scarcely be a dead stop, perhaps just come to a halt and then move on. We don't lose any time. Leastways we didn't yesterday. I guess it'll all be cleared again by tomorrow or next day, and we won't have to stop anymore. Bad wreck that was! Hear about it?"

"Why, yes, I believe I did read about it in the papers. Isn't that cleared off yet?"

"No, it ain't. But I guess today'll finish it."

"Where did you say the sidetrack is?"

"Just this side of Cranberry Crossing, about three miles—well I donno but it's nearer Cliffords. Just after you pass Cliffords."

"Cliffords," said Chan reflectively, taking out his timetable and running his finger down the list of stations, "where is that?"

The brakeman's grimy finger pointed out Cliffords.

"It's a dumb place," he said, "nothing but fields and trees."

"Say," said Chan, sitting up with interest, "I'm due at a house party off across the country not far from there. I wonder if I and a friend of mine couldn't just drop off when you stop? It would save me no end of time, not having to go clear in to Chicago and wait for a train to come out again. I'd miss nearly half a day of holiday and that means something."

"You're not supposed to do it, you know," said the brakeman doubtfully.

"But if I did and you didn't happen to see it, nothing would happen, would there? Nobody would have to suffer any?"

"Naw, I s'pose not," grinned the brakeman. "It wouldn't be any of my funeral."

"Well, I'm not taking any chances about funerals, buddy, so you needn't worry. But if I should decide to do it you wouldn't need to see us when we go off, would you? You wouldn't feel obliged to report it to the conductor?"

The brakeman grinned again and accepted the twenty-five dollars in crisp bills that Chan had manipulated across, putting them into a greasy pocket.

"Naw, I don't see nothing that ain't my business!" he agreed. "It's really nothing to me who gets off. You'll have plenty of time. I have to get off myself and run back, you know. The door'll be open, and I can't prevent your getting off."

"All right, buddy, I'll think it over!" Chan lazily arose and made his way back into the next car where he found a vacant seat and sat down to write another note to Rachel. When it was finished he snapped it together in his timetable with a rubber band and went on through the train, dropping it quietly in Rachel's seat as he stopped and leaned calmly over to take down her suitcase and carry it away.

He did not stop to look at her till he reached the front platform of her car and closed the door, then he turned and saw she was reading the note. She glanced up as he looked in, and he thought he saw a fleeting expression of a signal in her eyes, but he could not be sure.

He went on into the parlor car and was relieved to find that the two men had not yet returned to their seats. A glance into the smoking compartment showed them deeply engrossed in a game of cards, and he came back to his seat to get his belongings together and get out before their return.

As he sat down he noticed a torn paper lying on the floor at his feet, almost under his chair. He picked it up surreptitiously, glanced at the writing, and furtively put it in his pocket. Then without waiting for ceremony he gathered up his hat and suitcase and went back to the common car, taking a backseat where he could occasionally stand up at the back door and look into Rachel's car. She seemed still to be reading his note, or studying the timetable. The curtain was up and she kept casting anxious little glances out.

The note he had written was as follows:

In about half an hour we pass Cliffords. See timetable. Watch for it. When we pass there you go back to the watercooler and get a drink. Then go on quickly through to the last car, back platform. Shut all doors behind you. The train stops about a mile beyond Cliffords, only about a minute. Get off quick and *hide!* Look out for the down express if you have to cross the track! Stay hidden till I come. Don't get scared.

CHAN

Chapter III

In the parlor car the card game was not going well for the man with the heavy underlip and the diamond flashing upon his expensive tie. The other man, the one with the little shifty muddy-brown eyes and the unmoral mouth, was having things all too much his own way. In his vest pocket there crackled a small oblong bit of blue paper bearing the big man's signature. The man with the shifty eyes and the acquisitive fingers was figuring to have another such bit of blue paper in his inside pocket before this journey was ended. He was playing for large stakes.

The large man was growing restive:

"Oh, I say, Trevor, what about that little girl? Don't you think you've been a long time away from her? She might get suspicious or something. How about going in and asking her to the diner? You could introduce me as an old friend you'd just met. It's getting toward dinnertime, and I for one am ready for it. Suppose we cut this out now. It's getting horribly dull anyway. Let the cards lie. We can finish later and be the keener for a bite and a drink. I'd like to get this matter of the girl settled. It's getting on my nerves."

Trevor answered with a light laugh:

"Why, I take it that's all settled," and touched his vest pocket meaningly.

"Settled nothing!" growled the big man. "I can stop payment on that check, you know."

"Yes, but you won't," answered the other with assurance. "Remember, I've told the conductor!" His voice dropped with a warning accent, "Remember, I can put the police onto you."

"Thieves together, eh!" growled the big man facetiously.

"Well, have your own way and take your time, but go back now and see how that girl is. You can't tell."

"All right! Let's play this hand out first."

It seemed a century to the girl studying her timetable before the signboard bearing the significant word "Cliffords" flashed past her window, and she could close the little folder and slip it into her handbag. Her fingers trembled as she snapped the clasp, and she felt the need of steadying herself by a deep breath as she tried to rise to her feet like any casual passenger going back to the watercooler to get a drink.

Rachel had sat very quietly through the time that had elapsed since her would-be protector had come down the aisle, paused at her seat with a respectful touch of his hat, and reached up for her suitcase, bearing it away with him quite as a matter of course. She had managed to give him a casual glance and then direct her attention out of the window although her heart was beating wildly, and she simply could not keep from thinking that perhaps this was merely some diabolical scheme for robbing her of her few small possessions instead of rescuing her from a position that seemed, when she tried to realize it, almost absurdly impossible. Then a sober second thought reminded her that her shabby little suitcase could by no means be the object of even a petty theft, for it bore on its face the evidence of poverty. And anyhow, what was the chance of losing all it contained against the possibility of losing herself in a peril worse than death? She had not quite definitely visioned to herself just what that peril might mean, but all the horrible tales she had ever heard, all the veiled warnings that had ever come into her unusually sheltered life, all the newspaper stories she had ever read, flocked about her now and pointed menacing fingers till the earth fairly reeled beneath her faltering feet. Her whole soul seemed to be one great prayer that she might be protected and shown the way to go, yet her brain seemed unable to form any words of petition, nor even consecutive thoughts of what she should ask.

And then, just as she had half risen from her seat, and lifted her eyes to be sure she was not an object of special interest to any of her car mates, she saw a figure approaching from the car ahead, and her soul shrank within her and began to tremble. Even before he had opened the door, something in the slouch of his bearing, the cringing way he ducked his head to keep his hat from blowing off as he passed from one car to another, made her sure that it was Trevor and she sank back to the seat again with just presence of mind enough to turn her face toward the window and not appear to see him.

He came straight on down the aisle, and her heart beat more wildly with each instant until it seemed she would never be able to speak to him when he arrived. She was white as chalk. He was startled by her appearance, as she turned her face toward him appealingly, her eyes filled with trouble.

She did not have to dissemble to act her part well for her voice was literally shaking with excitement when she tried to speak.

The man was smiling ingratiatingly.

"I've come back to take you into the diner for dinner," said Trevor, smiling condescendingly.

"Oh, I couldn't, really, Mr. Trevor," said Rachel with new alarm. "I was just going to ask you if you would be kind enough to get me——"

But he interrupted her eagerly:

"I know, you think you can't afford it, but you don't need to worry, it won't cost you a cent. I've got a friend back there in the pullman has got all kinds of money, and he's nuts on pretty girls, and when he heard about you he sent me in here to invite you to dine with him."

The alarm in Rachel's eyes was changing to a deadly fear as she felt the slowing of the train almost imperceptibly. She had no time to waste. Her opportunity was at hand. In a moment or two it would be too late. Why had she not gone to the watercolor sooner?

"Mr. Trevor," she said, pressing her hand to her throat to steady the choking sensation that kept rising, "I feel ill, faint. Would you please get me a cup of tea or hot water or something—*quick!*"

She dropped her head over against the window, and her face was white. She did indeed look sick. The man started to obey, then turned back:

"I ought not to leave you," he said solicitously. "I can send someone else."

"No, *go!* I'll be all right! Oh, please *go quick!* Ask them to make it very hot and strong!"

He went and she forced herself to wait with closed eyes till he had passed through the car door and slammed it behind him. Then she raised her head and watched till she could see he had passed beyond the second car. She was in a frenzy of alarm, for now she was sure the train was slowing down and she must get back to the watercooler and appear to take a drink before she dared disappear into the next car.

At last she rose and made her way back to the cooler, but her feet seemed to be weighted and she dared take but a sip of water for now she could see that the objects outside the window were distinctly slower in their passage.

She had succeeded in getting out the door quietly and closing it behind her without apparently rousing the notice of any of her fellow passengers. She had a bit of a struggle, however, with the door to the next car which stuck and would not open, and as she turned to close it behind her she caught a glimpse of Trevor just entering the car she had left.

For an instant all strength seemed to have left her, and her feet refused to move. Then a power born of her desperation forced her on, hurrying down the aisle, trying to walk steadily, paying no heed to the curious glances of the sleepy passengers in the seats she passed, trying to look calm as if she were an ordinary passenger going perhaps to look up a friend or a better seat. People did walk from one car to another occasionally, she reflected breathlessly, as she reached the door of the last car and saw that her pursuer had almost gone the length of the car behind her now.

Her breath was coming short in tiny gasps, and her head reeled. She seemed to be moving in a nightmare. She remembered the dreams she used to have as a child, when her feet would suddenly be lifted up from the ground and she would be borne along with a feeling that she was too light to keep her balance on the earth, with the danger that she might at any instant be blown up a little higher, or that her feet might suddenly capsize her and get up where her head ought to be. Or that other dream that she was walking down the church aisle and without warning fell down and could not get up! It was terrific, the throbbing in her head, her eyes. She could not see anything about her. She could not remember ever having been so frightened. She was keenly aware of every possibility, of the fact that her pursuer might have instant power over her, and there would be no help for her if he quietly told people she was crazy. They would all be afraid of her and assist Trevor to make her a prisoner. She *must* get out and away, and the train was coming to a stop!

She was running now as fast as her strength would carry her. She did not care what people thought of her. It was her last chance. She must cast all caution to the winds and get away.

And then she was out on the platform, the last platform, with the blessed open country before her. But there was a brakeman on the bottom step. What would he think of her? Would he try to stop her? And she could see Trevor starting down the length of the last car! What should she do? She must do something now or it would be forever too late. Just then the brakeman dropped off and—joy!—the train was stopping!

When Trevor appeared at a stride back in the parlor car the big man had hailed him eagerly, apprehensively:

"Well, where is she? You don't mean to tell me you didn't bring her?"

"Be all right in a few minutes, I guess," placated Trevor out of breath from his hurry. "Says she feels faint and wants

a cup of tea. I'll just get the porter to bring it and then I'll go
back and get her. Haven't got something stronger with you
have you? Mine's all gone."

"Sure thing!" said the big man reaching in his pocket.
"Here, that'll fix her up. Don't need tea. The kid's probably
hungry."

Trevor found the porter and gave him the order to bring
the tea to the second car back at once. Then hurried back
with the silver flask which the big man had produced. But
when he entered the car where Rachel had been he stared
around bewildered and glanced back again. Why, she was
not there! Even her suitcase was gone from the rack where it
had been. Had he made a mistake? Was this only the first
car? Surely he had passed through one car, and this was the
second. He was certain of it. Then he heard the slam of the
next car door and caught a glimpse of her! What could she
be up to? Had she grown impatient and tried to come after
her tea? Got turned around probably and gone the wrong
way. That was it. He must catch her. If she really was faint
she might fall and get some injury!

He bolted on through the train with the handsome silver
flask in his hand exciting the interest of all the passengers.
But when he entered the last car and saw her still making for
the end of the train, he slowed down his speed a little. In a
moment she would surely discover her mistake, he thought,
and turn to come back!

But no, out the last door she went, and then he took
alarm. She must be really ill and had gone out there to get
air perhaps. He might get to her with the brandy quickly.
She might be dizzy and fall off, and then there would be no
end of trouble and he would have to beat it. He was glad he
had that check in his pocket. He felt a fleeting satisfaction
that the girl was bringing herself into the public eye. It
rather bore out his statement to the conductor that she was
mildly insane, and it would stand him in good stead later if
they had any trouble with her. He suddenly began to have
uneasy apprehensions about being able to carry out his pro-

gram just as it had been planned. The girl's eyes when she had declined to go to the diner had held a quiet strength, her lips set firmly together with a line of real character. She was nobody's dummy if she was green. Perhaps he had been a little mistaken in her. He must go cautiously and not arouse her suspicions. If they only could get her safely to Chicago and he could get away, he would take a chance that everything would be all right. There was a pal of his not far from the station who would railroad through the cashing of that check before the old gentleman had time to stop payment on it, and then, "he should worry." ·

Nevertheless he hurried solicitously out to the back platform after the girl, for the train was stopping most unexpectedly and she was nowhere in sight. She must have fainted. Rather a dramatic episode, but all to the good so far as his schemes went. And he opened the door and went out!

The big man had gazed after Trevor a moment, and then risen to his feet. He had a look of cunning in his jaded old eyes. It had occurred to him just at that instant that this might be a frame-up. The man had his check in his pocket, and the girl might be merely pretending to be sick to escape dining with them. Of course he could stop payment on the check—it was a large sum the rascal had demanded—but what was money if he bought a new toy? And the girl had been a stunner, all right! Yet he didn't trust Trevor. He had a shifty eye! And he had been fool enough to give him his flask too. A costly bauble! But he needed it right now. He felt the need of a stimulant himself! And by all that was unholy, wasn't the train slowing down? What did it all mean anyway? He had better go and find out. Where was that devil of a porter? Why didn't he come with the tea?

So the big man tottered unsteadily down the aisle; he had gout in one of his feet and did not walk as certainly as he had done a few years before. He had his cane to steady him, and he plunged on through the cars, managing to keep Trevor's back in sight most of the time, but pausing after each struggle with the car doors to get a new bearing on the situation. He was certain he had come farther than when Trevor first took him to get a glimpse of the girl. What was it all about anyway? Why, the train *was* stopping! It *had stopped!* He hurried, almost falling into an old lady's lap at the final jerk of the halt, but recovered himself with an oath and sprinted on again.

The porter had taken his time with that cup of tea. Trevor had forgotten to tip him. Trevor did not belong in the pullman car. He was merely occupying a vacant seat talking to the old gentleman with the diamonds. Of course the old gentleman was a frequent traveler and none too generous with his tips, but then he was to be considered. Still, for a girl in the common car, and a doubtful gentleman who did not belong in the pullman, one need not hasten overmuch.

The waiter who prepared the tea, grudgingly because he gathered from the porter that remuneration was doubtful, did not get the tray with the cup of tea ready until the train had almost come to a halt, and now the porter came down the aisle of the common car, scrutinizing each passenger inquiringly. He had no clue to the identify of the person who was in need of a cup of tea. He expected her to be eager enough to rise out of the multitude and claim it. But no one rose, and the few whom he questioned shook their heads, so he passed on. He came at length to the last car, a portion of the train that did not rightly belong in his precinct. He was cogitating how he might extract a large tip for his condescending service, when the train came to a halt. He did not really *have* to come back here with a cup of tea. Common folks had no right to demand such service. But here he was now in the last car. He might as well deliver his tea, for surely the lady must be here. Perhaps she had gone outside for air. He hurried on, slopping the tea irresponsibly. He had done his duty with it, and what more could be required of him?

Chan Prescott had laid his plans carefully. He knew just where the conductor and brakeman were located, and he

had so placed the two suitcases, his own and Miss Rainsford's, and arranged his ambush, that he could keep an eye
on Trevor's movements, as well as keep watch over the girl.
He did not feel altogether too sure yet of the girl. There had
been a reserve, he almost thought it was a frightened reserve, about the way she had responded to his overtures,
which seemed to remind him constantly of her father in the
background, and although he was aware that that father was
dead and buried he somehow could not shake off the feeling
that he was going to be accountable to the gravely kind professor for whatever happened in the next few minutes. It was
like a grown-up prank that he was playing, but playing with
tremendous odds.

Daring and fearless though he was, he could not help the
feeling of excitement that raced through his veins as the
wheels of the train began to slow down. If it had been himself alone that would have to suffer if his plans went wrong,
or if it had only meant a good fight with the two scoundrels
of the parlor car, he would stake his chances any day on a
free-for-all fight. But there was the girl, unprotected, in
grave peril, who would suffer worse than death perhaps, if
he did not succeed. Professor Rainsford's cherished daughter! A girl brought up in a holy protection such as Chan
could only vaguely picture to himself! And he knew from
the conversations he had overheard both between the two
men, and between them and the conductor, that he would
have little chance if it came to a showdown on the train.
No, he must get her off if he had to fling out the baggage
and at the last minute run with her under his arm and jump
off!

So he placed the two suitcases on the left-hand side of the
platform, and himself stood flattened with his back against
the end of the girl's car on the right side of the platform, entirely out of sight from either car, and apparently studying
the landscape and getting a little rest from the stuffy car. His
senses, like a regiment of soldiers, were at attention, under
full drill, for any contingency that might arise.

Chan had hoped against hope that Trevor would remain in the parlor car until the train had stopped and their maneuver was completed, but Trevor came with a breeze and a slam of the door that startled him and made him feel like a silly girl standing there.

It seemed to him at least five minutes before the man returned on his way to the diner, and he was maddeningly conscious of the slowing of the speed of the train. What if they should stop before he came back? Then, indeed, he would have to carry out his wild thought of a rescue. He kept a keen eye on the man till he started back for the tea, and then as soon as he had passed into the car ahead he sprang into action, stepping on the spring and raising the platform deftly. If only he could get off now before Trevor returned. But would Rachel get started? He must not leave the train till he was sure of her. Even if she should be afraid at the last minute to follow his advice he must not desert her. He stepped back and glanced into her car, relieved to see her rise and make her way toward the watercooler. Then he turned and placed the suitcases in such a way that they could be flung off in an instant when he was ready. Another glance back showed him that Rachel had opened the door of the car and was passing through. So! All was well.

Yet with the passing of the thought came Trevor again, carrying a silver flask, and almost knocking him down in his eagerness to get through the door! A new fear came to him, what if Trevor should give the girl some dope! He had not thought of that. But the train was almost stopping now, and surely she could make the back platform before he reached her! And he would get right back to the end of the train himself to protect her! The train was going slowly enough to dare to fling out a suitcase now. He chose his own sole leather one. Nothing could hurt that, and if it did, what matter? He must at any cost keep the girl's little cheap one intact for her. She could probably not afford to get a new one if anything happened to this.

Poised on the lowest step he gave a low quick whirl to his baggage and landed it neatly and deftly into a clump of elderberry bushes not far from the grade below the tracks.

He recovered his balance just in time to see the big man from the pullman lumber across the platform and push on excitedly into the day coach. This was an element of danger upon which he had not counted. Suppose now that he should get onto the situation and call in the conductor! What a mess that would be! Perhaps they would all be arrested or put in the insane asylum! Well, if Rachel was going to an insane asylum he resolved that he would go along and keep her company. She should not go alone!

For one flashing instant he wondered if it might not be a good idea to push ahead of the floundering old rascal and trip him, but just then the train halted with such a sudden jerk that any action on Chan's part became unnecessary.

Chan turned to catch up the other suitcase and swing himself to the ground, but in so doing came in sharp contact with the waiter from the diner, swashing his cup of tea irresponsibly through to the common car, and a few scalding drops fell stingingly on Chan's wrist.

Ah! The cup of tea! Another element in the situation. It would not take long now to rouse the whole train!

He paused on the platform, hesitating. Should he follow the fellow back and hinder him? Get off from another car? Could he make the back platform before the train started again? He must take no risks.

But the final jerk of the train in a dead stop warned him there was no time to change his plans. The brakeman had been most uncertain regarding the length of the stop. He had intimated it might be but a second or two, as the down express usually passed them on time.

Chan leaped down the steps and dropped to a little footpath that ran along beside the track below its grade, and put him out of the gaze of the ordinary observer at the windows. He hurried as fast as he could toward the end of the train. He wanted to be out of sight before the conductor had time

to begin investigations. Then he heard the roar of the oncoming down express and was filled with horror. Had Rachel had time to get out? Had she crossed the track in time?
Visions of her lying dead, mangled on the track turned him
sick. He glanced ahead. A flying figure was just hurling itself
from the last car and disappearing behind the end. Oh,
could she get across? Would she remember the train? And
would someone get her before she could disappear? Was
Trevor, even now perhaps, starting the alarm that a lunatic
had escaped? Should he try to rush on, or drop behind some
bushes till he could see where he was needed most and so be
better able to help?

A group of elderberry bushes a few feet away offered
screening and he slipped behind them, trying to discover
what had happened. A second more and the train he had
just left began to move, silhouetted against the blazing orb
of the setting sun. He thought he saw heads out of the windows and the conductor leaning out from the platform and
looking toward the engine, but the long slanting rays of the
sun blinded his eyes and black dots which might have been
men seemed to dance before them. Something large and
black and flabby flung itself from the back platform of the
train into the ditch below as the train lurched now into a
good gait and took up its way to the west.

Chan passed his hand over his eyes and when he looked
again the train was moving faster, the black dots were gone
and two figures only were on the landscape.

One was the man Trevor, slim, angry, bewildered, running around like a fox that was wounded, shouting and
tearing madly after the train with waving arms and flying
coattails, sleek-dyed hair ruffled to the breeze.

The other figure unfolded itself gradually from the ditch
where it had been flung, bruised and dazed, and turned
dumbly toward the fast departing train shaking an angry fist
of imprecation on which flashed a sparkling jewel, at the
grinning waiter who stood on the lower step of the last car
bearing a now empty cup and saucer.

Nowhere could be seen any sign of the girl!

Chapter IV

Across the tracks and a couple of rods beyond, there grew a woods of tall trees. The ground between was covered with tall coarse brakes or ferns, and in places, clumps of bushes and small trees dotted the clearing made by the railroad company. It did not make smooth going for the two gentlemen who were possessed of the idea that they would pursue and catch that train which was now well under way. Chan stood knee-deep in a meadow of buttercups and daisies and watched them stumble along, till the big man suddenly plunged and went down again amid the tall ferns. Chan could not keep from smiling as he watched. The man wallowed around and rose spluttering, having evidently sampled a little of mother earth in the interim, and being even more angry when he rose than before. But the fall had taught him the futility of his efforts and he paused on a hummock of land and gazed mournfully after the train which had rounded a wide curve and was now gliding into a cut in the woods to the northwest. The big man fumbled for a handkerchief, mopped his face and head, blew his nose, passed a shaky hand over his eyes, then shook his fist again at the retreating train, muttering loud words of which Chan could only catch an echo.

The man Trevor was still sprinting like a jackknife with his legs spread almost horizontally, and his arms working like pistons. He apparently was under some misapprehension that the train intended pausing again a few rods ahead and he meant to be on hand at the pause.

But Trevor presently arrived at a bit of marshy land and began to sink deeper with each leap forward into the oozy place. Soon he, too, began to realize the impossibility of his undertaking, and he struggled back to terra firma to look about him. Seeing the big man who began now to shout angrily at him, he came slowly forward attempting to assume his sleek habitual manner despite the slimy condition of shoes and trouser legs.

It was inevitable that they should see Chan. In such a wide and isolated stretch of landscape, shut in as it were by its very vastness and emptiness, Chan stood out in that meadow of daisies and buttercups like home and mother to a lost child. As the two men drew together, one blaming, the other placating, and began to gaze about them, he was the first thing they saw, the one bright hope to sudden prisoners on an empty desert. They made for him straightway.

During the brief interval before their arrival Chan surveyed the situation. Even if he had had the presence of mind to dash across the tracks and take to the woods when he first saw the men, while they were entirely immersed in catching the train, he could not have made it in time before they would have discovered him. Also it would have been a most unwise thing to do from the point of view of the young lady, if there was a young lady anymore, and if she had happened to hide herself in that scanty woods anywhere over there. It scarcely looked a thick enough woods to hide anything as bright as Rachel Rainsford. He scanned it from among the buttercups and daisies, and his heart failed him as he searched in vain for sign of her. What had happened? Had she somehow secreted herself on the train and escaped? Or was she close at hand? Whatever it was he must be exceedingly careful.

He glanced at the suitcase submerged in the bushes with two large white R's painted on the end. He parted the branches in such a way as to cover that end completely and then he stepped forth as if he had been coming to meet them.

"Didn't you get off that train?" shouted the big man as soon as he was near enough to be heard.

Chan waited tolerantly until they came up to him and said quite politely as if he had not heard:

"Beg pardon?"

"Didn't you get off that train?" shouted the big man again.

"Oh, why, didn't you *mean* to get off here?" asked Chan quite innocently. "It's not a regular stop, you know."

"That's quite obvious," growled the big man savagely.

"Now, now, Shillingsworth," put in Trevor, "that's not to the point. What we want to know is, did you see a girl get off that train? A girl with red hair. You couldn't have failed to notice her."

"Hardly!" said Chan dryly, giving a comprehensive glance about the vast expanse of sky and buttercups and ferns. "There are not so many girls around that I should have failed to notice her, even without the red hair."

Shillingsworth frowned angrily.

"Don't get funny, young chap. This is a serious matter. How far do you call it to the town?"

"Why, it ought not to be more than a mile, I should say," answered Chan flippantly.

"Which way do you go?" asked Trevor eyeing him keenly. "You live around here?"

"Not exactly," said Chan, "I'm here locating some property. Staking it out as it were, you know. You better follow the track. That's the shortest. When you've passed the woods over there you ought to be able to see the church spire, I should think."

The two men faced in the direction the train had taken and stared with dismay at the long stretch of gleaming tracks. Shillingsworth got out his handkerchief once more and mopped his brow. He looked around for his hat.

"I don't think I brought it with me," he muttered absently, "I came so hastily."

"Well, how are you going to get out of this devilish hole?" asked Trevor with a snarl. "Aren't you in the same box with us? Perhaps someone is driving out here for you?"

"Oh, no," said Chan hastily. "No one expects me. I just came to look after my property. You see, it is located somewhere between Cranberry Crossing and Cliffords. I could have got off at Cliffords, of course, but it is a trifle nearer to Cranberry, and I wanted to look it over thoroughly before anybody knew I was here." Chan seemed to have fresh inspiration as he went along. "I figured that I would have ample time to walk back to Cliffords before dark, and, as I say, I wanted to get a general idea of the property before I made myself known. You see, it is property that someone is trying to get away from me. I'll take it as a favor if you don't mention me when you get to Cranberry. It might put my enemies wise, you know."

Shillingsworth drew his heavy eyebrows down in a glower and eyed the young man savagely:

"Young man we have no interest in you or your property. What we want is an answer from you. Did you or did you not see that girl get off that train?"

"It's very necessary that we find her," put in Trevor. "She's insane, you see, and we must find her before night."

"No," said Chan, "I saw no girl get off the train. I was occupied in getting off myself. You see, when I found they were stopping I thought it would be a good opportunity to save a few miles so I got off. But that girl seems to have had more sense than some sane people. She seems to have stayed on the train. Couldn't you hike it up to Cranberry and telegraph the train to have her kept in custody till you can reach her? There must be another express along in an hour or two. Haven't you a schedule? I should suppose you might be able to flag a train at Cranberry. Got any influence back in New York? Just wire 'em from Cranberry to give you permission to flag an express and then wire the train to hold the girl, or wire Chicago or something."

He took out his watch and glanced at it.

"If I was you I would hustle, though. You want plenty of time for wiring before that express comes along."

Trevor and Shillingsworth looked at each other in dismay and then cast a sad eye at the perspective of the railroad track vanishing into the woods.

"Aren't you going to Cranberry, too, young man? I think
we all better stick together. You seem to know the ropes out
here."

Chan hastened to shake his head:

"Oh, no, I'm going back to Cliffords and foot it across to a
farm I know. It's only two miles across country."

He jogged his head in the general direction from which
the train had come.

"Well, that's all right for me," said the perspiring Shillingsworth. "I think we better go back to Cliffords and wire
from there. I don't see walking tracks all the way to Cranberry. It looks more to me than two miles just over to that
woods, and you can't tell how much farther it is beyond.
That's a pretty thick woods and it's liable to reach for some
distance. Besides, isn't that water I see ahead there? And no
bridge. I don't see walking across ties up high over water. I
get dizzy. I'm too heavy a man to run risks like that. Why,
suppose I should fall in?"

"Suit yourself," said Chan, taking out his knife and hack-
ing at a young sapling savagely, "but you may lose out in the
end. As I remember it, I don't think they have a telegraph
agent at Cliffords. Of course you can't get the next express
either from there. It isn't a flag station. I looked that up on
the timetable. However, it's up to you. If you want to wait
for me it'll be some time however. I've got to stake out my
property," and Chan set to work sharpening one end of his
sapling to a fine point. "You haven't either of you got a foot
rule with you, have you?"

Chan drove the sapling savagely into the moist earth with
a vigorous young strength, tied his handkerchief to its top,
and then began pacing off a distance westward, with long
even strides. When he had reached a distance of half a city
block he turned, squinted at his white flag, cut another sapling and proceeded to drive it into the earth, turned to sight
the two again, and apparently compare them with some
landmark toward the north, alternately consulting a bit of
paper which he took out of his vest pocket. At the distance

where stood the two uncertain and unhappy fellow travelers
it was not apparent that the paper he held in his hand was
nothing but a timetable. Chan was a good actor with long
experience, having begun while he was still in kindergarten
under mild and easily duped teachers. And withal he had an
engaging, convincing manner which impressed the two lost
men with the futility of trying to compel him into their service.

As Chan had figured, Trevor and Shillingsworth presently trudged toward him. His main desire was to get them
away from the place where the end of the train had stopped.
If Rachel were anywhere about it would be dangerous. They
might discover her if they remained there long. Disconso-
lately they picked their way over the humpy bed of ferns to
his side, where now he was sharpening more saplings with
long quick motions of his sharp knife. One would think to
watch him that he had come out to this part of the world just
to measure and stake out this particular piece of ground.

It was Trevor who reopened the conversation:

"Young man, what'll you take to come with us up to
Cranberry and see us through? This gentleman is willing to
pay you most anything in reason. You know the country
and it's important to get this thing through quickly. It may
mean life or death to this young girl, you know."

"Thanks awfully," said Chan briskly, "I could lend you
some money if you need it, but I'm not earning any today.
I'm here on important business I told you, and I've promised to get it through with before night. You'll have to excuse me. You won't have any trouble you know, just follow
the track. It's only a matter of patience. Sorry, but I have to
leave you now. I'm striking back into these woods. Wish you
success, gentlemen. You've plenty of time to make the next
train if you take it briskly. Good afternoon."

Chan picked up his bundle of sticks and strode with long
even steps straight back into the woods away from them
calmly measuring and counting his steps. The first time he
dared look back the two were scrambling up the embank-

ment to the track, and the second time they were plodding
excitedly along as if to make up for lost time. Chan drew a
deep breath and watched them narrowly, planning how he
must keep out of sight, at least until they had gone around
the curve. But he was not so easily rid of these unwelcome
companions. When he lifted his eyes once more he saw that
they had paused on the track and were gesticulating and
talking in loud tones that echoed back angrily. While he
watched, Trevor turned and ran back toward him waving
wild arms again, the big man standing still on the track and
waiting.

Trevor puffed up with red face and shouted at him:

"Say, young fellow, you're too fresh! You've got something up your sleeve. No man has property like that on the
track, and if you'd come to measure it up you'd have had a
tape line with you. You've had something to do with that
girl, and you might as well own up for we've got yer number. This guy Shillingsworth has all kinds of money and
he'll prosecute you in no time if you don't hand over that
girl. She belongs to us and she's out of her mind, see? And
we don't want any monkey business. There's two of us
against you, and Shillingsworth's in with all the big railroad
high-ups and he can jail you in no time for this. But if you
just tell me where you've hid her I'll say a good word for you
and get him to let you off easy."

For answer Chan threw back his head and laughed loud
and long.

It was a disarming laugh, so full of merriment and inno-
cence that even the two bullies were puzzled.

"Why, man alive!" said Chan when he could speak.
"Where do you think I've got her hid? In my pocket? I de-
clare to you I didn't see your young lady get off the train. I
haven't the slightest idea where she is at this minute, and
what do you suppose I would want of a red-haired girl when
I'm out to measure some land and incidentally straighten
out a matter for the people I'm working for? Say, I think you
people are wasting an awful lot of time. But it's none of my

affair, of course. If you don't really care why don't you both come here and help me? I've got a good two hours' work cut out before sundown, and perhaps more. I'll be glad to pay you for your services and then when we're done we can go back together and get a well-earned rest. What do you say?"

Chan realized that he was taking a chance. Almost for a minute he thought it was even too great a one, for these two men were afraid and lazy. They did not know what to do, and they did not have the nerve for the long lonely walk in the strange country. What if they should decide to stay and force him to go sooner?

Just for an instant Trevor wavered, a queer doubting look growing in his eyes. Then a glance at the sun showed him that the time was indeed short.

"Well, you're a strange one," he said uncertainly. "It sure looks mighty suspicious what you're doing, and I'm going to report you, the minute I get into Cranberry. See? So if you want to get away with anything you better come along with us now, for I shan't lose any time letting the authorities know just where you are and what you're trying to do!"

"Help yourself!" said Chan politely and went on driving in a new stake, a serene smile on his face. Perhaps the girl was still on the train. In which case every minute he could keep the men from the telegraph office was clear gain. On the other hand, the sun was getting lower and if Rachel had succeeded in getting safely off the train and was hidden somewhere, they ought to be clearing out of this part of the country at once, especially if this man carried out his threat and reported him. But Chan went on driving stakes at intervals and when he looked up again Trevor had joined his companion and they both seemed to be sprinting up the track in a lively manner. They evidently realized that they must get to the station as quickly as possible. And that meant that Chan must rustle around and find that girl!

As soon as the two men were far enough out of hearing so that their voices were not any longer distinguishable he began to hum a tune. He had a good tenor voice and he chose a popular tune that was heard about that time on all the radios and victrolas, but the words were the words of Chan, improvised for the occasion.

"I-am-waiting," he sang and one could fairly hear the twang of the mandolins and guitars in the lilt of the accompaniment. "Just-a-moment," he burst forth. "All-will-be-well!" The sound of long strokes as he drove in a substantial stick with a big stone, broke into the song. He could see the two men turn, pause, and watch him. It was too soon. He must not begin to search for her yet!

"I-am-going——" he crooned, and broke into a whistle for a note or two, "down-by-the-alders——" he cast a swift glance around with a sudden sense that she was near, but there appeared no sign of her. "Where-I-lef-f-ft——!" he swelled into song again, "our-baggaggaggag-age!"

He threw down his sticks all but one and turning toward the woods sang distinctly the last few measures of the tune:

"When I come ba-a-a-ack, be re-a-a-a-dy!"

He turned to walk toward the track and across to get the suitcases, but something suddenly dropped from the tree under which he was standing and struck his forehead, sliding down his nose.

He stopped, looked down, and picked it up. It was a tiny pinecone. He studied it an instant, cast a glance at the two retreating figures down the track, then looked up quickly.

The branches were thick and plumy. He could not be sure. Was that a bit of brown cloth very high up? Could she possibly have climbed so high? How did she manage it in so short a time? But he must not look up again for the enemy was too close yet. They might see him.

"All right!" he breathed softly under cover of a bit of a tune. "I'll-be-back-in-a-minute!" Then he paced on with his stick across the track and down to the elderberry bushes. Dared he take the suitcases across the track now? Would the enemy be able to see so far? Perhaps it would be better to wait a little. So he fussed about pretending to drive another stake, going through the motions at least. He reflected also that this was the main line of the railroad. There might be another train along soon. Passengers looking out of the window would notice. He ought to get the girl away from this region as soon as possible. It was even within the range of possibility that some other train might stop here. One train had, why not another? He must not risk any more complications. It did not of course seem likely that the two men trudging like two small beetles now in the distance would really take much trouble to recover for themselves a girl who was an utter stranger to one of them, and only a piece of property to the other, yet the denomination of the check that Shillingsworth had written was large, and he could see that the small man would not give it up without a fight. It was better to get away as soon as possible.

So Chan watched his chance when he was sure that the men were not looking and slid the suitcases, one at a time along the ground. The men in the distance could not see them there at least in all that deep grass.

When he had them safely across the tracks and up under the trees he straightened up and drew a long breath.

The two men had reached the curve of the track now and were only a few rods from the notch of the woods where the track disappeared. He went and stood under the tree where the pinecone had fallen.

"It is quite safe to talk now," he said in a guarded voice. "Answer me. Are you there?"

"Yes, I'm coming down," answered a voice quite near him.

"Wait!" he said. "Wait till they are out of sight. They must not see you. I'll just carry these suitcases into the woods a little way and park them. Are you all right and comfortable up there?"

"Yes, it's just a little sticky, that's all. I've got gum all over my dress."

"You should worry!" said the young man gaily. "There are other dresses in the world. We'll fix that. Don't try to get down till I get back and help you. That tree looks dangerous. The branches are not very well placed for climbing. I don't see how you ever managed it. Just keep perfectly still. I'll help you down as soon as it's safe."

She said all right, but when he came back he found her sitting on the lowest branch just above his head, her feet tucked somehow under her, and her arms clinging about the big resinous trunk of the tree.

"You oughtn't to have come down by yourself," he said sharply. "That last branch was a terrible drop. You might have broken a bone."

"Oh, I'm quite all right!" she said bravely, though there was a little shake in her voice that sounded like suppressed tears. He looked up and saw that her face was white, and her eyes were bright with a look almost like fright.

"Say, I guess you got pretty well shaken up that last drop, didn't you? Did you get hurt anywhere?"

"Oh, no," she assured him with a nervous little laugh, "I did drop some and I guess I was frightened for a minute. I came down really before I meant to. A branch snapped off and left me!"

He cast a startled look at the big dry branch lying on the ground:

"I'll say it did!" he exclaimed. "Say, that was a close call! I must get you out of here before anything more happens. Let's see if our friends have really left us!"

He stepped out from under the tree and looked. They were just entering the pass, two little black specks, crawling along laboriously. Chan hurried out in the open and began to pace off a distance. Their last look at him should find him still at work. He waited until he could see them no more, and then with a wave of his hat toward the cut in the woods he hurried back to the pine tree.

"Good-bye, brothers, your handicap is over. It's fifty-fifty from now on, and we're in to win," he said gleefully.

Chan went and stood close under Rachel's branch and looked up. She was still above reaching distance for him. He cast off his coat and threw it on the ground, flinging his hat after it.

"Now," he said, "we're ready. Do you think you can step down on my shoulder? I'll steady you."

"Oh," objected Rachel, "couldn't I just slide down?"

"You *could not!*" said the young man decidedly. "Hurry! We've no time to waste at this stage of the game. They might decide to come back at any moment. If they strike a trestle I'm sure they would. Their middle name is Coward. Put your foot right here on my shoulder!"

"Wait till I take off my shoes then. They are all gummy and will get you dirty."

"What's a little dirt between friends?" he laughed. "Hurry up, we've no time to waste!"

"But the heels will hurt your shoulder," she objected, beginning to twist around and get her feet down near him.

"What do you think I am, lady? A gum baby? Boy, I've played football and baseball for years! In the gym I've had a whole stack of fellows standing on my shoulders just to show off a stunt! Quick! That's right! No, keep it there, and don't be afraid to rest your weight. Now! Give me this hand! Steady! I'm holding you! Here we go!" and he swung her down to the ground beside him, a sorry little crumpled piece of girlhood, all shaky and trembling from her recent experience.

She looked down at herself in dismay and began to try to brush the dirt and lichens from her dress, but he checked her in a voice that startled her:

"Run!" he said, "a train is coming! We must not be in sight when it passes. That way! Straight ahead!"

She put down her head and scuttled away through the woods blindly, her heart beating wildly, and that sudden weakness coming again into her knees and feet. She could hear the train coming quite near now, and a glance back showed that they could still be seen from the railroad. She pushed anxiously on, and in her haste stumbled and would have fallen over a protruding root, but Chan caught her and swung her around behind a great tree and held her there, himself behind her while the thunderous train passed swiftly on. Rachel experienced a sudden feeling of being in a safe refuge for an instant, as they peered out from their tree at the passing train.

"That'll knock out those two boobs!" murmured Chan as he watched it. "Scare 'em stiff! But mebbe they'll flag it. I think that biggest slob would have the nerve to flag the President's Special. We've got to cover our tracks now. Are you steady? Then take my hand and we'll go! The suitcases are just beyond there in the clearing. All set?"

"All set!" answered Rachel, putting out her hand with a trembling little laugh, and they were off.

Chapter V

Out of the woods at last, they crossed two meadows and climbed a fence. Off to the right they could see an old stone house nestling under a hill, and a great barn looming farther on.

"It's too soon for us to strike out for a house," said Chan, eyeing the house speculatively. "I think we'll climb that hill beyond the meadow if you aren't all in." He looked at her keenly.

Rachel was panting but she lifted a game little face under the plain brown hat which was all awry and really looked much prettier that way.

"I'm all right!" she puffed. "But I'm going to carry my suitcase now. I won't go a step farther unless you let me."

For answer he swung both suitcases over the fence, and then turned laughing toward her:

"All right, see if you can get it first," and he lifted her to the top of the fence.

She scrambled over as fast as possible but of course he was there first with the suitcases in his hands.

"I really mean it!" she said soberly. "I can carry my suitcase perfectly well. It was packed so that I could. And I'm quite strong. Please! You make me ashamed and unhappy!"

"You're a good little sport!" he said admiringly. "But you see it's my job to get you to safety the quickest way I know, and if I let you use up your strength now why we'll lose out in the end."

"What about your strength? I really cannot accept all that you are doing anyway. It is an imposition. Here you have got off the train and stopped your journey, and no knowing how important the trip was and what you are upsetting by doing all this for me! And I've just been thinking how you may be letting yourself in for a lot of trouble and perhaps a lawsuit or something with those two awful men. I saw their faces when they were talking with you and I nearly fell out of the tree to think I might have been in their power if it hadn't been for you. I kept wishing my father could know what you were doing for me. He would have been so pleased!"

"Aw! Forget it! It's nothing!" said Chan with a sudden mistiness in his eyes and a strange tightening around his heart. "It's only what any fellow would do. Now look here, we can't stand here gassing. We've got to get under cover quick! I don't trust those guys one little minute and I'm not running any risks. If it was just myself I wouldn't care. I'd rather enjoy giving 'em a good walloping. But I don't want you mixed up in things like this, and those men are *mean!* I wouldn't trust 'em round the corner of a church! Now do as I say and let me manage this till we get over beyond that other hill. Then, if you want to, I'll let you take one suitcase for a little way. But we've got to hustle up this hill and *I'm* going to carry this junk! See?"

He dashed ahead among daisies and clover, and she had no choice but to follow, and indeed she had much ado to keep up with him as it was.

When they had climbed the second fence and crossed the brow of the hill they saw another little house, plainer and more weather-beaten, built of clapboards with the paint worn off. There was a hay wagon in the yard from which two men were pitching hay into a rickety old barn loft, and off at the side as if it were out of commission stood a seedy old flivver with torn curtains and a broken windshield. Chan stood a moment eyeing it, took a hasty survey of the landscape, then turned to Rachel:

"We're going down this hill along the dividing fence to that clump of blackberries down there, and you must sit down under that apple tree and keep behind the bushes while I go down to the house and see if I can get some kind of a conveyance. That wheat is tall and if you sit down in the grass you won't be seen. I'll take this suitcase down and you may carry yours."

"No, I'll take them both!" said Rachel, taking possession of them and standing straight and slim against the background of waving wheat. "I can carry them quite well and it's downhill and only a little way. Then you can go down along this fence and they won't know I'm with you."

He looked at her, hesitating, then twinkled his eyes with appreciation:

"All right. You win. But promise me you'll keep tight and lie low even if I'm some time. I may have to go to another house to get a conveyance, you know."

"Certainly, I understand, and you'll find me right here when you come back, if it's midnight."

"I believe you would," he said with a ripple of pleasure in his eyes. "Wasn't there somebody in the fifth reader did that? Yes, I remember, 'The boy stood on the burning deck, whence all but him had fled.' That's the only piece of poetry I ever did learn, and I stayed three hours after school to do it on account of sticking pins in Professor Belding's muffler. We'll have a try at that piece again when I get back and see if I remember it."

Somehow there was something about his breezy way of taking mutual old times for granted that quieted her fears and made her feel at her ease. She smiled shyly and turned to go down the hill, a suitcase in either hand.

"Isn't that a road just over there at the side of the barn? Wouldn't it be better for you to arrive at that house from the road, than to descend from the meadow? Less suspicious looking?" she suggested.

"It certainly would. You have a head on you, I see. And by the way, that road must run over below here, too. Just keep your eyes open and your ears. If you hear me whistling as I drive along and then suddenly stop you might reconnoiter a bit. If I give a long low whistle followed by two sharp ones, this way——" and he gave a sample under his breath, "you can just saunter down and find me, but keep close to that side of the fence and keep your eyes open. Don't take any chances. I don't want to leave any traces behind me. Well, so long! Don't worry. The sun isn't down yet!"

She started down the hill, then looked back and watched him disappear behind the wheat, his strong gray-clad shoulders under the fine panama hat swinging along as easily as if he were walking down a ballroom floor to ask some other girl to dance with him. She didn't know why that simile came to her as she watched him. Ballrooms were not in her line of life, but she seemed to know that they were in his. Still he looked not out of place among the wheat.

When he was out of sight she turned and stole down her hill, bearing the two heavy suitcases, trying to walk steadily and forget that her knees were trembling and her hands weak with excitement and hurry.

It was good to sink down in the grass at the foot of the apple tree, the suitcases parked unobtrusively behind her, rest her back against them and close her eyes, with the pale screen of the ripe wheat between her and the setting sun. She was tired and hot and a little breeze came and cooled her temples. She reached up her hand, took off the unbecoming brown hat, and let the breeze lift the red-gold of her hair and ripple about her tired head. A little brown cricket came out and chirped rustily at the edge of the wheat where she lay. A bird settled velvetly down in the apple tree over her head and chirped inquiringly, turning a bright beady eye sidewise to observe her and cheep to his mate of the phenomenon among the wheat. A cool drowsiness settled upon her as she tried to follow the steps of the young man in imagination, down the road, up a winding driveway to the barn, a driveway made in deep ruts and overgrown with grass. That was the impression she had got from her one brief glance down the hill. The sound of a pitchfork hitting against the wagon wheel rang out like a chime of evening bells, and a belated butterfly hurrying home brushed across her lashes with a breath and was gone. It was all sweet and quiet and safe, and she felt such gratitude and wonder for the way she had been saved! She would not let herself review the possibilities. She was shut in here for a brief rest and she would take it.

She must have drowsed, for she roused suddenly. A dog was barking sharply nearby. Men's voices rang out, and the chime of the pitchfork once more as it was flung down. She seemed to have the impression of the chug-chugging of an automobile and a sharp whistle, a long time ago! Where was she? There was a stirring in the grass beside her, and the ruby light of the sun shining through the wheat seemed to have been blotted out. She was afraid to open her eyes and the grass felt cool and damp under her hand. Then she looked and there stood Chan above her in the graying twilight, such a reverence upon his face, that she was reassured.

"You poor little kid!" he said softly. "Did you think I was never coming back? I couldn't help it, the old bus wouldn't run and I had to take her all apart and monkey with her, but she's all okay now. Lie still, I'm going to take you down. Don't talk. The men are not far off. They might hear us."

"Oh, I can walk!" whispered Rachel eagerly, trying to rise.

But he stopped and picked her up as lightly as a feather and strode off down the hill.

"Don't talk!" he ordered sharply in a whisper, and she subsided in his arms, ashamed that she had succumbed to sleep, and made him double exertion, yet wondering at the strength of his arms and the safety she felt.

There was an opening in the stone wall at the foot of the field and he carried her straight to the shabby little Ford and slipped her into the backseat.

"It isn't a very lordly chariot," he said in a low tone, "but it's ours. I bought it. Sit quiet there now. I'll get the bags and we'll be off. I won't be but a minute."

He was back in a minute, stowing the suitcases in the back of the car, then nearly down on his knees to crank the old machine, and presently they were on their way chugging along a rough country road.

"Where are we going?" she ventured to ask when they had gone about a mile and the gray of evening was changed into starlight and shadows along a wooded way.

"That's the fun of it," he declared solemnly. "I don't know. I didn't dare ask much back there. I'm trying to go the opposite way from what they directed me so if anyone asks any questions they'll be on the wrong trail, but I don't know whether I'm accomplishing it or not. I hope you're not worried. As far as I am concerned it's rather good fun, something like going on an expedition to the North Pole, or getting lost in the desert. But I keep forgetting that you may not take it that way. We're going to strike a town pretty soon I suppose, and then we can find some place for you to rest and talk over some plans. At present I'm having the time of my life managing this old ark of a car. She seems to have something wrong with her engine the way she sputters. I have a feeling she may lie down on the job any minute and I'll have to get out in the road and reason with her. It's a cinch she can't go far on the amount of gasoline she's got. I'll have to find a filling station before long or park in the woods all night. But at least she's an abiding place, and if worse comes to worst we can get out and push her somewhere."

Rachel was laughing merrily now at his comical tone, and the weary trembling feeling seemed to be gone. It was like a fairy-tale adventure. Somehow she was not frightened or excited anymore. She was having a good time! And she remembered that a few hours ago in the train she had reflected sadly that she probably would never have a good time anymore. Life was strange! Perhaps she was dreaming.

"But I don't understand," she said with sudden remembrance. "You said you bought it. How could you buy an automobile so quickly? And didn't it cost a lot of money?"

"Not this old ark. I got her for twenty-five bucks. The man wanted fifty, but I showed him it wouldn't run without a lot of work. He didn't know a windshield from a carburetor anyway, and said he was afraid of the pesky things. A man had left it on his hands for a debt, and he had had it three months and couldn't get anything out of it. I told him I would give him twenty-five bucks if he'd throw in all the gasoline he had. They had a gasoline stove in their out-kitchen, and I guess they'll have to eat a cold breakfast for I drained the tank. The man just jumped at the chance and grabbed the money as if it had been twenty-five hundred. I told him I left my car several miles back, flat tire and motor trouble, and I had to get to the next town tonight. So I tinkered her up and here we are. But where are we anyway?"

Chan drew up at a signpost and struck a match.

"Three miles to Cranberry Crossing," it read, and its finger pointed in an uncertain way toward the ground with a slight slant toward the right-hand road.

"Great Scott!" said Chan. "We can't go to Cranberry Crossing! We'll take the other road!" and he veered the rattly old car into the left-hand road.

It was quite dark when they drove into a little town. The lights were twinkling in pleasant cottages, and there was a long, thin splash of crimson lingering in the dark of the horizon, blending into the luminous sky above where a single star flashed out at them as if it had just been lit, and a slender moon sailed high.

"That looks like a good old-fashioned hotel over there," speculated Chan. "We might be able to get some supper. You must be half starved!"

"Oh," said Rachel wistfully, "do you think we ought? It will cost a lot, and I've only about enough money to pay for this car. Besides I look a sight to go into a hotel. Maybe we could buy a box of crackers somewhere if we could find a grocery open."

"What do you mean, ought? We ought to eat, oughtn't we? I should think we were far enough away now from the scene of our disaster. They wouldn't have got around to send the police out here yet. And what do you mean about paying for this car? This is my car, lady, and I don't let anybody pay for my cars. If you don't care to ride with me, all right, you can get right out and walk, when we get you to a safe place, but you can't pay for any car of mine."

Rachel giggled happily, and then grew graver:

"But you know I cannot possibly let you go to all this expense and trouble for me."

"Well, there may be ways of repaying anything you get from me. I don't know. Seems to me I'm getting a whole lot out of this expedition as I go along. And don't worry about the car. I'll be able to sell it for twice what I paid for it when I get done with it. But we haven't time to talk about that now. We've got to get some supper, that's one thing settled. I'll make a stab at this place and see what it's like. Wonder what they call this burg, anyway?"

Chan drew up in the shadow at the side of a big old-fashioned wooden building. The windows were bright with light inside and men were sitting on the hard wooden chairs on the porch, tilted back against the wall, their pipes glowing against the dark of the wall. It seemed a friendly, prosperous house, with a keen odor of roasted meat on the air that whetted the appetites of the weary, hungry travelers. There was a crude filling station just beyond the hotel and the road wound in front of it and curved to the side door of the hotel. The men on the front piazza were occupied with their discussion of the coming county fair, and gave little heed to the wheezy Ford that coughed around the deserted filling station and halted at the side door of the hotel.

"Let's go in here," said Chan, helping Rachel down. "Too many eyes around front. No need to give them anything new to talk about. Say, this smells like mother, home, and heaven, doesn't it? Gosh! I didn't know how hollow I was. We'll make a real meal, what?"

He looked at Rachel with a warm friendly glance as if he and she had been used to knocking around the world like this together for years, and she felt her heart warm toward him with a sudden childish desire to hide her face on his shoulder and cry. But Rachel was not a crying girl. Instead she gave him a shy little smile, suddenly aware, as they entered the lighted conventional world, of her torn dress and disheveled hair, and this utter stranger with whom she was about to take dinner.

Chan noticed in that fleeting smile, however, that Rachel was pale and that there were weary shadows under her eyes. She had been under a great strain and she had acted her part well. Something in her sweet womanliness appealed to him strangely. She was not like the girls in his crowd. There was a childlikeness about her that made him think of the little girl at the corner come to meet her father with the glad, trustful light in her eyes. She lacked much of the sophistication that he was used to seeing in girls, yet she somehow gave him the impression that it was not because she did not know the great truths of life. It was rather as if their knowledge had left her wise and gentle, instead of hardening her as it had done with others.

All this went through his mind with that one glance, and he felt a latent chivalry rise within him; a chivalry for which, in his day and generation, he had heretofore had little use. It stirred him to protection. It filled him with great yearning to lift the shadow from that face that seemed meant for joy and dancing lights, not grave serious thoughts. It gave him a strange ache in his throat as if he wished to cry for her who was too brave to cry. He wondered what it was about her that affected him so. A few hours later he would have laughed at his foolish fancies. His whole life had been one of lightness and trifling, of pleasure-seeking and daring. Even his mother had never bred within him such gentleness as had suddenly overtaken him. His own mother he scarcely remembered. His stepmother was a beautiful woman and he was proud of her, but she had always been sufficient to herself—too sufficient he had sometimes thought when he was a tired little boy and would like to have been petted. She had never petted him. She had always laughed at any such weakness on his part and put him aside for servants to deal with as if his wish offended her. So, he had grown up without tenderness.

And his sisters were worldly-wise women, old before their time; artificially youthful, lovely, untouchable, and sophisticated to the last degree. They had never stirred within him the slightest desire to protect them. Rather he had always been on guard against the sharp shafts of their sarcasm.

His face grew grave as he reached out to open the dining-room door for her.

"Poor kid!" he said gently. "You're all in, aren't you? We'll have to look for some place for you to get a night's rest pretty soon, when we get a little farther on. But we'll just swing in here and order dinner. Then you can sit still while I go to the office and register. Guess we better not give our own names, had we? I'll make up a couple. Just as well to be on the safe side."

He stepped aside to let her go before him and they stood within the threshold, for the instant blinded by the sudden light of the big white dining room with its glitter of cheap glass and silver. Rachel's mind was busy with the idea of fictitious names, not quite liking it, wondering if she ought to protest. Even in such a stress as this, it seemed in a class with anonymous letters.

Then she glanced about the room. Suddenly she stood rooted to the floor in horror that seemed almost to smother her. She could not even make a sound with her trembling frightened lips.

For in the center of the room at a table filled with food, two men, who had been seated there at either side, suddenly arose and faced her, with an exclamation in unison. She felt herself pinned to the wall by the look of Tervor's sharp, accusing, cunning eyes. Then like another barbed shaft close following, she saw the baleful, gloating eyes of the older big man with the flabby lips and the baggy eyes, who stood by him.

The floor seemed to reel beneath her feet, and her body began to sink, until she felt Chan's quick grip upon her arm, strong, protecting, reassuring, and his whisper in her ear, clear though seemingly quite far away:

"Beat it to the car, kid! Keep your head! I'll come!"

Chapter VI

Rachel, crouched on the floor of the backseat of the old Ford, listened agonizingly to the intermittent throb and whirr of the rusty engine as Chan tried in vain to crank it.

Chug! Chug! Whirr-r-r-r! it would go, and then suddenly die down. And hurrying footsteps inside the building were drawing momently nearer! Excited voices echoed outside the doorway:

"Which way did they go? Around the side? A girl, you said? I ain't seen no red-haired girl. Musta ben mistaken. Look in the dinin' room, did ya? Oh, where? Come out the side door, did they?"

The voices were distinctly approaching now.

Chan gave a final turn of the starter and groaned with helplessness. He dashed to the door of the car and opened it:

"I can't make her work. Beat it, kid, across the track. There's a freight coming. Maybe you can make it before she gets here. That'll cover you. Cut across behind those pumps and run. Don't be scared. I'll be close behind!"

Rachel darted on feet that felt strengthless, across behind the gas pumps, and into the shadow of an old barn, making for the railroad track. It seemed to her that she was simply treading a wheel which went round and round under her flying feet, and that she was getting nowhere. She could hear loud voices now, a big ugly voice swearing. Was that other one Trevor? It sounded like his high, thin tones. There was no sound now of cranking the car. Had they caught Chan? If so, she must go back and help him. No matter what the risk, she must stay by him. He had been simply wonderful the way he stuck by her. Oh, would she never reach the track? There was the oncoming train, such a little distance down the track! Could she make it? What if she should stumble and fall in front of it! But she must risk it. Such a fate would be no worse perhaps than the one which awaited her in the hands of the two unscrupulous men. It almost seemed as if the light from the engine scorched her face as she crept at last close to the rail, gave one desperate look and plunged across! How much her brain could do besides direct her faltering feet! Her whole past life went fleeting in review!

The engine screamed, but she had disappeared into the shadows. The engineer leaning from his cab and peering anxiously ahead and to the side did not discover her, because her white face was hidden in the grass where she had fallen as she slid down the slight embankment on the other side of the tracks. And there she lay, trembling and praying, not knowing what to do. Perhaps she ought to get up and run, but there seemed no power in her to rise. Every atom of strength had passed out of the ends of her fingers as she dropped into the grass. She was like an inert thing. Only her heart went pounding on with fearful rapidity that seemed to smother her.

Was the train slowing down? Perhaps they thought they had struck her and were stopping to find out. Then they would come with lanterns and search for her, and she would have no cover. Her tired eyes tried to pierce the gloom about her and search for trees or bushes, but it was all so uncertain and misty with little wreaths of fog rising above the meadow. Perhaps the fog would hide her. She made an impetuous little motion out with one hand with a fleeting vague idea of reaching a bit of mist and pulling it over her head like a blanket, and then lay still, quivering with fear.

She tried to summon her own natural courage, but it seemed to have fled and left her ashamed. She did not realize that she had fallen rather heavily and had really been stunned by the fall. She thought that she was simply frightened. She tried to reason herself out of her fear. What was there after all to fear so much? Surely with plenty of people about, there would be someone who would believe the truth! Chan would do something! But then, Chan was only human, and suppose they put him in an insane asylum, too! She did not stop to reason out and ask what motive there could possibly be for putting them both in imprisonment. She seemed not to be able to get beyond her fears.

Yes, the train was slowing down, it was just about like walking now, and she could hear voices and shouts on the other side. Then something dark dropped almost beside her and rolled a few feet. Was that one of her pursuers or a trainman? What should she do? Lie perfectly still? Perhaps he would not discover her. Or, perhaps it had only been a piece of freight or a mailbag or something. She lay quite still and held her breath. Then suddenly a match flickered and the flame wavered across her. She felt the light even with her face down in the grass. That was a step!

And the train was going faster again! In a moment its screen would be gone! She must get up and fly! She looked up. There were only three or four cars before the caboose with its twinkling red lights! Which way ought she to run? She staggered to her feet uncertainly and looked around.

Then suddenly Chan's arms were about her, Chan's lips at her ear:

"Come!" he said eagerly. "We've got to jump the train, kid! Just keep cool and do as I say. It'll all be over in a minute!"

Chan's strong arm supported her and seemed to put new strength into her. If he had said, "We've got to jump over the evening star that you see there in the sky," it would have seemed just as possible to her as to jump a train. Rachel had never practiced such sports. Yet she felt somehow that Chan would accomplish his feat, whatever it was, and she set herself to be facile to his movements, without in the least comprehending what was expected of her.

Chan ran with her a few steps ahead in the direction the train was moving till they reached level ground close to the tracks. Then he stood waiting, poised, with the air of an athlete who knows the exact crucial instant when he must be ready to act.

"Catch the handrail, kid, when I lift you, and be ready to spring. Stick, no matter what. Don't lose your head!"

The words were low and incisive, and steadied her while they filled her with a great awe. What were they about to do?

The freight came on, slatting its iron feet down on the rails with the air of an old, tired scrubwoman who was sick of her job and did not care for anything. Cruel, it seemed to the girl as she stood in that breathless instant waiting with the strong arm around her, waiting for the swaying, blinking red light to come.

It was all over in a flash and she was on her knees on the second step of the caboose, one hand clinging to the rude rail at her side, the other clutching the step. Another second and she was conscious that Chan was behind her, holding to the rails with both hands, his feet firmly on the lower step. She marveled how easily he had done it, like a bird alighting on a bough, as though he bore about him, somewhere, concealed wings that helped him poise in midair.

She laughed hysterically, a sorry little lilt that was almost a cry and he stooped instantly and warned her:

"Hush, kid! There are men inside! They mustn't know we're here!"

Instantly she grew grave and controlled. The danger was not over, then! And now she was conscious of the ground moving under them at a rapid jolt, and of the uncertainty of her position. She turned about and sat close to the wall of the car, leaving room for Chan to crouch beside her. He put his arm about her again and held her firmly. It seemed a strange precarious way to ride, yet somehow she felt safe, safer than since she had run from that dining room and the presence of those two awful men! She shuddered almost imperceptibly at the memory and Chan's arm went closer round her, as if to comfort and reassure her.

It came to her that this was a strange situation in which to find herself, for the daughter of such a father and mother as she had had, sitting on the step of a freight caboose with an almost stranger's arm about her. She had not been brought up to hold herself lightly. Yet there seemed no presumption in the arm that held her. Without it she would have been swiftly whirled off to the ground. She rejoiced in the strength that surrounded her.

Rachel's hair had come down in the flight, till not a single hairpin remained. She tried to put it neatly behind her ears, but the wind seized it and blew its fragrant softness across Chan's lips and eyes. It thrilled him like a caress, and in the darkness he half smiled and closed his eyes to feel its rippling touch as if a benediction had come to him unexpectedly. But though his arm involuntarily drew a little closer about her, it was with the utmost reverence. She was so different from other girls he knew, so sweet and wholesome, so shy and frightened and yet brave.

Her face was white against the darkness of the car. Poor child! How tired she must be! And hungry, too! To think that he should have been so careless after their first experience as to cast precaution to the winds and take her into that hotel without any investigation! Let her in for all this unnecessary trouble, too, and lose their Ford and their baggage and everything! He could have kicked himself for his stupidity. Yet he felt an exultant thrill to think they were here, safely away from it all, and that he might hold her so from danger. She seemed the most precious thing it had ever been his good fortune to hold, a trust that roused his deepest tenderness.

As they thumped along the fringe of the meadows, shot here and there with fireflies, or dark with a pool spiked with tall rushes and cattails, Rachel wondered that her fear was gone. It was like dying and suddenly finding that you liked it. There was something wonderful about being taken care of this way; they two borne safely along amid peril and possibility. And because her position was cramped and she could no longer hold her head up straight she let her forehead rest lightly against Chan's shoulder, yet did not feel the strangeness of it because of the necessity. And Chan bent over as far as one in his cramped position could bend and laid his lips lightly against her forehead breathing the words, "All right—Rachel?" as if it were a caress. Yet it all seemed quite natural. That was the strange part about it when Rachel thought it over afterward.

She only nodded then, mindful of the gruff voices from within the caboose where apparently a game of cards was in progress, and sat still enfolded in that strong arm, and resting after the stress, not even thinking about it, nor realizing what it all meant; only feeling safe and glad and dazed.

How long they rode thus neither was quite sure afterward. The firefly-dotted meadow fringes they skirted seemed endless, like space in a universe, and they were both there and safe. That seemed enough.

Then suddenly the wheels began to slacken. Lights appeared twinkling in the distance—a town ahead! Feet shuffled around on the floor of the caboose, cards were slapped down angrily, a man arose. They could hear the metallic twang of the lantern as it was swung down from its hook. The light blurred out through the door. Someone was coming! The train was almost stopping now.

"We've got to beat it, kid. Are you afraid to drop?"

"No!" she breathed with awed temerity.

"I'll drop first," he whispered. "You wait—wait till I catch up. Then jump. I'll catch you."

He was gone! The black meadows were changing into buildings just ahead. The steps were coming close to the door now. She must not be found here. She must jump—

"Oh——!"

There was a sudden startled gasp of daring as she poised upon the step and let go, and then she was caught as lightly as though she had been a thistledown, caught and whirled about a few steps in those strange arms again.

She clung like a vise about his neck for a moment. All her life seemed dependent upon clinging, and then the arms held her again and steadied her. Chan's lips were on her hair. Until afterwards, he did not realize that he had kissed it. She seemed so frail and young and frightened as she clung about his neck. Then as the clang of the train died away down the track, and they could hear the distant thud and chug of the halting and the shouts of the men swinging red lanterns up and down the tracks, she came to herself and drew away from him.

"I'm—all—right—now—" she said unsteadily. "I guess I was a little frightened!" she added in a more conventional tone.

"I guess you were," he said gently as one will talk to a very little child who has had a bad fall. "I wasn't so far behind myself for a second or two there when I struck my foot against a stone and almost went down. But we're off now, thank goodness, and I guess we better beat it. There's a road over there, seems to lead away from the town. We'll take that. It's safer. After we get out of sight we can sit down and rest a little and decide what to do."

He took her hand as if she were still the little child who had fallen, and together they walked silently under the far stars down a cinder road, until they had left the firefly meadows far behind them and the lights of the town gleamed off at the right in the distance.

An hour later they came to a little farmhouse set neatly behind a white fence with vines over the door and bushes about the yard. A light twinkled cheerfully from the windows and, as they approached, the front door was flung open and three people came out on the porch.

There were two women and a man. The man had a hat in his hand and one woman wore a hat. The other was a gray-haired kindly faced woman. She was bidding them goodbye. Their voices echoed pleasantly out to the road, bringing out a word or two in clear distinctness now and then, enough to show what kind of people they were.

"Aren't you afraid? Wouldn't you like me to stay all night with you?" called back the woman with the hat after she had got halfway to the gate. "I can just as well as not."

"No, I'm not a mite afraid," said the woman at the door.

"I often stay alone when John goes to town for a day or two. He'll be back late tomorrow afternoon, and the time'll be gone before I know it. Good night. Don't forget to tell Susan I want her to bring the baby out next time she comes."

The two callers climbed into a little roadster that stood before the gate and the gray-haired woman shut the door and went in. They could see her moving about in the rooms. The light in the front room where they had been sitting went out and she came over to the room on the other side and went about fastening windows and pulling down shades.

"Rachel," said Chan in a low tone, "I think we better see if you can stay here all night. Then I'll move on and get some kind of a bus and come after you in the morning."

"Oh, no!" said Rachel, shrinking back. "You can't tell when those men will turn up."

"They won't come here. Positive. It'll take 'em at least till noon to make out where we disappeared, and I doubt if they try. They'll put it in the hands of the police and let it go at that. There aren't any police around here tonight and I'll get you out of this early in the morning."

"Oh, must I?" said Rachel, beginning to feel a great trembling coming over her spirit.

"I think you must," said Chan firmly. "I can't keep you out all night. It's being done by some I know, but I don't think your father would like it."

"Of course," said Rachel, drawing a deep breath bravely, "I'll stay. But, how am I going to explain things?"

"Leave it to me," said Chan. "We won't tell her much, and if she pumps you afterward keep as mum as you can. Stick to your story."

"But we must tell the truth!"

Chan eyed her thoughtfully.

"All right! Come on! Here's for the truth. But not the whole truth! What's nobody's business won't hurt 'em if they don't know it. Hurry! The old girl is going up to bed. See, she's turned the light out downstairs, all but the hall."

They hurried across the intervening space and were soon

within the white gate and walking up the steps of the little
house. Suddenly after Chan had rung the doorbell Rachel
put a hand on his arm:

"But I'm afraid for you," she whispered softly.

He smiled and patted her hand:

"All right, kid, nothing'll happen to me. I gotta charmed
life, at least till I get you to a good safe place. Don't you
worry! Sh! Here comes your landlady."

They stood blinking under the porch light that suddenly
sprang out over their heads, an innocent-looking, but much
disheveled pair. Rachel had braided her errant hair in two
long braids and wound them round her head, tucking in the
ends securely and fastening them with a breastpin from her
little handbag, the only one of her belongings that had come
with her through it all, it having been slipped over her wrist
and held to by some unconscious sixth sense.

Chan looked handsome in spite of his tossed-up hair and
hatless condition. He stood forth with his engaging smile:

"I beg your pardon for disturbing you at this hour," he
said genially, "but we've had trouble with our car several
miles back. It stopped dead on us, and I must have missed
my way to the nearest town. This lady is about all in, and
hasn't had any supper. Could you possibly keep her over-
night and give her a bite to eat while I go on and hunt for
help? I'll pay you whatever you ask, and I'll be back for her
early in the morning."

The woman eyed them thoughtfully:

"Well, I suppose I could," she said hesitantly, "but it
wouldn't be worth my while under two and a half."

Chan smiled. He already had his hand in his pocket and
drew out a five-dollar bill.

"It's worth twice that to me," he said with a grin. Then
turning to the girl:

"This is Miss Ford," he said easily. "You all right and satisfied to stay here, Ray?"

Rachel smiled up at him with a twinkle in spite of her
fears. So this was the way he told the truth.

"I'm Mrs. John Davis," said the householder, eyeing the girl somewhat doubtfully.

"I'm rather a sight," apologized Rachel. "You see, we've been in the woods. And I'm afraid I've left my hat in the car. I didn't realize we would have to come so far!"

"Oh, you look all right," said the hostess with a relieved smile. "Young folks can't keep starched up when they are off having a good time. Young man, you better come in and get a glass of milk and some gingerbread before you go. It's quite a piece into the village, and you won't find anything open at this hour of the night except the garage. Just step this way and I'll get you something."

The something proved to be a very substantial spread of bread and butter, applesauce, cold ham, gingerbread, and a pitcher of creamy milk. The two sat in the neat little dining room and ate while their hostess plied them with questions which Chan was most skillfull in answering.

It was after Chan had taken his leave, promising to be back very early in the morning that Mrs. Davis as she bolted the front door after him, turned to Rachel and said:

"He's a nice well-spoken young fella. Is he your brother or your beau? He didn't give his name."

"Oh, he's just a friend," said Rachel. "An *old* friend," she added, as if that would make it more conventional.

"H'm!" said Mrs. Davis, studying her interestedly. "Well, he seems a good sort. And now, don't you wantta telephone your folks? Won't they be scared? How far do you live?"

Rachel felt a sudden desire to cry coming over her, but she smiled instead:

"My people are all gone," she said sadly. "I'm all alone in the world. I used to live over in eastern Pennsylvania, but I'm on my way west to take a position. I just stopped off."

"I see," said Mrs. Davis genially. She had quite a story now wherewith to enlighten the mite society next time it met with her to finish the quilting. "And this young man was showing you a good time. I know how it is with young folks. Too bad you had a breakdown. But I guess you got a good time out of it after all. Now, if you'll step right upstairs to the front spare room, I'll show you where the light turns on. There's the bathroom at the right. We think we're pretty fortunate to have water and lights out so far from town. We just got 'em last spring. My husband tries to make everything easy for me. This is your room. I guess there's plenty of covers, it ain't cold. And you can open all the windows if you like plenty of air. There's screens in every window! Now, I'll get the towels. And you ain't got a nightie with you either, have you? I guess you can wear one of mine. You're about my size. I'll get one."

When at last Rachel was alone in the little white room she stared about her on the immaculateness of everything and wondered at herself. How strange that she should be landed here, in a place whose name she did not know, in a stranger's house, without even her own night garments!

There was a comb and brush on the plain oak bureau. It was clean and immaculate like everything else. She took down her long braids and brushed them out, wondering how she was going to manage in the morning. No hairpins, no hat! Suppose she never got back her suitcase? And what of her trunk?

She got into the clean sheets and drew the homespun blanket and white Marseilles spread over her with a shiver, though it was not cold. She felt chilled to the bone, sick of life. How was she ever to go on and try to live again with all this behind her? Of course Chan Prescott was being wonderful to her, but he could not stay around always. She could not continue to accept his protection like this. How could she ever repay him now for all that he had done? And when he was gone, what? Life looked a sickening whirl in the future. It scarcely seemed worthwhile to go on. No job, no money, no place she dared go, and no one to care! How could she ever go to sleep with all that to think about?

Yet in five minutes she was fast asleep.

Chapter VII

Chan found himself suddenly weary and terribly sleepy as he started out once more alone in the dark. He recalled the story of a famous after-dinner speaker about a man who went into a dark room to find a black hat that was not there. He felt exactly like that. He was going through the dark to what? To find what? And when he got there would it be there? His tired brain found reasoning a hard matter. All he knew was that by morning he must have found some means of taking Rachel Rainsford into safety, and mighty early morning, too.

He tramped on down the road and began to wonder if the lightweight shoes which he had chosen for travel were going to stand all this wear and tear of climbing trees and jumping trains and tramping dark, rough roads. Still, that was a small matter. One could always buy new shoes.

And that brought him to the matter of Rachel's appearance. He had not thought of it until she spoke to the woman about it. But now he recalled that her dress was both soiled and torn, and how could a girl go a journey unsuspected without hat, or wrap to cover her dress? He ought to do something about that, but what could he, a man, do? And certainly the girl had no way of doing anything about it. He would have to work it out before morning somehow.

The stars were bright and near and friendly. He reflected that he had never before been out alone so near to them. Stars were distant lights that told when it was near morning as one was coming home from a dance. They had not been friendly nor interesting to him since the time when he was a kid in camp on the mountain and lay awake watching them blink while the other fellows around him were sleeping soundly. He looked up and experienced a sudden calm from their cool, clear shining. It steadied him. He had to take this thing seriously. Rachel was as much his responsibility as if she had been born in his family and were left alone on his hands. There was no one else to help her in this predicament, and his former connection with her father laid the absolute burden upon him. His breath came quicker at the thought, as he recalled the moments spent on the step of the freight train and the sweetness of her presence so close to him. He had not known a girl could make one feel like that. He had had his senses stirred by the sight and nearness of other girls, but never before this glow of holy reverence, this touch of something so deep and solemn in his soul that he almost was afraid to look it in the face and try to understand what it meant. It was enough now that he could help her, that he *must* stay by her and do everything in his power to put her beyond the possibility of those fiends to touch her. That was all he had a right to consider yet. But still there was in his mind a deeper sweeter something, a sense that this that was begun between them now was not to end with her mere safety.

But he must stop these flighty thoughts and decide what to do next.

About ten o'clock he began to enter a large town. He had no idea what its name was. He wished he had asked the woman, but concluded maybe it was better that he had not, for it would have shown at once his unfamiliarity with the region and have roused suspicions which might have reflected upon Rachel's character. Chan had been out many a time later than this with girls and had not been troubled lest they would be talked about. Girls nowadays did not mind gossip. It was nothing in their young lives. But this girl was different. This was Rachel Rainsford. Little Rachel of the haloed hair, who used to meet her father at the corner every night.

He had passed through several small villages, but when he came to this town he felt relieved. There would be shops here, and perhaps a place where he could get hold of a really good car that would make time and not go back on them in a crucial moment. He had plenty of express checks. There would be no trouble about getting anything he wanted if he could find it. Money was not a factor in this complication. He had always had all the money he wanted.

He was dog tired when at last he sighted a large garage, its lights still burning brightly, and a few loiterers sitting in the office smoking. There were two or three cars about the floor and one big new touring car in the window lighted up for display.

Chan sauntered along to the window and apparently studied the new model, while he reconnoitered. Then he strolled in idly and began examining the new car as if he were interested. An eager salesman shook off his sleepiness and came forward, exhibiting his wares exuberantly. It was not often they had a customer at so late an hour as this! Half past ten! He swallowed Chan's bait and showed him everything they had in stock.

Half an hour later Chan walked out having purchased a little secondhand coupe at a remarkably low price. They had promised to go over everything and have it in good running order by six o'clock sharp and also to fix him up in the matter of a temporary license.

Chan sauntered outside and eyed furtively a youth who leaned idly against one of the window frames. Chan liked his eyes—keen eyes, and his firm mouth that shut in controlled lines. He looked like the kind of fellow that enjoyed a good fight and could keep his mouth shut.

Chan came closer.

"Good hotel near here?" he asked casually.

The boy named it, without giving Chan more than a sweeping glance. "Two blocks over and three across," he added comprehensively inclining his head with the slightest possible movement in the direction that should be taken.

Chan waited a moment, looking the boy over, then spoke again.

"You work here?" he nodded his head back toward the garage.

The boy turned inquiring eyes briefly on him and looked away again:

"Help 'em out occasionally," he vouchsafed.

"How are they?" questioned Chan, lowering his tone. "Pretty reliable folks?"

"Fair," was the laconic reply.

"Own a car yourself?" was the next surprising question.

"Not yet!" There was determination in the firm lips, and clear intention for the near future.

Chan looked up the street and down before he ventured further.

"Left an old Ford down the road about seven miles," he said casually as if it were a common occurrence. "Couldn't make it run. Didn't have time to tinker it up. There's ten dollars in it if you wantta bring me the two suitcases I left in it, and I'll throw the Ford in."

The boy turned suspicious eyes on him now and looked him up and down coldly.

"No, you're wrong, kid!" said Chan laughing. "I didn't steal the old trap and I'm not a bootlegger. I simply got caught in a jam and had to buy the old can from a farmer who had taken it for a debt and didn't know how to run it. It went for a while but went back on me and I left it and took to walking. Couldn't of course carry two suitcases so I left 'em. I've got important business and can't stop now to go back, but there are a few things in those suitcases I'd like to keep. If you want the job of bringing them to that hotel you spoke of I'll see that there's another ten bucks waiting for you when you hand 'em in to the office. How about it? Wantta try to get 'em?"

"Got a license or anything to show it's your car?" The wise young eyes searched Chan.

"Oh, sure! Got an agreement of sale, and here. They gave me these where I bought it." Chan took out some papers and his fountain pen.

"I'll make the whole thing over to you and write an order for you to get 'em if you say so."

The boy studied the papers and handed them back indifferently:

"Awright!" he said as if he were agreeing to take a letter to the post office. "Where is't?"

Chan explained the position in which he had left the Ford.

"There's a coupla guys may make you some trouble," he added. "They were after the lady. I had to help her get away. They may tell you she is insane and they are taking her to an asylum, but it's a rotten lie. Anyway you don't know anything about the lady. She's far away by now. You were sent after the car by its owner. You don't know who left it there. See?"

The boy nodded, and gave Chan another keen glance.

Chan got out a ten-dollar bill and tendered it unostentatiously.

"Awright!" said the boy, accepting the challenge. He gathered in the bill as if it had been a piece of chewing gum or a cigarette, stuffed it indifferently into his trousers pocket and lounged up into an alert attitude. Placing two fingers in his mouth he emitted a bloodcurdling whistle that seemed to rouse the echoes, and almost instantly another young fellow appeared out of the shadows at the side of the garage.

"Get your motorbike, Tad. We're going on a ride. Gotta get this gent's car outta trouble. And say, Tad," as the other turned instantly to obey orders, "better wear yer uniform and badge."

The second boy disappeared with alacrity.

"Now," said Chan in a businesslike tone, "I'll give you a card to identify you when you come back to the hotel. I won't be there myself, but I'll leave word to have the baggage forwarded, and I'll leave the money to pay you and the other fellow. I'll make it two tens if you get both suitcases safely. It's worth it for the lady had things in hers that she thought a lot of. Well, so long! Good luck to you. Look you up next time I come this way. Hope the old can runs for you."

He put out a genial hand and the boy put a powerful paw into it and gave him a grip that made him want to yell. But there was something hearty in it, like the grip of one who understood, and Chan passed on into the shadows of the street, well satisfied that if there were any possibility of getting hold of that baggage that boy would get it.

After Chan had registered his full name at the hotel, Chauncey Gaylord Prescott, and his home address, he hurried to his room and put in a long-distance call for his chauffeur.

While he was waiting for it to go through he began to review the strange happenings of the day, and he found that whenever he thought of Rachel a strange thrill came over him. Here he was, Chan Prescott, the most irresponsible person in all the universe, with this pearl of a girl dependent upon him for safety! How amazing the day had been.

But most amazing of all the happenings had been that ride they had taken together on the freight train, his arm about her, her hair blowing softly across his face. Whenever he thought of it the memory gave him a suffocating sensation of wonder and joy such as he had never experienced before. It was as if something holy had suddenly come into his life. He had never believed that anything was holy. Not since the day when he found that his stepmother did not want to kiss him when he had fallen and hurt himself, because his face was all smeared with blood and dirt. Something bright and beautiful had seemed to die in him then, and he had taken it for granted that everything was disappointing: that men were meant to be hard and brave and have a jolly good time, and that gentleness and tenderness were weaknesses. And now, suddenly, he seemed to have discovered that he had been mistaken. He was almost afraid to think about it. It seemed too sacred for even thought to touch more than lightly. He was filled with wonder at himself.

His meditations were broken in upon by the tinkle of the telephone bell and presently he heard the voice of his chauffeur answering:

"Is that you, Jim?" he called. "Well, where is Andy? Right there? That's good. I want you both to start for Chicago right away in my new car. Yes, the *new* one. Can you do it? How soon? In an hour? The car all in good shape? That's right. Well, I figured if you spelled each other and kept right on going you could make it in thirty-six hours or thereabouts. Think so? What's that? Who has to get back? Andy? Oh—when does he have to be back? Well, if *you* figured on taking the last relay yourself, you could put him down somewhere and let him get the express back. He ought to be able to make that in time. Ask him if he is willing to do that."

There was a pause and then the voice at the other end of the wire assented and Chan went on with his directions:

"You better bring my other suitcase. The one I packed for the Adirondacks. And meet me at the same hotel in Chicago where we stopped last summer. You remember? That's right. Got plenty of money for the trip? All right. Don't take any risks. Even if you lose an hour or two. I want the car to come through in good shape. What's that? Do I want you to stay with me? No, that won't be necessary. I'll drive back myself. You can stay in the city a day or so if you like and get good and rested and then take a little bus I've picked up on the way and drive back. That is if it's fit by that time for such a trip. If not you can go back by train. You're sure the car is all ready for the trip? You had it all gone over this week? All right. So long! See you in Chicago sometime day after tomorrow."

Chan hung up the receiver and sat back, a big load off his mind. When he got his own car he would be able to take Rachel to any part of the continent with all the speed desired. That was one trouble out of the way. Now, what else must be settled before he slept?

He puckered his brows and set himself to the unwonted task of thinking. Why, what use would a car be if one had no place to go? Where was he going to take Rachel when he got the car? Well, that would have to be discussed with her, finally, of course, but really unless she had some definite destination would it not devolve upon him to suggest a refuge for her present need? And where could he possibly find a refuge? His mother? Chan turned from the thought instantly, realizing that Rachel in her plain little dress smeared with gum from the pine tree, and her plain little hat—why, she had lost her hat!—would cut no figure to appeal to his haughty supercilious mother. It gave him an unpleasant sensation to realize how uncomfortable she would probably be able to make the girl feel should he have the temerity to appeal to his mother for protection for this precious responsibility of his. Besides his mother was in Europe.

There were two or three aunts more or less involved in the social world, from the thought of whose sharp tongues he also turned without even considering them. There was a nurse, an old dependent of the family, but she was living alone in one room in a little village among the mountains. He could take Rachel there perhaps, and pay her board for a time, but where would she board? Old Hannah had no place to offer save the sharing of her own bed, and, respectable as she was, Chan shrank from the thought of placing Rachel even for a few days in the same room with a servant. Rachel was too fine to be thrust into unpleasant contacts and undue familiarity with one not in their own class, at least so thought Chan whose upbringing, what there was of it, had been one of much class distinction.

And even if there were no other refuge than old Hannah's room it was too far away for the present emergency, for Hannah lived up in New England.

What was neeeded at present was a place where the girl could rest and get her bearings, and find a way out of her present situation. Then when her pursuers had given up the chase and all was forgotten she could come out of hiding and go safely to wherever she wished. Also by that time he would have been able to think out a plan for her future that would put her out of reach of such adventurers as Trevor.

Suddenly there flashed into his mind a solution of the. problem so simple that it amazed him he had not thought of it before.

The house party! Why should he not take her along? There, if anywhere, would be absolute safety. And Mrs. Southerly was a lady. She could be depended upon to accept his statements absolutely and take Rachel in. He could say—what could he say? Why, that she was the daughter of a former teacher, a charming girl, on her way to California. That he had met her by accident on the train and found she was stopping over a few days in Chicago. Might he bring her with him for the weekend? And Mrs. Southerly would be only too delighted. He knew he was a favorite with her, and that his father's name and wealth would pave the way for anything he asked. He was fully aware that Mrs. Southerly appreciated his acceptance of her invitation, and would be cordial to the limit. Why, wasn't that just the right solution? Of course it was. Rachel might demur at first, but in the end he felt he could make her see that it was the safest and merriest way out of their dilemma. Then, wandering about the beautiful lakeside, or paddling on the mirror-clearness of its waters, or seated in some luxurious corner of the wide summer mansion, they would have ample leisure to discuss the future without fear of interruption.

With a smile of satisfaction Chan reached for his telephone once more and called for long distance. In another half hour during which he had done some rapid thinking and even written out once or twice what he was going to say to his hostess, he heard her pleasant voice at last upon the wire, and Chan blurted out his tale without using a single sentence which he had so carefully prepared. Still, what did it matter? Chan was always able to carry off a situation, and Mrs. Southerly was all that he had expected she would be. She was charmed to have Miss Rainsford. The daughter of a former professor! She mentally tacked on the prefix of "college" to the professor, and scented romance at once. She dearly loved romance, and her present household had only one budding possibility of that sort. One needed two or three couples with at least a show of interest in one another to give zest to a house party and keep things from becoming prosaic. Yes, indeed, she would welcome his friend, and the more so because one of her girl guests had sent word at the last minute that she had sprained her ankle and could not come for several days.

Chan was duly grateful and promised to let her know sometime the next day, as soon as he was able to see Miss Rainsford and convey the invitation to her. He would do all in his power to persuade her to accept, and he felt little doubt but that he would be successful unless indeed she had made some previous engagement of which he did not know.

When the conversation was concluded he hung up the receiver with a feeling of relief. He could enjoy himself once more, now that he had shifted the immediate responsibility upon Mrs. Southerly's shoulders. But almost at once he began to remember Rachel's firm little chin, and to wonder if after all she would be quite so easy to persuade as he had thought. Of course she had not met Mrs. Southerly. And the whole thing was a bit irregular. Still the circumstances were irregular, and he hoped to be able to persuade her that this opportunity to rest in a quiet safe haven for a few days until the enemy was out of sight was providential.

He began to question what objections she would put up against his plan and remembered her apology to the gray-haired woman. Her appearance! Ah! That might be a real objection! He could not take a girl to one of Mrs. Southerly's house parties without the proper clothes. She would feel most uncomfortable, and so would her hostess. Besides, it wouldn't do at all. It just wouldn't look right. What could he do? Go out and buy her something? But no, he wouldn't know what to get, and the girl wouldn't either, perhaps, and if he tried to tell her she would be all kinds of scared at the idea of going at all. No, he must manage it somehow and keep his own counsel. If only he were in New York now, there were two or three people he knew who would help him out! Aunt Fan would just love buying an outfit for a friend of his who had lost her baggage, and would ask him no questions. But Aunt Fan was in the mountains, far away from all the stores. Chan had many friends of all sorts widely scattered, and he presently remembered a young woman he had met in Chicago during the past winter, a girl with talent and brains who had renounced a social career for a business life, and occupied a fine position in one of the great department stores of Chicago. She had something to do with helping purchasers in their selections, or selecting goods for out-of-town buyers who ordered through the mails. The very thing! Her name was Caroline Robertson. Now if he could only find her. He reached for the telephone again, glancing at his watch as he did so. It was almost an hour past midnight, but if she had gone out for the evening she might be just getting home. He would try for it.

After some brilliant detective work, with the telephone operator and "information" to aid and abet him, he finally succeeded in getting her number and found to his satisfaction that she was still up, had indeed just come in as he had hoped, and greeted him in a friendly way.

"Say, what about doing me a favor?" he asked. "You still in business?"

"Oh, surely," said the girl crisply.

"Well, it's in your line I guess. Got a commission for you. Girlfriend of mine lost her baggage, and we're both booked for the same house party. Just happened to meet her on the train by chance and told her I'd see what I could do to help her out. She's too far from home to get anything sent in time, and she has nothing with her but the dress she has on, and that's pretty well messed up traveling. Can you get some things together by twelve o'clock tomorrow when I'll call for them? It'll be a coupla days anyway and maybe more before her own things arrive and you know about what she'll need. How's that for a proposition? Can you make it?"

"Why, I guess so," came the crisp voice reassuringly. "Do
you know her size?"

"Great Scott! I forgot that!" said Chan in dismay. "And I
won't see her till sometime tomorrow, but she's just about
your size. She's slim, you know. Probably wears a size eight
or ten. You can chance it on that I'm sure. She reminded me
of you in her build. Just fit yourself and I'm sure it'll be all
right."

"Did she say what she wanted?"

"Well, no, she didn't because she didn't see how it was to
be worked in time. She thinks she can't go. I'm trying to fix
it up for her. See? Then if anything isn't right she can
change it when I take it to her hotel, can't she? What's that?
Shoe number? Glove? Oh, yes, I can tell you when I call to
get it, but you have *your* size ready and I'll wager it'll be hers
to a dot."

"What kind of a girl is she? What's her style and build?
What's her coloring? Is she dashing or quiet?"

"Oh!" said Chan with a perplexed voice. "Gosh, that's
right, you have to know all that, don't you? Well, she's quiet
and refined. None of your flappers. She's a real lady.
Daughter of a professor. Good old family. Goes in for serious things and all that. But she's small and young, delicate
features you know, and clear skin. No makeup! Gosh, you
ought to see her! Do your heart good! She's the real thing!
Got eyebrows all her own, straight and fine, and glorious
red hair. What's that? Bobbed? Not on your life! Yes, got a
lot of it, and fixes it all right, too. Eyes? Yes, brown to go
with her hair. Oh, yes, she's fair—sure. You oughtta see her.
She's unusual."

"Well, about what will she want? Is it a country place?"

"Mountain lake place. Private, you understand. Very nice
people. Oh, she'll need sports things mostly and evening
things. You know she doesn't want to have to borrow. She
simply won't go if she has to, I know her. Just begin at the
beginning and get a suitcase full and a hatbox, enough for

two or three days at least. Don't forget a bathing suit. She'll
probably need that. And brushes and things. I tell you she
hasn't got a thing except what's on her back. What's that?
Price? Oh! Well, I don't imagine that matters. It has to be
suitable, that's the main thing. Suitable, but not flashy.
Think you can get an outfit for around a thousand or will it
cost more? All right, I'll mail you my check and she and I
can settle it up later. Yes, get what *you* think is suitable.
She'll be satisfied. I'll guarantee that. All right. Thanks!
Where'll I come to get 'em? Which department? I see. All
right, hope to make it by noon. You see we got stranded
here at a little backwoods town. Oh, didn't I explain before?
And if she stops to shop in Chicago we won't get there in
time. Think you can have the things ready by twelve? Yes,
that'll be plenty of time. Thanks awfully. Do you a favor
sometime. And I hope you get a big commission out of this."

Well satisfied Chan went to bed at last. But even there his
busy brain could not relax. It had occurred to him that Rachel needed a hat in the morning to travel in. If there were
eager detectives on their track a hatless red-haired girl
would be altogether too obvious.

He was still working on the problem when he woke up in
the morning hours earlier than was his custom. He felt like
an old man with great responsibilities. A sharp fear shot
through him. What if someone had been watching them,
had tracked them, and knew where he had left Rachel!
What if even now she was in the possession of the enemy?
What if he would have to spend the remainder of his life
searching insane asylums for her? For he knew with a great
assurance that if anything happened to Rachel Rainsford he
would never rest until he had rescued her. Why on earth had
he ever left her? He ought to have camped outside the house
until morning. Only how could he? He had to get a car and
get all those other things done, didn't he? What a queer mess
for him to be in anyway!

Meantime a call had gone out to officers of the law

through all the country, "Watch for redheaded girl in brown dress and hat, accompanied by young man in gray tweed suit. Both escaped from private insane asylum, both dangerous patients."

CHAPTER VIII

Rachel came sharply awake about three o'clock in the morning, her mind alert to much that had not been plain to her in the maze of the day before.

Among other things, the most important seemed that she must find a way at once to relieve Chan Prescott from the responsibility of getting her to a place of safety.

Morning had brought saner thoughts. Her cheeks burned over the remembrance of that ride on the caboose steps. It had been kind and wonderful of him to care for her so tenderly, and she would never forget his thoughtfulness; but she had no right to let her heart thrill over his courtesy. The arm he put around her had been entirely necessary for her safety, and it had been done in a most impersonal way, absolutely nothing about Chan's manner to make her feel that he was doing anything except render the plainest commonplace assistance to the daughter of his former teacher who happened to be in a predicament. She had been tired last night or she never would have had those sentimental feelings about it. She must guard herself. Chan Prescott was a most fascinating young man, but he belonged to a different world from hers. That he had stepped aside from his own path to help her for a few hours was no reason why she should presume upon his friendship afterward. It was her business as a self-respecting young woman to get herself upon her own feet and relieve him of herself as soon as possible.

That the lonely ache of both body and spirit should not get her in its grip she fell to planning what she could do. She would not go back to her home. It would be too humiliating. Of course she could explain to her old friends that her job did not prove to be what she had expected, and she must try again. But if she returned she would only be making herself a burden to them, and they could not afford to be burdened with her. That was out of the question.

There was an old crochety aunt of her father's with plenty of money to whom she might go as a last resort, but she had been so disagreeable at the time of her father's funeral that Rachel shrank intensely from further contact with her. Her tongue was like a scorching flame in its withering sarcasm. She had advised Rachel to take a position as child's nurse, and said she knew a woman who would give her board and three dollars a week. Rachel did not feel that she could turn to her now. It would not be pleasant to bear her scorn. She felt she would rather starve and be by herself.

As she lay still in the darkness she gradually came to the conclusion that she would ask Chan to drive her to some railroad station where she could get a train to New York. She had never been there but once but it seemed a good place to be lost in. Surely there must be plenty to do in a great city. She would go to one of her father's old colleagues who was teaching in a high school in the Bronx and ask him how to go about getting a position in a library or something. Or possibly she could take an examination and get a job in one of the lower grades of the public schools.

She had just money enough to take her to New York she thought, and she would ask Chan if he could lend her twenty-five dollars to tide her over until she could get a job, or maybe fifty. Fifty dollars would be plenty. She could live on very little. Then when she got a job she would save every cent she could until she got Chan paid back. Of course he wouldn't be in a hurry. He had plenty of money, and he was kind. He wanted to help her and this was the only self-respecting way in which she ought to accept his help. She certainly ought not to go traveling through the country with him, living on his bounty. It was not according to the code in which she had been brought up. She ought not to allow herself to be placed in situations where a young man who was almost an utter stranger would be compelled to take her in his arms to lift her out of trees, or hold her on freight trains.

She knew that her mother would advise her of this at once if her mother were still on the earth to speak to her. And her own heart told her that it was not for her good to be much in the company of this impetuously kind and most fascinating young hero. She was a poor girl with her living to earn, and she must not let her head get turned or her heart tangled up in a hopeless love affair right at the start.

As the light began to steal in on the edge of dawn her spirit rose, strong to meet the contingencies of the day. It no longer seemed probable or actual that two men were spending time trying to find her. What was there in herself to attract wicked men? Surely there was safety for her now in a clear bright day with the open world before her.

As soon as she could see in her room without turning on the electric light Rachel slipped softly out of bed and began putting herself in battle array. She had a needle and a few lengths of brown sewing silk in her handbag and with these she carefully mended the tear in the sleeve and skirt of her brown crepe de chine. But she could not mend out the long streaks of resin from the pine tree she had climbed, nor put back into place the sleazy threads that had pulled till the whole fabric of the front breadth was skewed and distorted in places.

She found three hairpins in her handbag also which helped somewhat, and carefully brushing her hair, she arranged it in bands with a caplike effect over the top of her head. After more consideration in front of the looking glass she finally removed the narrow girdle of her dress, and bound it around her head with a neat flat bow at one side. It did not look much like a hat at close range but perhaps it would pass for a semblance of one as she was driving along the road in a car. At least she would not attract quite so much attention as she would if she were entirely bareheaded.

She felt greatly troubled about her shoes. They were badly scuffed and streaked with mud from her long walk over the rough roads, but she worked over them with a bit of newspaper which she found in the wastebasket, until they were at least clean. And then, having done all she could to present a good appearance, she knelt down beside the bed and began to pray:

"Oh, Lord, I've lost my job and my baggage, and almost everything I have left in the world. I haven't any friends I ought to trouble to help me except this young man, and I know it isn't right to let him go on taking care of me. Please open the way and show me what to do. And please take care of me for I've no one else in the world."

She remained on her knees for some minutes after this simple request, and then added:

"And please help me to follow You and not to be a fool!"

There was a car coming along the road at last. It was stopping at the front gate. She hurried to the window. Yes, it was Chan and he had something in his hand. Could it be her suitcase Oh, if it was! How glad she would be! No, it was a box. Now what had Chan been doing? How was she to prevent his doing all these things for her?

Mrs. Davis knocked at her door and handed in the box.

"The young man thought you would want to put these things on before you came down," she explained interestedly. "And breakfast is ready as soon as you are."

Rachel stood for a minute looking at the box and listening to the retreating footsteps of Mrs. Davis.

She was much worried about this box. She must not let Chan buy things for her. Perhaps it would be better not to open the box at all. Just take it down and tell him she could not accept anything.

She half turned to go into the hall, but a sudden ray of light revealed words written on the box lid:

"Explanation inside!
                    C.P."

She stepped back and opened the box, trying to still the flutter of childish delight that went over her.

"Silly!" she told herself, "utterly silly!"

But she opened the box and there lay Chan's card with writing across the name:

"This is a disguise. I'll explain later. Put it on quick! We ought to get away. Chan."

There was something in the brisk command that stirred Rachel's fears once more, and stilled her objections. She put the little card safely into the pocket of her bag and with eager hands pulled away the tissue paper. On the top was a little green felt hat, plain and simple, and trimmed with only a rosette of tailored ribbon of the same shade. She caught her breath in delight, it was so like what she wanted and would have bought but for the lack of money. She lifted it out and there beneath it lay a pretty silk dress of the same shade of green, folded softly in tissue paper and showing a touch of ecru frills in the vest and a dashing line of black in the little string tie.

She closed her door and with swift fingers took off her torn, brown frock, unwound the brown girdle from her hair, donned the green dress and hat, pulling the hat far down over her hair, and adjusting it with innate grace as she had seen other girls wearing these new lovely felts. It was big enough to wrinkle into a generous fold on the crown, and one glance in the mirror showed it was wonderfully becoming. She could not help being pleased. Somehow she felt as if she had suddenly donned armor for the fight of the day. It was strange and exciting how clothes did that to you—made you feel fit to face hard things—when they were right and proper. She looked at herself again, drawing her breath hard. She ought not to accept these things, but perhaps, under the circumstances, it was all right. She could pay for them later when she got a good job. She would insist upon that. And she would only ask to borrow twenty-five. Then she would repay it all together.

Hastily she folded her old brown gown into the tissue wrappings, tied it into the box and hurried downstairs, trying to look as if this green hat and dress had always been hers and the young man had merely been to her home and brought them to her.

The breakfast was delicious. Delectable sausage, brown as velvet, hashed brown potatoes, and batter cakes, puffy and light, served with hot maple syrup and coffee rich with cream. The hungry fugitives ate eagerly, across the little round table from one another, while their smiling hostess came and went from the gas range nearby with fresh supplies of hotcakes. They could not talk much with the eager eyes of their hostess upon them and her ear alert for any clue she might catch to their identity, but long afterward if you asked either of those two what was their ideal breakfast they would tell you hotcakes and sausage.

Just as they were rising from the last cake they could possibly have swallowed, Chan said casually, casting a look of admiration at the girl:

"Did they get the right things you wanted? I told 'em you wanted the green ones."

And Rachel cast a twinkling smile at him and said demurely with a glance at her new garments:

"Yes, they are all right."

Mrs. Davis gave an approving glance at her young guest and added her word:

"That certainly is a fetching little rig. You look real rested after your long walk. You got your car going all right, did you?" to Chan, with a glance out the door at the little gray runabout standing by the gate.

Chan smilingly assented and paid her roundly for his breakfast and her kindness.

He handed Rachel into the car, sprang in beside her, let in the clutch and was off down the road. It is safe to say that the little car, though it may have had some wild handling in its time, had never before traveled at the pace that Chan drove it for the next hour. Down one road, up another, crossing and recrossing, until he shot into a wood and out again on a long smooth ribbon of pike and settled into a more steady pace. Then he sat back and surveyed his companion.

She had sat straight and silent, during the first breathtaking part of their ride, her eyes shining and her cheeks faintly pink with the pleasure of it, and now as he looked at her with the unveiled admiration in his eyes her cheeks grew pinker still.

"Say, you certainly are a stunner, Ray!" he exclaimed. "Got the right color all right, didn't I? Hadn't much choice it's true, but I liked that. It sort of went with your hair. Saw it in the window as I went for the car, and pumped the man who was washing the sidewalk till I found out where the proprietor lived and hailed him away from his breakfast to get it for me. I told him I wanted it for a present for my best girl!"

The color swept up into her cheeks once more and she lifted her eyes with a look almost as if the pleasure of his words hurt her.

"Oh!" she protested anxiously. "You ought not to have done that. It was very kind of you, Mr. Prescott, of course, and I just love them both, but you know you ought not to have done it. I am making you no end of inconvenience and trouble, and I'm very much worried about it."

"Trouble?" said Chan, looking down at her tenderly. "I haven't had any trouble. Why, I'm having the time of my life. Don't let yourself be disturbed on my account. I always did love a chase, and this has been a rare one, although I hope for your sake it is about over."

"But I *am* troubled," went on Rachel seriously. "It really is terrible, you going out of your way all this time, and buying a lot of things—going to so much expense. Of course, the expense I shall be able to repay you I hope very soon when I am settled in a job somewhere. But the upsetting of all your plans I never can undo, and I feel overwhelmed with obligation."

She had taken a tone, new in their acquaintance, so grave that she suddenly seemed to Chan to have grown years older, to be almost older than himself, and much wiser. He drew his nice brows together and turned to her.

"Look here, girlie, you're all on the wrong track. I hadn't any special plans. I was just off on a pleasure excursion, and if I find more pleasure in looking after you just now and seeing that you are safe, haven't I a right to change my plans without making everybody uncomfortable?"

A little trembling smile dawned about her lips.

"You are very kind," she said. "My father always said you were the kindest boy in his class."

Chan was deeply touched.

"Did he say that?" he asked huskily. "Well now, I feel honored indeed. Your father was a wonderful man if there ever was one in high school. But I was a regular scapegrace, I guess. Anyhow I know I was never very kind to him in the way of studying much. Say, Ray, what do you mean by that mister stuff? Can't you call me Chan? I don't want to be held off like a stranger."

"But—we *are* almost strangers, you know," said Rachel practically, looking down at the new green gown and smoothing it gently with her fingers, then lifting brave little-girl eyes that reminded him of her childhood.

"Not after yesterday," said Chan firmly. "Besides, we both loved your father. Isn't that introduction enough to bridge over the mister? Why, everybody calls me Chan. I don't feel at home when you stick on mister. Say, Ray, why don't you and I just get married and get over all this trouble? Nobody could touch us if you belonged to me. I could have them jailed in no time if they laid a finger on you. What do you say?"

CHAPTER IX

Rachel turned a startled look on him, thinking at first
that he was joking, but he went on eagerly:

"Say, that would be great! We could just drive on up to
Chicago and get my car. I've had it sent on—telephoned for
it you know last night—and then we'll go wherever you like
on a honeymoon."

But Rachel laid a frightened hand on his arm to interrupt:

"Don't, please," she said gently, "I can't bear you to joke
about such things. You have been most kind, but I really
must get on my own now, you know. I was going to ask you
if you would be kind enough to take me to the nearest railroad station, and then if you could lend me money enough
to get back to New York State I will go to an aunt who lives
there and stay till I find a good position. I shall soon be able
to repay you. No, please let me finish before you speak. I
thought it all out last night. I really couldn't let you carry
me all around the country this way. It isn't the right
thing. Mother would be horrified at me, not finding a way
to relieve you sooner. If I had remembered all that mother
taught me I wouldn't have been in such a mess as this
anyway. I ought not to have trusted that man! I have learned
a lesson."

"You mean you don't trust me?" Chan asked sharply.

"Oh, no! No, indeed!" she hastened to explain. "I trust
you perfectly! You have been just wonderful! Nobody could
have been more——" she hesitated for a word, "more beautiful!" she finished shyly.

Chan smiled and put one hand briefly over hers in a warm
clasp.

"But I really—you know yourself—a girl mustn't go
around this way and let herself be dependent on a man, no

96

matter how fine he is. It's up to me to take care of myself now that it's daylight. You know it isn't right."

She appealed to him with a look.

"It's being done quite a good deal, little girl," he said gently, "but it isn't your style, I'll admit. Most girls don't care nowadays what people say or think about them; but *I* care for *you,* and that's why I suggested we get married right off the bat without waiting for any preliminaries. That'll satisfy all the conventions and make it no end of pleasant all around. Can't you see it that way?"

Rachel drew away in a troubled silence, then looked up again shyly as if she did not want to hurt him, yet knew she must speak the truth.

"But—Chan——" she spoke the name gently, using it for the first time to help him see that she appreciated his greatheartedness, and his heart gave a queer little leap that brought a sparkle to his eyes—"but, people ought not to marry, unless—unless they love one another very much—unless they are *perfectly sure* that each one is the only one the other could ever put in that place in the heart. And *we* are just—well, practically *strangers!* It wouldn't be right no matter how much we like each other to jump into a sacred thing like that—and for life! It was meant to be a holy relation!"

He was watching her now with a dawning reverence. They had come to a little stretch of woods and he stopped the car by the roadside and turned toward her.

"But, Ray, if it was a matter of practically saving your life."

Rachel shook her head.

"I ought not to do a wrong thing even to save my life. My mother taught me what a holy thing the marriage relation was, and how terrible it could be unless there was the right kind of love behind it. No, if it came to a matter of life or death I think God would have to look out for me. I don't think He would want me to do wrong just because I was in a panic."

She had lifted earnest eyes to his, and was talking in a low voice, a lovely glow of earnestness in her face. Chan had a sudden wild impulse to throw his arms about her and strain her to his heart, covering her face with kisses. But instead he leaned a little nearer to her and spoke in a low earnest tone, himself quite grave now and almost pleading.

"Ray," he said, very gently, and laid a reverent hand once more on hers, "you don't understand, quite. I do love you. I've loved you ever since I saw you in the train. Before I knew who you were, when there was just a vague memory, I wanted to shove the man out of the seat behind you and take his place where I could sit and watch you. I almost fell over the people in the aisle twisting my head to look at you, and when I found out who you were, then I knew that I had loved you away back through the years. I know in my soul now—I found it out last night—that I had loved you ever since you were a little kid coming to meet your daddy with that golden light in your eyes and the sun on your glorious curls. Now, do you understand? And, kid! didn't you feel it too, last night? Didn't something pass from your hand to mine when I held you close on that frightful ride on the freight? Didn't it seem dear to you as it did to me? Tell me, was I all alone in thinking that you and I were somehow one and that it was the greatest thing on earth for both of us? Answer me, please!"

Rachel was a full minute waiting with eyes cast down, her hand quivering in his, half ready to slip out and away from his clasp. Then she lifted clear eyes to his face and her voice was low and sweet as she answered:

"Yes—Chan—I felt it! It was beautiful! I've been thinking a lot about it all night! But, Chan, my mother taught me that it takes something more than just that to make a happy life together. That's very important, of course. But it is just one third of the whole. That was the senses, and it was very sweet. But we don't live in our senses alone—or at least we oughtn't to. We've got minds and spirits, and two people whose minds or whose spirits are at variance could not be happy for long together on just the senses. My mother and my father, too, took great pains to make that very plain to me."

"Well, and how do you know but our minds and our spirits are alike? If we feel like that together, isn't it likely?"

Rachel looked troubled.

"Not necessarily," she said slowly. "You see, this house we live in——" she slid her hand out from under Chan's and lifted it to show him what she meant, "this house of flesh, is full of electrical currents, like the wiring of a house. That's how father explained it to me, and when we bring the wires together the current is bound to flash along the whole circuit. And we have no business to bring them together unless we really belong. That was why father objected to dancing. He said it gave license for too much personal contact, and young people especially were misled and took it for a deeper feeling. They thought it meant mind and spirit too, when it was only just the senses. And then when it was too late and they had spoiled their lives they found out it was only the flesh deceiving them. He said that these feelings were not the main thing in lives. They were meant to come after and add beauty and light and glory, just as the lighting system of a house is not the place we live in, but only an added beauty; a thing to rejoice in, but not a thing to shelter us."

Chan looked at her as if she had been speaking in an unknown tongue, which however he was somehow dimly comprehending.

"Your father was a wonderful man," he said at length, his eyes lowering almost as if he were abashed in her presence. "I—never heard any talk like that before. Especially not from a girl. Most of the girls I know are all for petting parties. I've always taken it for granted all girls liked that sort of thing, and it was a part of life—at least till you settled down."

Rachel was silent for an instant, then she said, lifting earnest eyes:

"Mother used to say the lights of the house were not for

everybody to turn on. They are for the master's hand only. They are the crowning glory. She said that for anyone else it was uncleanness, impurity." She paused again abashed at her own temerity.

Chan was sitting like a statue looking straight ahead, his handsome brows drawn, his firm lips set sternly, a look of almost consternation in his usually merry face. He did not answer nor stir for a full minute. She began to be afraid he was offended. He had the attitude of one who had been rebuked.

At last he drew a long breath like a sigh:

"Gosh!" he said earnestly. "Why didn't I know a mother like that? You're right! I don't match you! I don't even fit in the flesh. I never heard of standards like that. You're a wonderful girl. As for my mind, it's a cinch I couldn't match up there! I never did study much. Your father must have told you that. He wrestled many months to get me passed from one grade to another. And I don't even know if I've got a spirit. If I have it's a wild one, I'm sure of that! You win! I'm no account!"

With that Chan threw in the clutch and was off with a jerk down the road as if they were going to sudden destruction.

Rachel watched him for several miles, his eyes set sternly, his gaze ahead, the look on his face of a man thrashing out a terrible situation. He seemed to have forgotten her existence. At last she could stand it no longer for he looked as if he was hurt, rebuked, rebuffed. And he had been for a whole twenty-four hours going out of his way to do everything imaginable for her! She put out a timid hand and laid it on his sleeve.

"Please," she said, lifting troubled eyes to his stern face. "Please don't look like that! I did not mean to criticize you! I was only giving you my reasons!"

For answer he stopped the car and looked at her:

"Look here," he said. "Isn't there any way back for a fellow that didn't know—that never understood? Can't we get a second try? I've never been what you'd call *bad*—but——!"

"Oh!" said Rachel eagerly, a light coming into her eyes. "Yes, there is a way for sin to be forgiven."

"*Sin!*" said Chan aghast. "You call it *sin?*"

Rachel grew grave.

"Well—isn't it?"

"What *is* sin?" asked Chan sharply, "according to your code?"

"Sin is any want of conformity unto or transgression of the law of God," responded Rachel quickly.

Chan turned a quick glance at her.

"Where did you get that?" he asked keenly. "You never made that up on the spur of the moment. Did your father say that?"

"Oh, no," smiled Rachel. "That's the Westminster Shorter Catechism. I was brought up on that."

"I should say you were! So you think petting parties are breaking the law of God, do you?"

"Don't you? He said our bodies were the temple of the Holy Ghost, and we must keep them pure."

Chan was still a long time and then he said:

"I guess you're right."

He started the car and drove thoughtfully for some minutes. At last he turned to her again:

"Well, if I'm not fit to marry you I'll have to find some other way to take care of you. I sure am not going to leave you alone in this part of the country on some railway train for those two beasts to devour, and I guess it's about up to you to do what I say till I get you where you are safe. See?"

Rachel smiled with a breath of relief. He was almost like his former self again.

"I didn't say you were not fit to marry," she said wistfully. "I just said such things were—sacred and not to be rushed into hurriedly. You don't really know me, nor I you."

"I know you well enough to be sure I'd like to spend the rest of my life getting acquainted," said Chan stubbornly. "But of course I can't expect a girl like you to feel that way about me. I'm not really worth much. I suppose your father told you that. If I'd known there was *you* in the world I'd have spent my time trying to be worth something. But I see you're right. My proposition can't work out in a day, anyway, and we've got to get one that will for the present. But you needn't think I have forgotten because I don't talk about it. We're not more than an hour's drive now from the outskirts of Chicago and we haven't much more time left to decide. The question is: Are you willing to go where I say for a few days till everything is safe for you to go wherever you like? I can't see leaving you around on trains for those fiends to snap up, even if you do want to be independent."

Rachel looked up with troubled eyes.

"But where do you want me to go? I really can't go on indefinitely letting you take all this trouble and spending all this money."

"Forget it! Money's nothing! I spend more than this on folderols every day of my life somehow or other. If it hadn't been this way it would have been something else not worth half so much. As for the trouble I figure I'm enjoying what I'm doing now better than anything I ever did in my life. I'm enjoying it so much that I'd like to go right on doing it all my life. Just figure that you're giving me pleasure. Won't that cut any ice with you? Pay me back for what you think I've done in letting me do a little more, that's all I ask."

Rachel gave him a look that fully repaid all he had done, but the trouble was still in her eyes.

"But it isn't *right*, you know. It isn't the right thing for a girl to let a man do all this for her. You have helped me while I was in danger and I shall be grateful all my life, but the time has come when I should be self-respecting and take care of myself."

"You're not out of danger yet by a long haul!" said Chan, facing her squarely with a straight true look. "Young woman, I suppose I might as well be frank with you. I saw that old rascal sign a check for a thousand dollars and give it to the other man to help him get possession of you! Do you understand what that would mean, or do I have to explain further? Where would your self-respect be if that happened? He's got all kinds of money and all kinds of pull, and he could put you into some place where you could never get out. And he would keep you for his plaything! Do you understand?"

Rachel's eyes were wide with terror. For a moment she looked at him white to the lips, then she buried her face in her hands with a shudder and shrank into the corner of the seat.

They were driving along a country road with very little traffic, and Chan was going slowly. His heart was broken with the sight of her. As if she had been a little child he reached out and drew her to him with a comforting touch, and she turned her face and hid it against his shoulder, another shudder passing over her.

"Oh," she said after a moment, lifting her face up, still white and filled with horror, "I can never thank you enough. You think I don't understand what you have done for me, but I do, *I do!* My father always said you were true and wonderful in a trying time, and I know what he meant now. Yes, I will do what you want me to do. I did not realize that there was still danger."

"Well, I don't want to frighten you," said Chan, his arm still protectively about her shoulders with yet a respectful touch, his face full of unwonted tenderness, "and of course I may not be the wisest person to guide you, but it strikes me that man isn't going to let a thousand bucks go for nothing even if he is rich, and the other little rat is going to hold on to that bit of paper pretty darned tight. He won't stop at anything if he gets on our tracks. He wants to make good his bargain so that he can do business in future."

Rachel sat up with a brave little smile now, as if she would reassure him.

"I'm all right now," she said, "I really am. It just all came over me how terrible it was. My mother and my father! They would have felt it so! They always safeguarded me. It seems so strange that I should have come into this as soon as they left me! I suppose I was too proud to ask advice. I know now I should not have answered that advertisement without finding out who the people were."

Chan looked at her sharply.

"You answered an advertisement?" he questioned. "Tell me all about it. What paper was it in?"

"I don't know," said Rachel with a troubled look. "It was an advertisement the washerwoman brought me. She said she found it in a paper where she worked, but she did not bring the paper, just tore this out and there wasn't a mark on it anywhere to tell. Only she said it was that day's paper, and it sounded so fine I tried it."

"Where did you have to go to answer it?"

"Why, that worried me some," said Rachel, looking more anxious now. "It was on a little side street down below Third Street in the city. It was called Lillian Street. I had trouble finding it. Nobody had ever heard of it. I had to go into a side door and go up a flight of stairs. I was rather afraid, but the salary was so good it tempted me. I knew I must face the world sometime and it was foolish to be frightened."

"I'll say it was not foolish," said Chan vehemently. "That district down around Third Street is the toughest neighborhood in the city. It's a wonder you didn't start something before you got on the train. Well, go on. What did you find?"

"Why, I found Mr. Trevor. He was in an office, a sort of an office. It did not look very luxurious. It just had a table and some chairs. But he said he was only there temporarily."

"I'll bet he was!" said Chan with set lips.

"He said he was a friend of this woman in California, knew her intimately, and that he must have references before he could take me positively, but that the contract was all ready, and as he liked my appearance so well, if I would like to sign it then he would look up the references after I was gone, and it would save time. He said he wanted me to start the next day as she was in a hurry for me, in fact he suggested that I might be willing to go right along that day, and send for my trunk afterward."

"The hound!" said Chan. "But contract! Did you sign a contract?"

"Yes," said Rachel, "I thought I had to. He said it was necessary because he was advancing the money for my fare."

"But didn't you read it?"

"Well, yes, I glanced it through. He didn't give me much time. Said he had an appointment with a man in five minutes, and he simply must go. He explained it to me that it only meant I was to stay a year at least in consideration of their having paid my fare, or else I was to refund the money. He said it was a mere technicality."

"Don't you know you must never sign anything which you do not thoroughly understand? Didn't your father tell you *that,* too, as well as to be careful whom you married? Now you don't know what you've let yourself in for. That man may make all kinds of trouble for you."

"That was what worried me after I got back to the house. I could scarcely sleep that night before I left. Father had told me I must never sign things without reading them through and I really didn't get a chance to read that contract through."

"That's what he meant then, when he said he had you hard and fast in black and white," said Chan thoughtfully. "I tell you, Ray, we've got to clear out of this part of the country and get you in a safe place. There is no use mincing matters. That man is a professional and he's not giving up easily. He would find it dead easy to clap you in some institution for a little while till everybody had forgotten about you and I'd have the very dickens of a time getting you out, you know. Yes, I'd get you out," he said vehemently answering a sudden lighting of her eyes, "of course I'd get you out if it took my last cent and my last breath. I may not be good enough to marry, but I'd find a way to put you where you were safe."

"Oh!" said Rachel, her eyes full of mingled admiration and fear. "Oh, I'm making you so much trouble! Yes, I will do what you want me to do, if I possibly can. What is it you think I ought to do?"

For an instant Chan hesitated. Why was it that he wanted so much to take Rachel with him to that house party? What mingling of motives was struggling within him? Was it merely that he wished to see her in the environment that was home to himself? Did he want to prove to himself that she would shine in such a setting? Was it merely that he wished to prolong their companionship? Or was he truly convinced that this plan was the best one for her safety?

With a motion of impatience he swept the thoughts from his mind and turned to convince her and himself at the same time.

"I want you to go with me to a friend's house for a few days. It is not far off, and she is a delightful lady, always with charming people about her. She will welcome you to their circle and make you forget that there ever has been anything unpleasant, and while we are there you and I can make plans. I will have time to telegraph, or telephone to some of my friends, and find just the right place for you."

"Oh!" gasped Rachel with troubled eyes again. "But how could I go to a stranger's house that way? She would think it strange of me. Do you mean you would tell her all this miserable story? I was hoping no one need ever know. I feel so humiliated by it."

"There is no need for her to know," answered Chan quickly. "I have already told her all that is necessary. I called her up to explain why I was not on hand at the hour I had promised to arrive. I told her that I had accidently met you on the train, an old friend, the daughter of my best beloved teacher, and that I found you had some time in the city before you must go on your journey, and that as an old friend I felt that it was absolutely necessary that I remain and help you to pass the time pleasantly and safely as you were alone and a stranger in Chicago. She was charmed and

invited you at once. I knew she would! I remembered that
you wished nothing but the truth told. I think I stuck to the
truth. You are an old friend, are you not? Didn't I bring you
a box of chocolates once when you were a little kid, meeting
your daddy?"

Rachel swept him a warm look of acknowledgment.

"You certainly did." She smiled. Then her eyes clouded
again.

"But, really, I don't see how I could visit a stranger under
these circumstances. You practically asked for the invitation, and she does not know me at all."

"No, but she knows me," said Chan with assurance, "and
she wants me at her house party. I made it plain she couldn't
have me without you."

"But that's not fair!" said Rachel, her eyes all worried
now with lifted stormy fringes. "I have been thinking. There
is a YWCA. You could take me there and tell them to watch
out for me. Tell them the whole thing if necessary, and they
will look after me. Or some minister. Or some teacher. Let
me think. I know there were several of Father's friends who
lived in Chicago. I could go to one of them. Of course, that
is the thing I ought to do. I simply couldn't think of being a
burden to you after all that you have done for me. And you
must leave me at once and go where you were expected. It is
awful I have kept you away so long."

"But I don't want to go!" protested Chan stubbornly,
"and what's more I won't go a step unless you will go with
me. House party be hanged! I'm not going to leave you until
I see you safe. The kind of safe that satisifes me, not you.
You are much too naïve to take care of yourself, and besides
you promised!"

CHAPTER X

They argued it for miles, Rachel feeling more and more that she was hindering this friend from pursuing the even tenor of his way, and Chan settling back stubbornly, mile after mile with set lips over the declaration that he would not go to the house party, if she would not go with him.

In a silence that had grown from sheer exhaustion, they entered the outskirts of the city. Chan paused before a fruit shop where the wares were displayed out to the curb and purchased apples, bananas, pears, and grapes.

"You see, it's this way," he said as he peeled a banana and handed the fruit to Rachel, "I just can't and won't leave you alone a minute till I get you out of this infernal neighborhood. I took a big chance leaving you at the woman's house last night. I wouldn't do it again. As it was I heard some talk on the street about the police looking for two crazies. So I'm going to stick by. But I've got a hunch this way we're traveling isn't quite okay in the world you come from. It's being done I know, and in this instance there certainly isn't anything wrong, but your mother wouldn't consider it respectable and I'm thinking what your father would have expected of me in the way of protecting your name. If you don't mind I'd like to land you in Respectability for a few days, and get things all straight."

Rachel was still several seconds before she answered.

They had been driving through traffic for a long time, and she had withdrawn behind the curtain of the car as far as possible, the little new, green felt hat drawn low over her face. Her eyes were full of trouble. She shrank inexpressibly from the ordeal of visiting his friends. She instinctively felt and continued to feel that she should somehow take herself

out of the way. Yet a measure of deference was due her rescuer. It seemed as though she must submit.

But after Rachel had given that quiet word of consent to
go to the house party a great elation arose in her breast. It
was as though the terror of the past twenty-four hours, and
the uncertainty of the future, were suddenly given an inter-
mission, and she was to be happy, really happy as other girls
were, for a little while at least.

Rachel's life had been a quiet one, perhaps some girls
would have called it drab. There had been sweet compan-
ionships of an almost unique type with her father and
mother, both souls of rare depth and richness of nature. And
there had been rich study and some travel, limited always by
lack of funds. There had been her college training of course,
but that too had been a bit lonely, owing to the fact that she
had been a day student merely, and had always hastened
home at the close of classes to spend all her time near the
couch of her invalid mother. She had grown up into the life
of these two mature beings who loved her and whom she
loved deeply, and when they were gone she was lost. Yet
there had been times when she longed to see the young life
of which she read, and of which she had had very few
glimpses save in books. It therefore filled her with a fine an-
ticipation, now that she had really decided to go.

They threaded their way through the thronged streets of
the city, and at last drew up before a great department store
where Chan addressed himself to a portly individual in uniform. He handed out a bill and a letter and said he would
wait, and the uniformed person bowed respectfully, and sent
a smaller uniformed person with the letter.

"It won't take long," explained Chan. "Just sit back out of
sight. We're all safe."

By common consent they did not talk, and Rachel, her hat
well drawn over her face, peered out of the crack between
the side curtains and glimpsed in the show window a gorgeous evening dress of rose satin, with scarf of tulle, though
she drew back almost instantly remembering that it was as

well not to be seen. But she carried in her mind the vision of the rosy gown, and glancing down at the little green frock she wore knew a new uneasiness. She had nothing but this to wear! Wouldn't that be strange, at a house party? But of course she would have to explain that she had lost her baggage, and had to come as she was. Of course Chan wouldn't think about clothes. Men didn't care about clothes, and anyway, what did it matter? She could keep in the background, and perhaps go to bed early.

The uniformed person presently appeared with a couple of suitcases and a hatbox, swinging them into the back of the car as Chan directed, and Rachel scarcely got a glimpse of them. He presented a receipt for Chan to sign, accepted with a grin Chan's goodly tip, and they drove away through the throngs once more and out into the suburbs and so to the highway.

"Can you get along without stopping for food?" asked Chan. "Perhaps I'm foolish, but I don't care to run any more risks stopping to eat. Here are plenty of grapes and pears."

"Lovely!" said Rachel. "What more do we need? It's like being cast on a desert island, isn't it? Only I'm afraid you'll miss your lunch. Men always want coffee and things, don't they? I just love fruit."

They rode along eating the fruit and talking happily about school days. Chan began to tell some of his own escapades in the Beechwood School, with a touch of wistful praise for her professor father. Now that they were really on their way to the house party he seemed anxious not to talk about it at all, and when Rachel tried to ask a few questions about where they were going he turned her thoughts away by plunging into another story this time about a trip of his through Arizona and an encounter with a rattlesnake.

Evening began to draw down about them, and they had a cozy intimate sense of being apart from the world in a beautiful place of their own. Chan had a way of making her feel as if she were the only one with whom he had ever talked this way, and he were enjoying the experience beyond anything else he might have been doing. She wondered once whether that was just a part of good breeding, and whether all well-bred young men had a habit of making anyone with whom they were thrown feel happy and at home with them.

As the dusk grew deeper she caught herself watching the outline of his profile against the dark of the evening landscape through which they were passing, and thinking how strong and manly he seemed, not like the boy she had always named him in her thoughts, and something thrilled shyly through her of pleasure and pride in the possession of him for this little while at least. Always in the years to come no matter how hard things might grow, she would have this pleasant time to remember, this gay friendly converse of youth to youth.

And they found so many things in which they agreed. He did not like bobbed hair, and hated fish, and liked the woods, and a sandy beach without a boardwalk. She found he had read her favorite authors, and couldn't abide purple or jazz music. When they got on the subject of music then they were at home together, for Chan had attended all the symphony concerts from the time he was a kid, and Rachel's one great luxury had been the occasional orchestra concerts to which she had gone as a part of her musical training.

It was quite dark when they at last drew near to a little summer place of beautiful estates set about individual lakes that shone with a reflected glow left over from the sunset, and the thought of the house party to which she was going set Rachel's heart suddenly to beating fast once more. For when she glimpsed the stately summer homes of these favored ones, and began to remember her present destitute state it quite frightened her.

But before she could protest Chan drew up before a tiny village drugstore, set down quite casually on an otherwise rural road.

"Just a minute," he said, "sit back out of sight. I must tele-phone!" and was gone before she could say a word.

He was back in a couple of minutes with satisfaction on his face.

"She's expecting us all right," he said eagerly, "and we'll have plenty of time to dress for dinner. It's about a mile and a half farther on, right over there behind those trees. Can you see those stone towers and gables behind the trees there to your left? That's the house. Gee, I'm hungry, aren't you?"

But Rachel was plunged in the depths of despair.

"Dress for dinner!" she weakly echoed and stared help-lessly ahead.

"Oh, yes," said Chan studiedly as if he had just thought of it. "I knew you'd need a few things and I just phoned a friend of mine in that department store to get a few together. I hope they're all right. They ought to be, that's her business, picking things out. But if everything isn't just right they'll understand. I told her some of your baggage had gone on ahead and I didn't know what you had with you. And any-way, if you need anything just tell the maid. She'll fix it up. Mrs. Southerly will understand perfectly."

Rachel sat aghast.

"Oh, but, Chan! You shouldn't! I *can't!* You really mustn't!"

"That's all right, Ray, don't you worry! And if I were you I wouldn't talk now, while we're going up through this woods. You can't tell who might be about listening. Here we are, we turn in here. Those are the lights! Sh! It'll all be over in a minute, and you'll be safe!"

It seemed to Rachel's frightened heart that it was not even a minute before they drew up before a great rambling stone cottage with wide verandas reaching all about, shut in by shrubbery and vines, luxurious with deep comfortable seats and hammocks, and brilliant with light and color against a background of dark pines sloping away at one side to a mir-ror of water below in which a slender moon was reflected silverly.

Mrs. Southerly received her graciously, called her a dear child, and it was so sweet of her to come! Rachel felt small and awkward as she stood a moment upon the wide stone step and received a perfumed salute from the exquisite hostess slim and lovely in something thinly black that set off her perfect arms and neck to a dazzling whiteness. The small shapely head was sleekly black and the gleam of diamonds elusively darting here and there seemed akin to the brightness of her dark restless eyes. It was all disconcerting. Rachel suddenly felt very tired and old-fashioned and strange and wished she were back in her father's shabby study lying on the couch reading about it all instead of having to live through it.

But her hostess made the way easy. Were these the bags? Take them right up to Miss Rainsford's room, Hopkins, and tell Marie to lay her things out.

"You see, my dear, I'm rushing you a bit, but you've plenty of time. One of the other guests hasn't arrived even yet. But I want you to come down as soon as possible so I can introduce you before we go in to dinner. Yes, go right up with Hopkins. Marie has your bath all ready. That will rest you. I knew you would be tired after the ride from Chicago, such a warm day, too. I'm so glad Chauncey brought you. You are lovely, and I'm going to enjoy you a lot I know. Now, run along. And, Chauncey, my dear, the same room you had last year, and don't you dare take an age to dress. I'm dying to ask you hundreds of questions, and Lila and Tom are crazy to see you, but I wouldn't let them meet you now lest it would make you late."

Rachel found herself in a great airy room with soft flowery draperies, shaded lights, and luxury. A door opened into a white-tiled bathroom and a capped and aproned maid was already taking garments which Rachel had never seen before from an open suitcase. It seemed to Rachel that the maid was the finishing touch to her embarrassment and unhappiness. She paused in the doorway and glanced behind her as if to flee, but her hostess was standing there smiling, and shut her in with that terrible maid. Rachel had not been half as much afraid of the two men in the swamp by the railroad as she was of that maid. And the worst of it was she knew it was perfectly silly and unreasoning, but she found herself trembling from head to foot.

But the maid knew her business and her place most thoroughly and was a thoroughbred. She was taking Rachel's hat and helping her unfasten her dress before the child fairly realized what was going on.

"Now, if you will just step into the bathroom, the bath is all ready," she said with that impersonal command that perfectly trained servants know how to assume in crucial moments, and Rachel felt her self-respect returning.

"There isn't much time, and dinner will soon be served. I will hand you your things when you are ready," and Rachel found herself retiring into the white-tiled bathroom with a charming kimono of pale green silk about her shoulders. Its texture and color seemed somehow to lift her tired frightened spirits, and the sight of the waiting water looked good to her weary young flesh. She emerged from the water refreshed, and more ready to meet the next trying ordeal.

If only that maid would disappear and let her get dressed by herself! There was no telling what Chan's friend had put in that suitcase, but if she could only have a few minutes perhaps she might be able to work out a suitable toilet.

But the maid had not disappeared. She was handing out exquisite silken garments for Rachel to put on, and Rachel, remembering Chan's last whispered admonition as they drew up at the house, that she must not act as if anything was strange, meekly took the gossamer fabrics and put them on, feeling that at last she was really Cinderella, even down to the silver slippers which were presently upon her feet. Marvel of marvels that they fitted comfortably well! Rachel looked down at her feet as the maid fastened the slipper straps and wondered.

"I have chosen the yellow for this evening," said the maid.

"It seemed most suitable, unless you would prefer the green?"

Rachel in a daze eyed furtively the mass of pale yellow gossamer the maid was holding to slip over her head and assented, wondering what the green was like, and where came all this grandeur? Could Chan have done it all? And how had he managed it? Or was she indebted to her hostess? She must get a chance to ask Chan somehow before she had to talk to Mrs. Southerly again.

She found herself seated before a dressing table having her hair done by a French maid for the first time in her life, and the reflection in the mirror looked back with strange wondering eyes. Was that herself, that vision in the yellow draperies? She had never known she could look like that. She watched herself, amazed while the deft fingers of the maid manipulated the rich bands of hair about her head.

"Miss Rachel has such lovely hair!" she said respectfully, and then:

"And you need no make-up, unless just a bit of powder if you wish. No? It is better so. It does not belong to your type."

She threw open the door into the hall:

"Now if you will just go down the stairs. Mrs. Southerly is waiting in the living room. I think they are quite ready to serve dinner, and—Miss Rachel is—perfect!"

Rachel went down the stairs feeling as if she were some new creation which the maid had just perfected, and which she must in no wise spoil by any awkward movement. Yet feeling strangely easy in her mind and ready to meet the ordeal of the dinner. What a difference clothes make, clothes that fit the environment! Rachel inwardly rebelled at the idea that she was not just as self-respecting and worth knowing in green jersey as she was in yellow chiffons, and put the thought aside to be reckoned with at a more convenient season, while yet her soul rejoiced just now in the chiffons.

"Ah, here she comes!" chimed the pleasant voice of the

hostess. "My dear! How quickly you have done it. You have
not kept us waiting an instant. And how darling you look!
One would never know you had been on a journey. Let me
introduce my friend Mrs. Warren, and Miss Warren, Mr.
Percival Warren, Miss Rainsford, and this is Mrs. Shillingsworth, my dear, and her daughter, Miss Gladys Shillingsworth, my daughter, Lila, and my sons, Tom, and
Archibald. Archie, dear, hasn't Mr. Shillingsworth come
down yet? Oh, there you are, Mr. Shillingsworth! Now,
we're all ready to go out. Mr. Shillingsworth let me introduce my little friend Miss Rainsford!"

And Rachel looked up to face the little, sharp admiring
eyes and voluptuous smile of her enemy of the day before!

CHAPTER XI

For the instant her heart seemed to stop beating, and she could feel the blood draining from her face, leaving it startlingly white, even in the gracious candlelight that pervaded the beautiful room. All her strength seemed oozing from her hands and feet, and she felt that in an instant she would crumple slowly and sink down to the floor. If only she might go on out of sight like water sinking through the ground.

It is curious what similes will present themselves to our minds in sudden stress of circumstances.

And then she suddenly felt sorry for Chan; terribly, terribly sorry. She would not see his face. He was standing behind her, but she somehow felt the tenseness of his body, his quick horrified drawing of breath. He had brought her here for safety and had run right into the hands of the enemy again! He would never forgive himself! His judgment had been wrong, and she had an instinctive feeling that Chan was not often wrong in his judgment. But how could he know that this particular despicable person from whom they were fleeing would be here at this house party? Of course it was the last thing he would expect! And he would feel so terribly cut up! He had blamed himself for hours the day before because he had been so careless about taking her into that hotel dining room and causing her that unnecessary fright and exhausting ride on the freight train. And now he would never forgive himself having thrown her right into the hands of the enemy again!

These thoughts raced sharply through her mind like a flash of lightning, and instantly she knew that somehow she must save the situation, and keep him from self-condemnation. This thought gave some measure of strength, and brought back a faint color into her cheeks. She was able to give her enemy back a steady cool look without any sort of recognition in it as she acknowledged the introduction with the slightest inclination of her head, graciously, with the poise of a young queen.

If she had stopped to think about what she should do she could not have been more unconsciously lovely in her attitude, but her intense desire to shield Chan from his own reproaches and to save the situation till there should be a way of escape, gave her power. She was not thinking of herself, but of Chan. It helped her, too, to remember, after that first frightened instant, that her garments were all new and beautiful, and that she could not possibly look like the little red-haired girl in brown who had entered the hotel dining-room. Perhaps he would not recognize her, not at first, anyway. But, what were they to do now? Run away again? How could they manage it? Would Chan have to explain to Mrs. Southerly? How dreadful! The thought of it brought the color fully back into her cheeks again. To have such things connected with herself! How her mother and father would have felt it all! If only there were some way for her to carry it off and get away without being recognized!

She cast a furtive glance around. A rich glowing room with a picturesque firelight at one far end vying with the candlelight from a score of candles deftly disposed. There seemed no way of escape except through the doorway where they all stood. The windows were draped in long silken folds and did not seem made for egress. She had a wild idea of perhaps slipping in behind these curtains, until they had all passed into the hall, and then making her escape, but at that instant they all seemed to close around her and make it impossible, and suddenly she felt Chan's strong hand close about hers in one quick reassuring clasp, and her own fingers answered the pressure for just an instant as they passed through the door. But when she glanced furtively up, his face was turned away from her and he was speaking deferentially to Miss Warren who held his arm, and whom he was apparently taking out to dinner.

Then she suddenly became aware that her own hand was being drawn within someone's arm, and a voice was speaking to her, in pleasant conventional tones. In wild alarm she looked up, fearful lest fate had thrown her as the dinner comrade of her enemy, but instead she met a pair of nice brown eyes and a very kindly though youthful smile, and remembered that this was the younger son of Mrs. Southerly. Tom they had called him, and she drew a deeper breath. Was it possible that she must sit through a dinner and behave as if nothing had happened? Could she do it? And, oh, if she had to sit next to that awful man! She cast another wild furtive glance about the company as they emerged into the spacious dining room and met his eyes, little twinkling wicked eyes with baggy flesh underneath, and they were looking straight at her appraisingly, studying her, although the man himself was smiling and talking to his hostess.

Involuntarily she shuddered as she met his gaze and turned her own eyes quickly away as though she had not seen him. She could not be sure whether he was recognizing her or not, or whether he was just gazing impertinently at her as he might to any strange girl who took his fancy. Perhaps it was just her lovely frock. She remembered that Chan had called it a disguise. Could it be possible that just clothes could change her enough so that she would be safe, at least for a few hours? She glanced down at her yellow draperies with sudden wonder. She had never had a dress like this. She hardly felt she knew herself. The memory of her one brief glance into the mirror before she left her room gave her confidence to go forward to the chair where her escort was leading her.

"Do you know," he was saying with the enthusiasm of youth, "do you know you remind me of a daffodil! A lovely golden daffodil! You don't mind my saying that, do you?"

She laughed a faint little ripple of amusement, and her own voice sounded strangely to her. Perhaps, after all, she was disguised so that Shillingsworth would not recognize her. There was also the fact that he had never seen her many times, and then only briefly. How could he know that she was the same girl he had been pursuing? Now if it had been Trevor! She glanced anxiously, furtively, about lest Trevor too had somehow crept into this company ready to accuse her, and was reassured to find he was not present.

Shillingsworth was seated next their hostess with Mrs. Warren, a stout woman in flowery brocaded velvet, on his right and Tom Southerly, her own escort, next. She was thankful that he was where he could not easily look at her. At least the evil moment of recognition was being put off, if indeed he did not already know her.

Chan was far down the table on the other side, and never looked her way. She caught her cue from him and did not let her eyes stray his way again. She sat and attempted to talk lucidly with her young host, meantime trying to think what she could do.

The time for action would come after dinner. That was plain, but what should the action be? One thing she was resolved. It should not include Chan. Chan had done enough for her, and must not be further involved. She must manage her getaway by herself, and in such a way that Chan should not suspect, until she was gone, and should not be disturbed from following out what he had come here for. This was his natural element. It was not hers. She had never been much in society, and while she might have enjoyed it greatly at another time, just now she felt mightily out of place and unhappy. But Chan belonged here. Through the fringes of her eyes she could see his head bent interestedly toward his table companion, a pretty girl with a painted face and daringly coquettish manners. These people were Chan's natural companions, beside whom she would be something like a plain brown sparrow among birds of paradise. Were it not for her lovely borrowed plumage, she would not even be al-

lowed in here. And Chan's kind heart had allied him with
her, even carrying him so far as to offer to marry her and
take her on permanently, but it must not be allowed. She
must be self-respecting and take herself entirely and satis-
factorily out of his life so that he would feel no further responsibility.

Between such thoughts she managed to smile and sweep a
pleasant glance toward her escort keeping him happily employed saying nice things to her which she hardly heard.

Now and again she saw with a tumult of her heart, that
the great shaggy head of her enemy had leaned forward and
was looking across the two between, staring at her, with his
little beady eyes glittering above the baggy flesh, as if he
were reflecting what he would do after dinner. She saw with
horror that he was pleased with her. Whether or not he recognized her as the girl whom he had been pursuing, he was
evidently especially attracted by her, and she must somehow
manage after dinner was over to escape or he would surely
try to talk with her. And if he did she felt sure her courage
would all desert her and she would be absolutely paralyzed
with fright.

Gradually as the meal progressed and she grew accus-
tomed to the surroundings and realized that nothing would
happen until it was over at least, she was able to form a plan,
and she thought it out in every detail over and over again, as
a person who is to make an after-dinner speech will be living
it over beforehand while he is smiling and talking and trying
to eat the good things that are put before him.

And so she came at last to the moment when they rose
from the table and in the brief stir and confusion she said
quite casually to her young host:

"I wonder if I might use the telephone? There is something I am anxious about."

The young man led her through a little back passageway
to a telephone booth tucked away under the stairs, and left
her telling her to come straight back to the living room as he
was going to get out the pictures of his trip about which he

had been telling her and he wanted her to have the first glimpse of them.

What Rachel did was to ask Central to give her a taxi stand, and then to order a taxi to come for her at once. While she was still in the booth she wrote two hasty notes with the pencil and pad she found lying there:

My dear Mrs. Southerly:
    I find I shall have to leave at once, and as I do not wish to disturb Mr. Prescott who will think he must accompany me to the city, I have ordered a taxi to come for me. Please forgive me for going this way, but I have only time to catch my train. I will write further explanation when I reach my destination. You have been so lovely. Thank you.
                                        Hastily,
                                        RACHEL RAINSFORD

The other note was even briefer:

Dear Chan:
    Forgive me. I had to do this. Don't try to follow. I shall be perfectly all right. Will write when I get there.
                                        RAY

She folded the notes and crumpled them in her hand, stole forth cautiously from the telephone booth, listened for an instant to get her bearings, and then slipped up a back stairway, which she figured would somehow carry her to her room.

She arrived at the top without meeting anyone and located her room at once, but was dismayed to find the maid there going about, turning down the covers of her bed, laying out a night robe, and turning the bed light on. It cast a soft pink glow over the room, and gave dusky shadows everywhere. Rachel was thankful for the dusk, for she feared the maid would notice her embarrassment. She wondered what do do now. Should she wait until the maid was gone? Then suddenly a new thought came to her.

"I have just been telephoning," she said with a little catch in her breath at the daringness of her scheme. "I find that it is very necessary that I go back to town tonight. I have sent for a taxi and it will be here almost at once. I do not wish to disturb either Mrs. Southerly or Mr. Prescott. I wonder if you will put my things in my suitcase after I have left, and they can send them after me? No, I won't have time to wait for them. The taxi man told me there was just time for me to catch the train. I have written two notes, one to Mrs. Southerly, and one to Mr. Prescott. Would you give them to them after I am gone? I would not want Mr. Prescott to know sooner because he would think he ought to accompany me, and it isn't in the least necessary. You can tell them that I will telephone later in the evening when I have reached the city, and let them know that I am all right."

Rachel handed out a precious five-dollar bill which she could ill afford to spare, and the maid gave smiling promise and accepted the two little notes. Moreover she seemed to enter into Rachel's plans saying it was very good of the young lady to be so thoughtful of everybody's plans, and offered herself to accompany her down to the station. Rachel declined with thanks, and even refused to let her accompany her down the stairs, saying she wanted to get away before anyone knew it, and would like her to remain behind and deliver the notes at once in case anyone noticed the taxi going away. She asked the maid please to impress it upon her hostess that she went in this hasty quiet way because she was afraid Mr. Prescott would feel he must accompany her and it would upset all the plans for the evening.

It was almost incredible that she was able to accomplish it, but she did. She worked with feverish fingers lest someone should discover her absence and come in search of her. She slid off the silver slippers and stepped into her own tan ones while she was having the yellow chiffons unfastened by the deft hands of the maid, and she slipped into the little green jersey dress before the maid had had time to hang up the delicate frock she had just taken off. In a moment more she had drawn the green hat down firmly over the soft arrangement of her hair, poked its rich redness out of sight, caught up her handbag, and started for the door.

"That is the taxi," she said breathlessly. "I'm sure I hear it. Thank you so much. You won't forget to deliver the notes as soon as I am gone, please." And she vanished out the door while the maid was still peering into the darkness out the window at the approaching lights of a cab from the village.

Rachel had a little trouble with the fastening of what seemed to be a door into the side yard. She had come down the back stairs once more, safely so far, without seeing anyone. That night latch was on this door, and it seemed to have a peculiar catch, or else her hands were unsteady. But she could hear the throb of the taxi engine as it came to a halt, and she worked feverishly, finally discovering a key, which unlocked the door. Quickly, with a furtive glance behind her, she stepped outside and closed the door. Yet in that one quick glance she had caught a glimpse of the door at the far end of the hall opening, with a flare of light and a burst of music and voices. Someone had been coming out. She had not noticed whether man or woman. What an escape! Now, if that was her taxi she could be off and safe in a moment more. She drew a soft breath and took a step out into the darkness, blinking the light from her eyes. She must cross that patch of brightness from the windows, and, yes, that must be the taxi, that dark shape just ahead. She could see the driver standing uncertainly beside the path.

She took one step out into the edge of the light and cast a quick glance behind her at the wide window where the bright light showed moving figures. In that one glimpse the pattern of Mrs. Warren's brocaded velvet seemed to stand out as she sat in a great, deep chair under a lamp. And was that Chan, the one in the evening clothes, just beyond her? His head was turned the other way, and she could not be sure. The lampshade was in the way. She paused a second longer, her heart suddenly constricted with the thought that she would probably see him no more. And he had been so good to her! And they had been through such a wonderful day together! Chan, who had said he loved her, and wanted to marry her. Bighearted Chan! Chan—and she was leaving him! Yet it must be right for her to go, to take care of herself and not to hamper him longer. It would be hard, but it was right. If he only would turn his head and let her get a glimpse of his face to remember!

Then suddenly as a finger snuffs out the flame of a candle, something big and soft and suffocating enveloped her, imprisoned, and overpowered her, she was lifted from her feet and borne swiftly into a blank smothering nothingness. Snuffed out!

CHAPTER XII

Chan had not seen Rachel leave the room because he had been watching Shillingsworth. There was a furtive look about that old rascal that made Chan sure he had some deviltry on foot. He wanted to be sure that he was not up to anything new.

Shillingsworth slipped slyly out into the hall, with a cunning look in his old eye, cast a quick surveying glance about, and went into the smoking room. Chan did not follow him, but stood where he could watch the door, and when he did not return immediately he stepped where he could glance casually into the room without being noticed. Shillingsworth was slumped in a big leather chair enveloped in a cloud of smoke. It looked as if he was safe for the moment. Chan went swiftly up the stairs to his room. He wished to write a note to Rachel which he planned to hand her sometime during the evening. His mind was busy with what he should say. He did not notice Rachel's door closing softly as he reached the top of the stairs. His object was to get to his own room without arousing notice. He felt that Rachel was comparatively safe for the moment in the living room with their hostess, and that during those few informal moments immediately following dinner he could count upon no one's noticing his absence. He felt that what he had to do must be done swiftly. He was plunged into mortification at the way his plans had turned out, for here, instead of putting Rachel in a safe place he had brought her into the very center of danger. It was up to him to save the situation at once. He was not used to making a mess of things like this. Something decided had got to be done.

He took the precaution of locking his door before he went to work, and his first act was to go to the telephone which stood on a little stand beside the bed. But to his surprise, when he took down the receiver he found that someone was talking, and the big asthmatic voice was familiar. This instrument, then, must be an extension, perhaps of the one he had seen in an alcove down in the smoking room, or else of the little booth in the hall just off the dining room.

His naturally honorable nature prompted him to put back the receiver, annoyed that he would be delayed until someone else had finished but just as he was about to slip it on its hook a sentence caught his attention. "Well, our little redhead is caught at last! She's walked right up and is eating out of my hand. You've only to come and bag the game now and our little bargain will be complete. What's that? Yes, she's here. Yep. Ate dinner with her. And she's all you said and more of 'em. She can wear the rags all right. I don't know where she got 'em, but she's all dolled up and looks like a million dollars. I'm satisfied all right with my bargain. Now, what you've got to do is to get up here with your men on the double jump. You can't tell how soon the girl will clip out. The man's here too! Seems to be thick with the folks and all. But I'll not say anything till you arrive. Then I'll come out and say what I know about her being insane and all. You're an old friend of mine, see? And I know you to be guardian of this insane girl. Better make the boy innocent. He seems to be the son of an old friend of the house. She has just played on his sympathies, see? He never saw her till she got on the train. That'll be a plausible story and fix things up all right. Then you can take her right off to that address I gave you. Got it? No, I mean the other one. Number Ten Barberry Row, Littleton Crossing. It's about ten miles from here on the pike and turn off at Barberry Row. Yes, you can't mistake it, it's an old estate a little bit off the road. Yes, I'll phone 'em to expect you. All right. You beat it up here quick as you can, and we'll see about more pay."

The receiver clicked off and Chan sat grim with fury. He longed to plunge down into that smoking room and take that old fox by the throat. He ached to expose the creature before the whole house, let his fat wife and daughter know what he was, let his sweet gentle hostess understand what kind of people she was harboring, let the world know that the wealthy and honored old Shillingsworth was rotten, rotten, rotten!

It would have been the way of the old Chan to have rushed down instantly and performed all these things, taking chances on being believed. He had used this policy all his life.

But, on the other hand, he had never had the responsibility of a girl like this one before, and he could afford to run no chances. True, his father was powerful both socially and financially, yet he reflected that he himself was not very well known to his hostess, and perhaps his word would not weigh against the word of an older man whose daughter was all too evidently interested in a son of the house. He must run no risks. What should he do?

But first, he must get hold of a telephone line where no one could listen in. He could hear Shillingsworth trying now to get a number which his mind registered mechanically, and in a moment more he heard arrangements made for the reception of a patient who would presently be brought to the sanitarium. This was old stuff and he did not need to listen. Time was the important thing. If only Jim had reached Chicago now, and he could get him on the wire, things would be easier.

Chan went out in the hall and reconnoitered, finally discovering the back hall booth where Rachel had telephoned for the taxi. Having assured himself by questioning the butler that this was a private wire Chan put in a call for the Chicago hotel and most unexpectedly got it within a very short time. Yes, the chauffeur had arrived, came a couple of hours ago, and after a brief delay Jim's voice answered on the wire.

"Yes, sir. Arrived safe. Andy came with me. Got his other engagement changed. Had a good run. Car all in good shape. Just been going over it. Yes, sir. It's ready to run again. I was just having her washed. What's that? Yes, sir. We could be ready to start in ten minues. Andy too? All right. Meet you where? At the railroad station? Yes, sir. I can find it. What, sir? Oh, how long will I take? I oughtta make it in a few hours, oughtn't I? All right, sir! I'll beat it!"

Chan was startled by the sound of a suddenly suppressed scream of terror, and there was something self-contained about its quality that made him think of Rachel. He started to his feet forgetting to hang up the receiver and dashed out into the hall.

All seemed quiet. There was a sound of a car at the back of the house, but there were many cars there of course, with all those people. He hurried wildly into the living room, studied the groups a moment and failing to find Rachel dashed across the hall to the smoking room. He was somewhat reassured to find Shillingsworth, his eyes half closed, a wreath of smoke surrounding his head, as he leaned back in the big leather chair enjoying his cigar. He disappeared from the doorway before Shillingsworth had seen who it was, and made for his room again coming almost in collision with the maid as he reached the top of the stairs.

"Oh, excuse me," he stammered. "Have you seen Miss Rainsford? I—that is—there was a telephone call."

He fumbled madly around in his mind for an excuse for his anxiety.

But the maid was handing him a note.

"Yes, sir," she said calmly, "Miss Rainsford has just gone. She left this note for you."

"Gone!" he said wildly. "Gone! But I——"

"That's all right, sir. She said she did not wish to spoil the evening for you, and she could just as well go in a taxi. They have just left. She did not wish the note delivered till I heard the cab drive away, sir. She said there was just time to catch her train, and she did not wish Mrs. Southerly's company disturbed. She said the note would explain." And the maid put the little folded paper in his hands.

He read it feverishly with a sinking feeling at his heart, such as no experience of his youth heretofore had brought him. Gone! Rachel was GONE! She did not trust him anymore for her safety. He had brought her twice straight into the presence of the enemy and now she was going out on her own! And the enemy was hotfoot on her tracks!

"But she must not go alone," he said to the maid. "I must catch her if I can."

Suddenly he remembered that smothered scream.

Without waiting for anything further, without hat or coat, he dashed down the stairs and out the side door. He paused for an instant listening intently. He could hear the distant throb of an engine making toward the village. With a wild hope that she was still in the yard waiting he made a hasty detour around the house, and wound up at the garage.

All was still there. The servants were eating their evening meal. He had much ado getting out his car. Somebody had left a big car standing in the driveway in front of the garage door that sheltered Chan's small roadster. He had to move it by main force before he could get out. But at last he was free of the driveway, having apparently escaped the notice of the house, and was burning up the road toward the village, his mind in torment over the possibilities. Could it be that Trevor had been near enough at hand to have arrived so soon after Shillingsworth had telephoned?

This thought was made further tormenting by the arrival of a taxi from the station, bowling emptily toward the Southerly house. He stopped the driver, demanded his destination, and found that this was the taxi ordered by the young lady. And yet the maid had said that she had heard the car that took Rachel away! Gradually the conviction came that Trevor had arrived and kidnapped Rachel! He groaned aloud as he pressed the accelerator and shot down the road.

It was a wild-eyed young man that sprang from his car at the little suburban station, and left his engine running while he strode furiously around a dark building hunting for an agent. But there was no agent about, and from a boy who was crossing the tracks he learned that the only train that stopped at that station in the evening had passed there an hour and a half before.

He stood for a moment looking desperately up and down the dark track so calm and inscrutable under the faint light of the slender thread of a moon. If Rachel had not gone away down that track where was she? Oh, why had she treated him so? Yet why indeed should she not when he had taken her twice straight into danger?

In fierce anger at himself he threw himself into his car once more and started on. Perhaps if he drove to the limit he could catch the car in which she had gone, Trevor's if it was Trevor. Or perhaps he should go back to the house and watch for Trevor, make sure—what was it he should make sure of? He felt as if he were losing his mind. If only Jim and Andy were here now. He could leave one of them up at the house and go in search of Rachel himself.

But it would be two hours before Jim could possibly arrive, even with the high-powered car. He must do the best he could alone.

At the next corner he slowed down and inquired the way to Littleton, and then shot out on the pike again at a speed that would spell catastrophe if anything got in his way. He knew he was taking tremendous chances with a car that he had not tried out, but he felt it was a chance that he must take.

Once he was held for several minutes at a railroad crossing while a long freight train passed, and he questioned the flagman concerning recent passers. The flagman said there wasn't much traffic this time of night. There hadn't been but four cross the tracks in the last two hours. A couple of trucks, a Ford roadster and Eli Bennett's Chevrolet. It had a flat tire and monkeyed round quite awhile getting patched up. Had a sick lady aboard going to the hospial, Eli said, and they were in a terrible hurry. Just got off about five minutes ago. Lucky they did or this freight would have held them still longer.

Chan drew a long breath. He was on the right track then. Could he possibly catch them before they reached Littleton? If he could only somehow double-cross them and hold them up in a lonely place it would save a lot of trouble. He could easily handle Trevor single-handed. But this Eli Bennett might be more than a handful, and no telling how many others Trevor had with him. It would not do to get knocked out himself, and thus leave Rachel unprotected. He must play safe for her sake.

He shot across the track as soon as the caboose of the freight was passed, a pang in his heart at the thought of the ride he had taken on another freight, with her safe beside him. Oh, why had he been so foolhardy as to take her to Southerlys'? All because he was anxious to put the stamp of respectability upon her. But he ought not to have tarried in this part of the country. He ought to have—and then his mind would come up against a blank wall as it were and he would frown into the night and send his car ahead faster, and still faster.

Several miles ahead he sighted the red taillight of a car, and set himself to overtake it. Of course, there were plenty of chances that Trevor might have turned off the pike, but all the roads he had passed had not seemed good roads, and Trevor would scarcely be worried about being overtaken. He could not know that anyone had overheard Shillingsworth telephoning. He had been long enough with his flat tire to be sure no one had immediately followed the girl's scream. He would feel comparatively safe. And the chances were that the old car he had hired would not be capable of great speed. So Chan bent to his race once more, trying to think, as he flashed along through the darkness, what he should do when he caught up. And now he began to think what a foolish thing he had done in not stopping long enough to take a police officer along with him. He might have arrested Trevor for kidnapping the girl. There were dozens of possibilities! And just because his head was filled with the thought of this lovely girl he had acted like a scatterbrained kid. Well, he wouldn't be that from now on. He would get on the job like a regular and see this thing through. If he ever got possession of Rachel again, bless her precious little heart, he would stick by and take her to the world's end, if need be, till he was sure he had a safe place. The very idea that that beast had followed him to the spot he thought was safest! He never had such luck in his life before. And here, for the first time in his life, he had been absolutely trying to do the right thing! Well, it was strange! But he wasn't going to be beaten yet!

The red light ahead ducked over the top of a hill out of sight, and Chan spurred up to keep it in sight, but it persisted out of sight, and when he reached the top of the hill the whole landscape was swept clear of any red light anywhere. In vain he searched this way and that, and shot down the hill in a hurry. It seemed incredible that anything could absolutely disappear in that short time. Down in the far valley there were the lights of a town, and when he arrived the various signs here and there showed him it was Littleton. But when he inquired for Barberry Row, they pointed up the road he had come, and told him he would find a driveway almost at the very top of the hill which led through the woods to a castlelike building set deep among trees. He could see faint lights twinkling, but the darkness of woods between seemed ominous as he quickly climbed back to the top of the hill again, and discovered at last the road where the other car must have turned off.

Anxiously he pulled out his watch and noted the time. He had been more than an hour on the way. Andy and Jim would be arriving soon if they had good luck, and he would not be there to meet them! Yet he must find out, now he was here, if Rachel was really in this region.

He turned his car into the wooded road, which was by no means so smooth as the pike he had been traveling, but his face was grim and his hand was steady as he pushed his way on, and by and by around a curve, and up higher on the hill he saw the gleam and twinkle of a red taillight once more, and heard a car stop, its engine still running.

There were lights in the windows of a big stone house, and a door opened around to the side, with a stream of light rushing out and making a bright pathway. Figures were silhouetted against it, and someone was being carried in. Voices were echoed intermittently, though he could not make out any words.

After watching a moment he turned his car straight into the woods, ran it behind some bushes, stopped the engine and turned out the lights. Then he got out and scrambled up through the woods till he reached a point where he could see the house clearly.

Lights had appeared at the upper right-hand corner of the building where he thought he remembered it had been dark before, and the front door still stood open. In the wide pathway of light that flowed out stood the car, its engine at rest now, and two men, an old one, and a half-grown boy came sauntering down the steps of the house and got into the car, with an air of having finished a disagreeable task. They talked in low growling tones. Chan could not make out what they said, only one word from the old: "pity!" or had it been "pretty!"

Chan crawled a little nearer and waited behind some shrubbery. He could see through the open door that someone was coming down the stairs. A woman's white skirts, probably a nurse—yes, a nurse with a white cap. And behind her came Trevor! He knew him more by his attitude of slyness, than by being able to distinguish features at this distance. But he knew him, unmistakably. And it was a relief. Because now he knew where Rachel was! And it was better to know even that she was held a prisoner here in what was probably a private sanitarium than not to know where in the wide world she was, and into what danger she might not already have gone.

Trevor was standing in the open door now, pulling on his gloves, and he could hear his words distinctly:

"Yes, Mr. Shillingsworth will be over in the morning, or at least as soon as he can possibly get away from very pressing business. This is only a deposit you know, until he gets here. He will arrange it all. He would have come himself, you understand, only that he was suddenly called in another direction by the illness of someone very close to him. Yes, I shall see him tonight and tell him how she came through and you will let us know by telephone, of course, if there are any developments. But I imagine she'll sleep through the night. No, she is not violent in her attacks. There is nothing to fear from her. She will not do anyone harm, but herself perhaps. You must watch that she cannot get hold of anything to harm her. Well, good night, and I hope you won't have any trouble with her."

Trevor came briskly down the steps and got into the car, slamming the car door with a bang of satisfaction as of a disagreeable duty well done. Chan crept back under shelter and stole down through the trees, pausing only for an instant to look back at the room where the light appeared. But the shades were drawn and he could see nothing but moving shadows, one wearing a stiff peaked cap. That was a nurse.

He waited until the other car was well down the hill and into the road before he pulled out of the woods and got his own car under way. Not for the world would he reveal himself now. His job was to get to the rendezvous as quickly as possible and meet his own car. After that it might be clearer sailing. Only, how was he going to work it to get Rachel out of what looked like a stone fortress? He was even sure there had been iron bars at the windows, though perhaps that was imagination.

As he drove along through the night, cautiously at first, because he did not wish to have his identity discovered by Trevor at present, and madly later, after Trevor turned off toward the town and there was no longer need for caution, he felt as if the spirit of his old professor was with him in the car, upholding, encouraging, helping him to think. He could almost feel his kindly hand upon his shoulder as it had been once long years ago when Chan was very angry at someone who had done him a wrong, and wanted to fight. His strong, kindly voice had spoken low words, with a touch of command in them, and a yearning friendliness that had made the angry boy listen and heed:

"Steady, son, steady! You know you lose half your power when you give way to anger, because you can't see what is the right thing. Steady! Don't let this fury get the better of you. Be the stronger of the two men when you go out there on the field again."

And Chan had never forgotten those words. Often it had helped him to control his hot temper and think through a thing before he acted. So now, he felt that presence of the man beside him, the only man who had ever seemed to care about what he did from a moral standpoint. His father loved him, of course, and gave him all the money he wanted, but his father was hotheaded like himself, and never stopped to think, never indeed had counseled him about his actions. But Professor Rainsford had lifted a standard in his young life, which although he had not always followed, had yet remained an ideal. And now as he rode, perplexed, angry, terrified at the situation he had brought upon that man's little girl, he found the memory of the father steadying him, giving him cool, sane thoughts in this crisis.

And now at last he was coming to the little station dark against the sky where the late little thread of a moon was sinking low in the west. Would Jim be there to meet him, and would Andy have decided to stay and come along? Or would there be a long wait before he could be free to go and rescue her, his darling, his little Ray! Oh, why, why when he had her safe didn't he know enough to keep her, and not let her go through all this danger and horror! Could he ever forgive himself?

Then he swept across the railroad track and round the

curve into the pool of dark shadows by the station. Was that his car that stood over beyond that far shadow? No, it was only a pile of boxes on the platform. His heart sank, as he slowed down his engine to a stop and got slowly out of the car. Then out from the shadows that enveloped the front of the station there stepped a silent figure in the dark, laying a firm hand upon his arm, and looking up he saw behind him two other figures standing closer to the building with guns upon their hips like silent images set there to guard the night.

Now Chan had terrorized many an evildoer in his boyhood days himself, having been a great friend of the police, and liking nothing better than to go with them on a raid after a stolen automobile, or a recreant lawbreaker, but he had never happened to have been met in this way before, and his heart stood still. Not for himself, for he was naturally courageous, but for the girl whose safety was in his keeping. With a fierce light in his eyes he turned to meet his challenger.

CHAPTER XIII

When Rachel came to herself she was being borne along in a car at what seemed to her like a terrible pace, but when she tried to cry out she found her mouth was filled with something big and soft that felt like woollen cloth, which seemed to be tied about her face and head firmly, and furthermore her hands and feet were tightly bound with cords.

After the first instant of gasping horror she lay still trying to remember what had happened. She could go back to the moment when she stepped from the side door into the dark yard and started toward a dark car. She remembered turning her head to look back at the house, she distinctly remembered Mrs. Warren in her bright brocaded velvet sitting in the great armchair under the lamp, as plump and well-upholstered as the chair itself, and she remembered the back of a sleek head above a well-fitting evening coat, and now as she revisualized the picture she knew the man had not been Chan, but the young son of the house. How strange to be lying here in a car going swiftly away in the darkness, when a moment before she had been standing in the grass looking back at that window filled with light and people! Or was it but a moment before? She had a dazed feeling in her head and, now she thought of it, there was a pungent burning sensation in her nose and throat. They must have given her some sort of strong anesthetic.

She lay perfectly still. There was a strange inertia upon her. She did not want to stir. She seemed not even to have strength enough to be frightened, although her mind was alive enough to make her sure she would be frightened if she were not too tired.

Gradually she made out that there were three men in the car with her, and by watching carefully whenever they passed a light she discovered that the man sitting in the backseat beside her was Trevor. A shudder passed over her when she made this out, but she had sense enough to try to control it. Better let him think her unconscious. At least she would be ready to act if there came an opportunity. Still, how could she act with both hands and feet tied, and this awful thing in her mouth that almost choked her? No, she was helpless. There was only one thing she could do. Only One Person to whom she could now cry for help. Her parents were gone. Her friends were far away and could not hear her. Chan was gone! She realized now that she had done a foolhardy thing in going away from the rescuer whom God had sent. But she had put herself where he could no longer come to her assistance. There was nobody who could hear her but God!

Suddenly into that horrible situation came back to her mind a story which she had heard in her childhood of a consecrated young missionary caught and tied to a stake with a fire kindling at his feet, and taunted by his tormentors that now he could not get away.

Shining-faced, he bravely replied, "There is always the way up!"

The story had impressed her as a child. She had admired the courage of the young Christian, but it had never occurred to her that she could ever be put into a situation where her only possible help could come through God. Of course, in a sense everyone was dependent upon God for everything indirectly. But suddenly to realize that unspeakable things were staring her in the face and there was no one in the wide universe upon whom she could call but God was a new way of seeing it. And here she was, she and God, and *these devils!* And the trouble was that she realized she didn't really know God intimately.

Chan, she knew a little; she had seen him before, often had admired him from afar, had heard of him through her father, but she had considered Chan a stranger; had felt shy about accepting help from him, had even run away from him. How then could she ask God to help her; God, a stranger?

True, her father, and mother too, had known God, and had tried to teach her that God was her Father, and she had always considered that He was; but now in her stress she knew that He had never meant anything tangible to her, never anything to lean upon.

"Oh, God," she tried to say in her heart. "Dear God, please——" the old prayer words that had been upon her lips often as a little child. There had never been much thought behind them; she always felt that He was very far away, farther than Chan would have been if he had sat in another car and known nothing about her predicament, and she had had to go to him and explain the situation and try to make him believe her danger and find a way to help her.

Then like a miracle in her helplessness there came to her words that she had learned as a little child, words that were a mere formula to her through the years, that she had never thought about, or realized as meaning anything special for her individual needs:

"Fear thou not, for I am with thee, be not dismayed, for I am thy God . . . I will strengthen thee, yea I will help thee; yea, I will uphold thee with the right hand of my righteousness . . . Call upon me in the day of trouble. I will deliver thee . . . and will show thee my salvation . . . The eyes of the Lord are upon the righteous and his ears are open unto their cry . . ." went on the words that had been stored in her memory for years and were now released for this, her time of need.

Was she righteous? Could she claim a promise like that? She decided she was not, but perhaps it only meant people who wanted to do right, who were trying their best . . . "This poor man cried and the Lord heard him, and saved him out of all his troubles," went on Memory, ringing out the promises like treasure hoarded away and found in a time of need.

"When thou passest through the waters I will be with

thee, and through the rivers they shall not overflow thee."
What did it mean? Was God reminding her of His own
words?

"The angel of the Lord encampeth round about them that
fear him and delivereth them." Ah! She could claim that!
She had always feared the Lord, in the sense of reverencing
Him. That had been in her heart for worship, instead of loving, instead of nearness. She saw now in her need that there
should have been more than fear of displeasing Him. There
should have been a closer relationship. But even so she had
a claim, and now her soul began to cry out to the God who
could hear, and somehow He seemed to come nearer. Not a
God afar off, but a God with an encampment all about her.
The flutter of her waking heart, which had been growing
more intense as she came to more keen consciousness, was
quieter now. A kind of peace settled upon her, even in the
midst of her alarm. God was there. He would do something
about it. She had only to keep still and wait. There was not
anything she could do but wait and keep praying.

Later she made out that the two men on the front seat
were neither of them the big man, Shillingsworth, whom she
feared more than Trevor, and the burden lifted a little. One
of these on the front seat was a mere boy. Perhaps if worse
came to worst she could appeal to him. She would not be
afraid of him. He was merely someone hired to take her
somewhere. And the other man, as his profile shone out now
and again against some sharp streetlight, seemed kindly
enough, a farmer perhaps who had been pressed into service. She tried to think how she could put her case coolly to
them so that they would believe, or try to help her somehow.
If only she could get her hand into her pocket and get a
pencil and a bit of paper, she might write a few words telling
them how to send for Chan, or for some of her friends back
at home to rescue her. But her hands were firmly tied. And
the worst of all was that she had cut herself completely off
from any hope of anyone discovering her soon, for she had
told Chan in her note that she would write when she got set-

tled again, and he might think she did not want to communicate with him and so never know. How terrible! And he would think her ungrateful, too!

Gradually all the little details of her situation picked themselves out clearly against a dark background, and she knew that she had reached the depths, where only God could save her. She saw her own self in her foolish pride, taking things in her own hands. She saw, too, now that she was utterly cut off from him, that her soul cried out for Chan in her distress. What a wonderful friend she had found in him, and to think she had so easily slipped away to take care of herself. How had she dared? It was as he had said, she did not at all realize what she was up against.

Such thoughts as these whirled idly through her dazed mind as the car drove on, and the men, her keepers, sat silent, for the most part only stopping now and again to discuss the road. However, there was one stop in which the men seemed annoyed. From the remarks passed between them, Rachel guessed it was a puncture which caused the delay.

At last they turned into a wood road, went up a hill and stopped. Lights flared out. She found her heart almost stopping its beating when they lifted her out and carried her in. Under the fringes of her eyes she saw the building. It was of stone, like a castle. Was she going to a prison? Would she ever come out save as a prisoner to that other awful man whose face came back now to haunt her?

She kept her eyes closed until they carried her through a hall and up a wide staircase into a room. It was a large room with a look like a hospital, but there were bars at the windows behind the white holland shades, and there was very little in it save a bed and chair and bureau.

They had taken the gag from her mouth when they stopped and had thrown it back in the car. She might cry out now, but who was there to cry out to? Chan was miles away and no one else knew. Only God, and God could hear without a whisper.

It was a relief to get the cloth out of her mouth. She could breathe better now, and the strangling sensation was almost gone. She opened her eyes and looked up into the eyes of a tall, thin nurse. She had an angular nose and an expression of disillusion. She looked down at Rachel as if she had been a new specimen of bug or beetle in a laboratory which she was expected to spike with a pin for further examination.

"Is she dangerous?" she asked placidly, as if it made little difference.

"Well, she gave us a good deal of trouble when we first started out," said Trevor anxiously like a sad relative. "Of course, she doesn't realize what's wrong." He rubbed his hands together sorrowfully. "You see she's been in an asylum before, and whenever one of those spells comes on now she thinks she's all right and we are trying to put her away. But it isn't safe of course to keep her at home. She takes strange dislikes to people and thinks they ought to be killed."

"I see," said the cold voice of the nurse. "Do you think it would be safer to use a straitjacket at once?"

"Oh, I don't think so," said Trevor, shifting from one foot to the other uneasily as he suddenly saw Rachel's wide-open eyes upon him. "She has never been actually violent yet, it's mostly in her mind, but I would have one at hand in case she becomes unmanageable. This spell seems to have worn off some. She may sleep now."

The nurse stooped over and gave Rachel a cold critical look.

"Those cords are binding her," she said unsympathetically. "I think they should be loosened. Will you lie still if I untie your hands?"

Rachel opened her eyes wide and looked back, a steady beseeching gaze. Was there any hope from this woman? She was a woman. Perhaps after the men were gone she could make her understand. But the cold eyes of the nurse gave back no answering spark of sympathy to her appeal.

"You can't trust her too far, you know," warned Trevor.

"Better get some handcuffs, or keep the door locked. She's as cunning as they make 'em."

"All right," said the nurse, "we better come out now. The quicker she gets quiet the better if she's to rest any tonight. The doctor's out for the evening. He won't be back till the late train, but we've plenty of nurses and a couple of strong men attendants. You needn't be afraid. I've seen them like this many a time. We'll look after her. You tell Mr. Shillingsworth she'll be all right and we'll keep him informed."

The men stepped out in the hall and their voices rumbled away into nothingness as the door fell shut. The walls seemed to be soundproof. She could scarcely hear a word now as they stood in the hall outside her closed door. It would do no good to scream. She glanced toward the windows which she could see were barred. She was a prisoner!

But neither doors nor bars could shut out the great God who had promised to be with her. She remembered the childhood story of how He walked in the fiery furnace with the three Hebrew children, and stayed in the lions' den with Daniel to shut the mouths of the lions. She was awed with the thought. What would have seemed to her a vague tale of the misty past, impossible in these days at least, became suddenly a credible thing. Here she was alone except for God. If there was a God and He cared, He would surely be there. He would not let her get into the clutches of that awful man. He would save her somehow. He had promised. She believed it. A feeling of assurance and peace came to her and stilled the fright of her heart.

Presently the nurse came back and spoke in a cold, dictatorial voice:

"Will you lie still and behave yourself if I cut those cords and make you more comfortable?"

"Yes," said Rachel quietly with gratitude in her eyes.

The nurse came and untied the heavy cords, wrapping them up and putting them in her pocket.

"You know it won't pay you to make a fuss," she said sharply. "There are two men in the hall. They can overpower you in an instant if you try to put anything over on us."

"Thank you," said Rachel pleasantly, "that feels better." The nurse seemed surprised.

"I am going to undress you and get you to bed," she said, "and then I'll send for something for you to eat. Which would you rather have, a glass of hot milk or a cup of tea?"

"Thank you," said Rachel, "I don't care for either. I've been at a house party and we just finished dinner before I started away. And I would much rather not be undressed if you don't mind. I'll lie quietly here if you want me to, but I prefer to keep my clothes on."

"That's nonsense!" said the nurse sharply, turning to pull down the shades. "You're a patient here and you've got to be put to bed. I shall lose my job if I don't obey orders."

"But I thought I heard you say that the doctor has not come yet. You can't have had orders about me if he isn't here."

"Yes, I've had very strict orders about you from your guardian and I'll have to carry them out in a way you won't like if you make me any trouble!" said the nurse shortly.

Rachel was still for a minute, thinking, praying.

Oh, God, show me what to do!

"Of course I don't suppose it will do any good to tell you," she said quietly after a minute, "but I haven't any guardian, and I'm not insane or sick or whatever it is they have said about me. Those men who brought me in here threw something over my head and caught me and carried me off, as I stepped into the path to take a taxi from a house party where I had been having dinner. I don't even know the men nor the Mr. Shillingsworth who has hired them to bring me here. It's quite a long story and I can tell you all about it if you are willing to listen."

"They all have interesting stories when they come here," said the nurse knowingly. "I can't take time to hear yours now. I've got to carry out my orders, you know. Even if it were true it wouldn't be my business to judge anything about that."

"Yes, I can see that," said Rachel reasonably. "Of course I wouldn't want to get you into trouble, but if you would be willing to send one or two telegrams for me to my friends I would be glad to pay you for your trouble. I haven't very much money, but I'd gladly give you all I have if you will just let one or two of my friends know where I am. They will come and make it very plain who I am."

"Look here!" said the nurse sharply. "Mr. Shillingsworth is the president of our board of directors, and he gave me his orders over the phone a couple of hours ago. There's really nothing I can do about it even it if were true. But I'm sorry for you, for you evidently think you're telling the truth, and if it will make you feel any better I'll write some letters for you tomorrow in my time off. You can see yourself that's all I could possibly do even if you paid me a fortune. It wouldn't be honorable."

"I see," said Rachel, "But I'm afraid that would be too late. I guess I shall have to depend on someone else for help."

The nurse eyed her sharply.

"You won't find anyone in this institution that will help you that way. We're all loyal to the place. It would be as much as our job was worth if we weren't. Now, you let me undress you and you drink your hot milk like a good girl and go to sleep. In the morning we'll see what the doctor says."

"I will be good," said Rachel, "and will lie still, if you will let me keep my clothes on, but I will not drink anything nor eat anything in this place. It would choke me. And I do not want to go to sleep. I would like to speak to the doctor when he comes even if it is the middle of the night."

The nurse eyed her uncertainly.

"All right, I'll trust you to lie still for awhile," she said, "But you've got to keep your promise. No trying to pull anything off!"

"All right," smiled Rachel, "but won't you let me give you

the addresses for those telegrams before you go? It would be worth a good deal more to me if you sent them off tonight, at once."

"No," said the nurse sharply, "I can't do anything tonight! I'm on duty and we've got some troublesome patients. There'll be time enough!" And she walked out of the room.

Presently she returned with a glass of ice water. Rachel had heard the ice tinkling as if it were being stirred with a spoon, but the water looked clear enough. Perhaps they had put something into the water to put her to sleep!

"Thank you," she said pleasantly, "I don't care for it just now."

"But this is your medicine," said the nurse crossly. "You have to take it. You don't want me to call in the attendant, do you?"

The nurse held the glass out to her lips but Rachel turned her head away.

"I'm not taking any medicine until I see the doctor," she said.

The telephone rang sharply and the nurse hurried out to answer it. She had left the door open and Rachel could hear what she was saying. It was evidently the doctor and he was not coming back until morning. It would seem from what the nurse was saying that he had advised her to let the new patient alone as long as she behaved herself. This would have given her some hope if the last sentence of the nurse had not filled her with fright. She said:

"You think Mr. Shillingsworth will be over with you in the morning then. All right. Good night."

Then there would be no chance with the doctor if that terrible man came along! And he was president of the board of directors! How impossible seemed her situation! She closed her eyes, pressed her hands together over her heart and began to pray quietly in her soul. The nurse came and looked in and went away again softly, thinking she was sleeping. But when she came back again Rachel was sitting up by the window looking out.

"Here, what are you doing?" she reprimanded. "You promised me you would lie still!"

"Do you mind if I sit here and look out a little while?" Rachel asked gently. "I can't seem to lie still."

"But you ought to be asleep. You're a sick girl, you know."

Rachel looked at the woman with steady eyes.

"I'm not sick. There's nothing at all the matter with me except that I am worried. Can't you see that yourself?"

"I see all kinds of things in this place," answered the nurse crossly, "and you're just like the rest. They all have their stories. Come, be a good girl and lie down. I'm tired out and I can't be bothered with you."

"I'm not going to give you any trouble, but I'm going to sit right here by the window," said Rachel firmly. "This can't possibly be doing any harm. I couldn't jump out of the window even if I wanted to, which I don't, for I see there are bars. You'll have much less trouble with me if you'll let me sit here. I promise you I will not try to do anything that will annoy you if you will just let me alone."

There was something quietly commanding about Rachel's voice, a sane, firm quality such as the nurse herself knew how to use at times when she was not as tired as she was tonight.

"Well," she hesitated, "I'll let you sit there for half an hour if you will go to bed like a good girl then."

"I'll see!" said Rachel quietly. "If I feel like sleeping then I will. But I can't possibly sleep now. I want to get this air, and I want to look out."

The nurse stood the door open and went out, talking in low tones with one of the attendants who was reading the sporting news by the desk.

"Better let her alone as long as she's quiet," he growled. He, too, was tired. "That party down the hall has subsided for awhile and I'd like to be able to hear myself think. I've had a dog's life for three days with that old man, till Doc doped him. For heaven's sake don't let's get another one

started raving. Let her have her own way as long as she's
quiet. Let sleeping dogs lie, I say."

"That isn't what we're here for," reproved the nurse
primly. Nevertheless she stood the door open and let Rachel
alone.

Hour after hour passed, Rachel looking down into the
cool, quiet night, till she knew every shadow and twinkling
light of the village below the hill on which the institution
was built. Again and again she saw with alert eyes and
quickened heartbeats, the lights of a car come into sight far
down in the valley, twinkle and gleam fitfully, as it passed
along unseen roads, out of sight behind the trees, and into
sight again, only to pass on to the left or the right and away
out of sight. Till at last the night grew old, and the lights of
travelers grew fewer and farther between, and finally there
were only the stars shining steadily above, like old promises
long unheeded, and Rachel looked up and repeated over
once more those promises she had learned so carelessly, long
years before.

Then sharply into her thoughts came the ring of the telephone bell. She heard the nurse lift the receiver, and heard
her sleepy answer, cross and low:

"She's all right so far, only she won't go to bed. Just sits
by the window looking out. No, she wouldn't eat anything,
and refused to take any medicine. I thought best not to stir
her up till the doctor gets here. He always likes us to use
persuasion till he gets a case in hand. Yes, I'll let you know
if there are any developments. I know, Mr. Shillingsworth
told me it was a very special case. Who are you? Are you
Mr. Shillingsworth's secretary?"

But there was a click as if the one at the other end of the
wire had hung up, and presently the nurse clicked her receiver into place and yawned, remarking in a low tone to the
attendant:

"The fools aren't all dead yet. There's no fool like an old
fool. Why can't he trust her in our hands, now he's put her
here, and go to bed and to sleep like a sane man, instead of

having to call up in the middle of the night to see how she is!
As if we wouldn't let him know!"

But Rachel's heart was standing still with a new horror.
Shillingsworth was pursuing her even over the telephone in
the middle of the night! She put her head down on the win-
dowsill and began to pray once more, and the nurse peering
in by and by found her so and thought she was asleep.

"We ought to put her in bed, I suppose, but I'm too tired
for a fight!" she remarked as she sat down with a sigh.

The night wore on, and the stars looked down with their
old faithfulness, and Rachel lifted her head and looked up
at them wistfully, her heart full of prayer.

Then off in the distance one of the stars began to move, at
least it seemed that way, and to shoot through the trees, and
blink nearer and nearer until finally the long searching rays
of two headlights became distinct, coming on up the road
and in among the trees below the window. Her heart stood
still again with fear. Was it Shillingsworth come himself so
soon? Or the doctor? She had ceased to hope for rescue, for
how could Chan possibly know where she was, or know she
needed him? If he were hunting her at all doubtless he was
away off to Chicago making hopeless search. Oh, fool that
she had been to run away from the only protector she had
on earth!

She put her hand on her heart and tried to quiet its beating. Tried to listen painfully, as the car swerved into the
drive and came round in front of the house, quite a way
from the window.

She heard a car door open and steps on the gravel drive.
She started to her feet, hoping to get near the door to listen
and know if anyone was coming to her. If the doctor had arrived she meant to put in a plea to see him at once. It was
important that she should see him before Shillingsworth had
a chance to talk to him.

But the door to the hall was drawn shut quickly from
without, and she heard a key turn in the lock! She was a
prisoner! And who, who was coming?

She went wildly toward the door. She wanted to beat on it with her hands and cry out, but realized that this was futile. It would only confirm them in the idea that she was insane. In fact, there seemed hardly anything she could do that would not confirm them in that. How helpless was one in her situation!

Then suddenly she dropped upon her knees beside the bed and began to pray in a soft, wild little whisper:

"Oh, God, You take care of me. You save me! For Jesus' sake!" The sweet old formula she had learned when she was a child.

And outside, the nurse was coming up the stairs with two visitors.

CHAPTER XIV

The man at the station stepped further out of the shadow and Chan saw there were brass buttons on his coat. It was too late to get away. He had to face this whatever it was.

"Name Prescott?" asked the officer gruffly.

"What's that to you?" asked Chan, eyeing the other man calmly. His old effrontery served him in good stead now.

"Well, if you are I gotta message for you from yer man, name of Andy. Says to tell ya he's got a puncture about eight miles below here on the pike. If it suits you you can come on to meet him, otherwise he'll get here as soon as he can. He phoned the station house. Said you'd be here."

Chan's hand was in his pocket and relief upon his face.

"Thanks awfully," he said, putting a five-dollar bill in the officer's hand. "Saved me a long wait I guess. If he phones again tell him I'm meeting him." And Chan slid the car off down the road once more.

"Well, that was a narrow escape!" he mused. "You never can tell what's coming next! This country is hoodooed. We'd better get out of it. A puncture! Can you beat it? And every minute counts."

Five miles down the pike he came upon his car shining even in the darkness, and Jim down upon his knees, his task almost completed.

"Had bad luck on this last trip up," Jim explained. "Got a flat tire just outta Chicago and didn't wantta stop to patch it so I put on one of the spares. But this time I thought I better not use the other spare, we might need it later, so I hadta patch her. Get my message? I figured the cop would be safe enough. He find ya all right?"

"All right," said Chan contentedly. "All right now?"

"All right," said Jim, straightening up.

152

"Where's Andy?"

"Back there tightening a loose nut."

Andy appeared with an easy lurch and greeted his employer with a grin.

"Heah yoh gotta raid on, Mr. Prescott."

"I sure have, Andy. Glad you came along. I need you. Know any place you can get a disguise? I need a disguise."

"What like?"

"Old woman. I want to fix you up like an old woman, Andy. It's an absolute necessity."

Andy flashed another grin.

"How about the old woman back whah we got the doughnuts, Jim?"

"Yes, you might get something there."

"How far back?" questioned Chan anxiously. "We ought to get on our way."

"Bout two miles."

"All right, Andy, jump in the little car and run back. See what you can get. Don't forget anything. Shoes, hat, a bonnet would be better, a veil, and a shawl or cloak. Guess you'd have to have a dress, too. You've got to be fixed so nobody would suspect, see? Tell the old lady you're going to play a joke on somebody, and pay her anything she asks."

Chan handed out a roll of bills, and asking no further questions, Andy, who had had experiences with this young daredevil before, cheerfully jumped into the roadster and drove off down the road. In five minutes more the work on the tire was completed and Chan and Jim climbed in and followed him.

They found Andy just getting back into his car with two large newspaper bundles under his arms and a grin on his face.

"Chuck 'em in here, Andy," ordered Chan. "Take your car to the garage over there. I guess it's open. There seems to be a light. Tell the man you'll be back for it sometime today or tomorrow, and get a hustle on. We've got to burn up the road in a hurry now. We'll wait for you at the next corner."

Andy was soon back, climbing over the door into the backseat limberly, and they swung off into the night.

"Now," said Chan, when they were out in the open country, "we've got to rescue a girl from a private insane asylum! No, she isn't insane. She's been kidnapped. She's a friend of mine. I'll tell you more about it later on. For the present we've got work to do. She's about twenty miles from here, and the old beast that put her there is coming for her in the morning, so we've got to work fast. Andy, you're her old nursemaid come to condole with her, and see if you can't quiet her, see? Think you can play the part? I'm bringing you. You're brokenhearted to find she's lost her mind and had to come to her at once. You don't need to say anything. Leave that to me. All you need do is get out your handkerchief and cry a little. Did you get a bonnet and veil?"

"I reckon, Mr. Prescott. She got out her best things for me."

"Well, then when we get up to the room I'll manage some way to get the door shut and you shell off the costume and hand it over to the lady, see? Then I lead her out to the car, and you slide out any way you can. You'll have to manage to secrete your cap in your pocket somehow so you'll look like a chauffeur, and you can be wandering around the halls trying to find us, see? If anybody meets you and interferes with your getting out, say it's almost time for our train and you came to tell us. Think you can play the part, Andy?"

"I guess so. Any guns?"

"No, no guns."

"I gotta gun in my pocket," said Andy in a tone that showed he was not unwilling to use it.

"No, Andy, this is a peaceful raid. We use strategy this time. Savvy?"

"I get yah."

Andy and Jim had been in Chan's company in France which explained their mutual familiarity.

An hour later they arrived, and there got out from the car in front of the big stone building a gentleman and an elderly woman, attired in neat black dress, long black shawl folded cornerwise, and a black silk Quaker bonnet, somewhat the worse for wear, a little dented on one side, but still respectable, black cotton gloves, and big flat-soled shoes. The lady carried a handkerchief which she pressed to her face from time to time, and she leaned heavily upon the arm of the young man.

In the darkened car Jim sat, alert, ready for any emergency.

The reluctant attendant opened the door after the second ring. The nurse hung over the balustrade and listened.

"I have come from Mr. Shillingsworth," said Chan, politely raising his hat. He took great credit to himself that he was in this opening sentence adhering to Rachel's wish for nothing but the exact truth to be told. He had come from Mr. Shillingsworth. He had no desire to stay near Shillingsworth.

The attendant opened the door a little wider at the magic name of the president of the board of trustees.

"He is anxious about Miss Rainsford." That, too, was strictly true.

"She's all right. She ain't making any fuss so far. Just won't get into bed, that's all."

"Well, I've brought with me an old nurse." Chan indicated the lady on his arm. "We feel that she may be able to soothe and quiet the girl and perhaps make her able to sleep. Is the doctor about?"

"Nope, but the head nurse is up there. You c'n come in if you think it's worthwhile, but I think she's asleep."

Chan stepped in, the lady beside him, her handkerchief held tremulously to her lips, and covering a good portion of her face.

"We feel," said Chan vaguely, "that it may do wonders for the young lady to see this old nurse. There is much fondness between them. I have traveled a good many miles since dark to get this woman and bring her here, and I think it is important that she see her."

The nurse spoke from the head of the stairs, sharply:
"Did you say you came from Mr. Shillingsworth?"

"Yes," said Chan, raising his voice clearly, "I said I came from Mr. Shillingsworth."

"In that case they'll have to see her of course, Tom," said the nurse reprovingly to the attendant.

"All rightie, walk right up," said Tom, yawning.

Chan and the lady went up the stairs together, Chan assisting her, the handkerchief much in evidence. The nurse eyed them as they came forward, and was much taken with Chan's handsome face and courteous manner.

"It certainly was kind of you to come all this way at this time of night," said the nurse in her most flattering tone. She knew on which side her bread was buttered with the president of the board of trustees.

"Nothing is too much trouble," spoke Chan, purposely raising his voice, hoping it might penetrate to Rachel's ears. "Nothing is ever too much trouble if it will help the poor little girl."

"I had better prepare her for your coming," said the nurse fluttering to Rachel's door. "It might frighten her to waken her out of her sleep."

She opened the door softly, but Rachel was standing in the middle of the floor, her eyes wide with fear, her hands clasped at her throat.

"Somebody has come to see you, dearie," she said to the girl in honeyed tones. "Somebody who loves you very much and has come a long way through the dark to speak to you. You'll be a good girl and sit down quietly to talk with her, won't you? It's your old nurse, dearie, who has known you all your life."

"My old nurse?" Rachel's eyes growing wider with fright looked beyond the Quaker bonnet of the weeping nurse, to the smiling face of Chan just within the doorway, and Chan's eyes looked back at her steadily, gravely, reassuring her. Then he smiled and spoke:

"You remember your old nurse Mary, don't you, Rachel?

Tell her how glad you are that she has taken all this trouble to come and see you."

Suddenly the fear went out of Rachel's eyes and a smile played about her mouth:

"My old nurse!" she exclaimed. "Oh, yes! I am glad you have come! My old nurse Mary!" and she dropped her face into her hands in sheer relief and laughed hysterically to hide the tears that were springing to her eyes.

Chan turned to the nurse:

"Don't you think it would be a good plan to leave them alone for a few moments? It will be good for them to have a little talk together. Suppose you and I step out into the hall, and then you can give me any report which you wish sent back."

The nurse assented eagerly. It was an innovation to have a good-looking young man to talk to for a few minutes, a break in the terrible monotony of her job.

"I will come back for you in a few minutes, Mary," said Chan as he left, and the black figure of the old servant bowed assent.

Chan and the nurse stepped out in the hall.

"You have a beautiful building here," said Chan, looking about on the grim painted walls that wore the air of a hospital. "I've never been in here before, though of course I have passed. Have you many patients now?"

"No, not so many as in wintertime. Two were discharged last week, and several of the milder cases have been allowed to go home to their friends for a few weeks. You know we do not take the more aggravated cases here."

"So I understand. It is a very interesting old building from the outside. I should like to see more of it. Is that your parlor that I saw downstairs opening from the hall? Why, yes, I should like to see it. I know Mr. Shillingsworth would be interested to have me see it."

"Thomas," called the nurse, "just come up here and stay on the stairs, so you can hear in case anybody calls. I'm going to show the gentleman the dining room and parlor.

We have a sleeping porch, too, divided into compartments so that it is perfectly safe," she offered. It was not often she had an opportunity to show off the buildings. The day nurse usually had that duty.

"This must be very hard work for a woman," said Chan in a deeply sympathetic tone as he walked by the nurse's side through the halls and looked down pleasantly into her sour disappointed eyes. "Don't you sometimes yearn to get away from it?"

"Indeed I do!" said the nurse eagerly, surprised into naturalness by the unwonted sympathy. "Sometimes I think I will go crazy, too, staying here so long."

"Why do you stay?" asked Chan earnestly, counting the seconds off with a nervous finger and thumb inside his hat which he carried.

"Oh, I have an old mother to support," sighed the nurse. "I dare not give up here. I am in good line for promotion and a better salary someday. It is not nearly so hard to have the daytime shift and I'm hoping to get the position of manager someday."

Chan drew her out to tell her longings and ambitions, and even took her name and address, saying he would remember her if he ever heard of a better position, and all the time he was noting that the attendant who had been sent upstairs was lolling over a newspaper halfway up the stairs where the light from the ceiling was good for reading.

At last he looked at his watch and snapped it shut in surprise.

"We are staying too long," he said. "Mary will miss her train if I do not hurry her away at once. I must go and call her. No, don't go up the stairs again unless you have to, I can perfectly well call her. Well, then, if you think you must. You have been most kind. I shall not forget."

As they mounted the stairs the attendant rose and came down, mindful of a coffeepot he had put on the gas heater a few minutes before. He disappeared into the region of the kitchen.

As they approached the door of Rachel's room a figure in black issued forth tremulously, one hand holding the handkerchief to its face, the other feebly groping for the stair rail.

With quick gallantry Chan sprang to steady her, and bending spoke to her in a low tone. The bonnet bowed assent, and Chan explained to the approaching nurse:

"She's falling asleep. Mary turned out the light. Perhaps you better wait a few moments before going in to make sure she's sound. Now we must hurry or Mary will miss her train. So grateful for your kindness, and I'll not forget my promise about that position if it comes about as I suggested. Good-bye. I hope the poor child will soon be out of her torment. Such a pity that mental troubles have to be, isn't it? And—oh, I almost forgot!" He handed her an envelope. "Just a little token of Mr. Shillingsworth's confidence, you know. And I hope the remainder of the night will be more restful. I don't believe you'll have any more trouble with Rachel tonight. I'd take a little rest myself if I were you. You look tired. You owe it to yourself, you know."

And all the time Chan was edging the black, sorrowful woman toward the stairs, and edging the nurse farther and farther away from the door, luring her down behind him as he talked, until they were almost down to the front door.

"Thomas," called she, "Thomas!" with an annoyed tone. "Where can that man be? Thomas, come here and open the door for them. Turn on the light so they can get down the steps! It's very dark tonight!"

But Thomas was just searching in the refrigerator for cream for his coffee and did not come at once, and Chan, protesting that he could perfectly well open the door for himself and needed no light, got his lady out the door, closing it after him with a quick clip; even while the nurse was hurrying to find Thomas and reprimand him, for she could smell the coffee now, and wanted some herself.

Mindful of her duty she hurried back upstairs after having told Thomas to bring her some coffee and a bit of the cinnamon bun that was left from supper, but when she reached the top step she gave a frightful scream, and almost fell backwards as she came face-to-face with a man in livery.

Andy reached out and placed a helpful hand upon her arm and saved her from falling.

"Sorry I scared you, ma'am. I didn't go to do it. I just come up to find my man and lady. Ain't you seen 'em?"

"What do you mean? How did you get in here?" said the nurse, assuming her nurseliest eye and her manner of command, the eye and the manner that subdued unsettled minds.

"Why, I'm just hunting the folks I brought. You seen 'em, didn't you? I come up just afore you went down and I ben going around from dooh to dooh, listenin' to see if I heard 'em. I didn't want to disturb no one. I most got lost back theah in that back hall, so I had to get back to the stairs again to get my bearings. I seen you just going down as I got here, so I waited till you come up. Where are my folks? They oughtta go. They'll miss that train, an' then I'll have to caht 'em back to Chicago, and I'm about beat out! But Mr. Shillingsworth would have it I should bring 'em, night or no night. There's no saying no to him."

"Mercy! Are you Mr. Shillingsworth's man?" said the nurse. "Why, they've gone! They must be out there now! Go quick. They were in a terrible hurry. You had no right to come in after them. You should have waited out in the car. Quick! Down those stairs! Out that door!"

Andy made one wild dash for the door, while the nurse stood at the top of the stairs and listened, and Thomas appeared from the back regions with a tray.

Meanwhile a well-trained motor so expensive that it knew how to move without a sound, had been slipping, sliding softly away down the drive, and when Andy threw open the door and slammed it shut with a resounding bang there was no car standing outside the steps, nor anywhere in the driveway, and though the nurse listened for a whole minute not a sound did she hear.

"Turn on the porch light and see if they have started!" she

commanded the indifferent Thomas. "We shall hear from this I'm afraid. That was the Shillingsworth car, and the Shillingsworth chauffeur was up here hunting them. If you had been doing your duty he couldn't have got by. It was all against rules to allow that servant up here anyway. You ought to have brought the message up for him. Why didn't you?"

"I didn't see any man," said Thomas. "I guess you're getting dippy yourself. Here, take some coffee! I'm not going to open that door again tonight. Those folks went away a long time ago. I heard 'em go. What's the matter with you?"

When the nurse finally prevailed upon Thomas to open the front door and turn on the light, Andy was far down the hill through the shrubbery, just springing on the running board as it passed around the curve of the hill and slid out into the open road. A moment more, and the car, still coasting downhill silently, was almost at the end of Barberry Row, leading into the highway.

Thomas came in and shut and locked the door. He was disgusted. But before he could remonstrate with his superior officer a scream rang out from upstairs that froze even the heart of a Thomas, and he rushed upstairs three steps to a bound.

"What's the matter?" he cried, expecting to see a raving maniac trying to kill the nurse. But instead, there stood the nurse in the upper hall in front of the new patient's door, weeping and wringing her hands.

"She's gone! She's gone!" the woman moaned. "Oh, why was I left with a fool like you to help me, this night of all nights. And the other man sick and as sound asleep as the dead! Go! Go quickly! Catch them. They can't have got far yet. I tell you go! Call up the police! Stop them! Stop them, I tell you! You and I will be to blame! And now, just when I thought I was going to get promotion! Oh, you fool! Won't you go?"

"Where'll I go?"

"Go down and look through the yard. Take the dogs and

catch them. Listen for a motor. They can't have got far away. I'll call Mr. Shillingsworth. That's the first thing to do. He will at least know that I reported to him at once. You search the yard. Wake John and the servants. We can't help it if John is sick! Wake him, I tell you. Don't waste a minute! Central! Central!" and she began clawing at the telephone like a wild woman.

And far below on the highway, that scream had rung out, and echoed down to the little group dashing madly eastward.

"Ah!" said Chan in a low voice to Jim who was driving. "Ah! They've found us out! Now we must go like thunder. It won't be long before every cop in the county will be on our heels! We've got five minutes' start. GO!"

CHAPTER XV

Miles away in a little moon-swept village on a quiet, maple-lined street there stood a little cottage, white with green blinds and a big glass door. Vines crept over it and window boxes filled with geraniums dripped delicate vines to the breeze. Small evergreen trees nestled about it, their pointed tops fringing the little terrace on which the house sat. The house that had been Rachel Rainsford's home.

Back of the house was a garage that used to be a barn, but had been turned into a garage to eke out the salary of a teacher who had the greatness to stay in a school that loved him even though he was in need of the larger salary that his ability might have brought him somewhere else.

The garage had a loft, and in that loft was stored all that was left of the furnishings of the home that had been Rachel's for most of the happy years of her girlhood.

There was a great old walnut desk with capacious drawers, and ink spots over the top, and a great deep scar of a pinhole like a miniature well that was dug by Chan Prescott himself one bitter day, when he had been caught redhanded meting out justice to a fellow student. The kindly professor had showed such genuine concern that this student had broken rules and taken matters in his own hands, that Chan had seen for the first time in his life that he really had been wrong. And he had stood there minute after minute driving that pin deeper and deeper into the rich old wood of the professor's treasured desk, waiting to get the consent of himself to acknowledge his wrong. What it had cost the professor to see his desk so mutilated Chan would never know; but something of the fineness of the nature that cared more for a boy's character than for even a treasured possession stole into the soul of the boy, and bound him to the teacher through all the years. And now, as he rode along through the darkness, accusing himself as he had not had time to do before that night, he remembered the night in the professor's office, when he had come to bluff it out and take what was coming to him; remembered the mellow old desk with the professor's papers set in neat piles, and a row of books across one end; remembered the pin that he had driven deep, and twisted about till it made a blemishing hole, and the words he had finally spoken bringing a shining light to the teacher's eyes, and a quick grasp of the warm scholarly hand.

Suddenly he leaned over close to the little trembling figure in the big black bonnet sitting so straight and frightened beside him, watching the shadows with tired eyes as they flew along in the darkness.

"This was all my fault," he whispered in a a low tone that could be heard only by Rachel. "You were right. I should not have taken you to Southerlys'. Will you forgive me?"

Rachel's little cold hand stole quickly over to his with an eager pressure, and he caught and held the hand fast in his big warm one.

"You did it all for the best," she whispered. "It was no one's fault but mine perhaps. I bungled things. I had no right to go off without consulting you. I knew that as soon as I came to myself. I have suffered so about it!"

"They didn't hurt you, did they?" asked Chan in quick alarm. "If they dared to lay a finger on you——"

"No, no," she shuddered.

"There! There! Darling!" he soothed and did not know that he had breathed the endearment. "Wait till you are rested before you tell me. Put your head down on my shoulder. No one can see. It will be easier for you. Give me that other hand! Why, you are trembling! I'll put the robe over you. Take off that hideous bonnet. We are safe now. We shan't need that again! Now, put your head down so. Is that comfortable? No, don't worry. Jim and Andy can't see you. Now, rest. What's this on your head? Why, you managed to bring along your hat, didn't you? That was clever. Wore it inside your bonnet. Clever child! All right, now shut your eyes. I'll waken you when it begins to get light."

Rachel obediently laid her head against the strong shoulder, surrendered her shaking hands to the big warm ones, and closed her eyes, but she did not go to sleep. She felt as if she should never sleep again. Such a warm, safe, happy feeling nestled round her heart, that even though she was shaken so that she could scarcely move her lips to answer him steadily, she was glad. Glad, not only with a great relief from the horror that had been over her during the first hours of the night, but just glad that she was here, with Chan, who had cared enough to go to such lengths to rescue her. And now she knew that she had known all along that he would come, would find out somehow and be there, would drag the depths if need be to protect her, and her soul rejoiced.

She was too tired to try to analyze what this meant. She just let her soul sing to itself as she laid her head against his shoulder and was borne along to safety.

There might be other dangers and difficulties ahead. There doubtless would be. But she was glad now, singingly glad!

It occurred to her to wonder whose car they were in, and who Jim and Andy were, but it seemed not worth bothering about. She was tired, so tired! And she must rest before it was time to wake up and go at the problem of her life once more. She knew now that she must not do anything rashly again. That was enough for now. Every minute was taking her farther away from that terrible asylum where they thought she was crazy. She would stick now to the strong hand that was holding hers till he told her she was safe. And though there might be other difficulties she knew now that God was guiding her case, for did He not answer her prayer, almost at once, and send deliverance in her time of need? And here was not only one strong deliverer, but three, all guarding her as if she were a queen.

And all the way Chan sat with that precious head against

his shoulder and it seemed to him that new strength was pouring into his veins and new power coming upon him as he felt the gentle weight of his responsibility. Chan did some deeper thinking than he had ever done in his life before.

He went back to that pinhole in the walnut desk a good many times and seemed to see himself a raw youth, living only to please himself, stalking through life with little thought of others unless they pleased him. He did some intensive thinking on the matter of his own character, and decided that he was utterly unfit for the honor that had been granted him of saving this sweet young life. Who was that lad the professor was always having them study? Sir Galahad, was it? Chan remembered only a sentence or two: "His strength was as the strength of ten, because his heart was pure," and that other, something about a gardenia in his buttonhole, wasn't it? Oh, yes, "Wearing the white flower of a blameless life." Oh, not that he had ever been so bad, of course, but he wasn't blameless by any means. And could he by any stretch of the imagination be said to have a pure heart? Why, he hadn't *ever* been really *bad*, not to say Bad! Of course Rachel had said breaking God's law was sin, but he'd never heard any talk about sin before, not that way. In the world where he had grown up sin meant getting caught at something.

Well, supposing he could pass on that. What was that old rule Galahad went by? "Live pure— Live pure——" There it was again! There seemed to be so much stress put upon that. Why, compared to many fellows he knew he was what you might call spotless. He had always looked upon himself that way. But in the light of this girl's new standards he had his doubts. Well—and what was the rest of that? Oh, yes, "Live pure, right wrong——" There you had it. He had done a lot of that all his life. This that he was doing now was righting wrong. A terrible wrong. Why, wasn't that enough to make up for any lack in the other direction? His sense of justice swelled into notice. He had righted numberless wrongs ever since he as a boy of ten fought to save a little girl in the back alley from being frightened by a dog. His self-respect rose. He could qualify on that one anyway. Now, what was the rest?

"Live pure, right wrong, and follow the King."

The long forgotten words came back to mind with swift condemnation. His self-esteem vanished. He shrank into the corner looking down shamedly at the girl by his side. No, he hadn't ever followed any King but himself. All his good deeds had been done to satisfy his own sense of the fitness of things. Very often he had visited justice as his vagaries dictated. If he liked a man he helped him out, and sometimes the man was not always in the right either. A newly roused conscience got up and told him that to his silent amazement.

Well, follow the King. What King? If there had been a real visible King who merited following, none would have joined His train quicker than he. He would have ridden over miles of mountains, trod rough roads and valleys uncomplaining, have gone without food and rest, have suffered no end of tortures, to set a real King on the throne, to see that He was made King and honored. But a spiritual, intangible King; that was what they all meant by it. He had only the vaguest notion of a heavenly King. It was vague enough to be beyond him.

He looked down at the small dark shadow on his shoulder that was Rachel's head, and for the first time in his life wished that he knew what all this meant and could take hold of it and make himself into the kind of man that she could honor and respect and love.

His face grew gentle and tender in the darkness, and something moist came upon his lashes as he regarded the quiet little shadow there beside him, and reverently held her small hands that were warm and relaxed now within his grasp. Oh, if he could somehow prove himself as the knights of old did, prove himself as one worthy of her love! Love had never meant much to him till now. A disease he had called it in idle jest among his comrades, and expected it to strike him for a season just as had chicken pox and whooping cough and measles.

But this was different. This made him search all the realm of his being, and like a searchlight brought out traits in himself that he had never dreamed he possessed.

The King! Oh, if there were a real King, he would go and join himself to His army tomorrow morning, and follow wherever He might lead, if in so doing he might prove himself worthy of this sweet child and her precious love.

Then suddenly a thought occurred to him. Perhaps there was someone else. Perhaps, young as she was, she had already given her love! It seemed appalling. For an instant he shrank and wavered from it. And then as if some test had been put to him his soul answered:

"Yes, even if that were the case, I would still want to follow the King, because I have known her."

It came to him that all women ought to be that way, to bear with them an atmosphere that made every man wish to be pure-hearted, to right wrong, and to follow the King. He had a vague idea that following the King might involve a good many matters which he did not at all understand. Matters of theology for instance. Things about God and the Bible. He could not have been in Professor Rainsford's classes for several years without getting an inkling of what he as a teacher had meant by following the King. Chan looked grave in the darkness and wondered if in this age of the world there were ways of finding out that simple sweet philosophy which that great quiet teacher had known. People laughed at such things now. Jeered as if they belonged to a forgotten age. He wondered if Rachel still believed as her father had? He wondered if there would be a way for him to find out about that King.

Then the dawn came up faintly.

They were skirting a great lake and the rosy flush of dawn was marvelous upon it, giving almost a shock of sudden light as they shot out from a covert of trees and were full upon it.

Rachel came suddenly wide awake and sat up, retrieving her hands, straightening her little hat, tucking in close her vivid hair, sitting primly to her corner, small and shy in the dawn.

They were passing through a summer colony where everything was still asleep. Even the streetlights looked pale and sickly in the rapidly growing rose of the dawn.

Andy was driving now, and it was all downgrade. They slipped down the wide boulevard, past the luxurious cottages of the summer people almost silently. Even the milkman and the bread man had not begun to stir. And then they whirled out to the open country again, slipped through woods and out once more into highways, sometimes taking an obscure side road that would cut off miles from their distance, and keeping always as much out of the towns as possible.

"You must be very tired and we ought to stop and let you rest for a few hours, but I do not dare take any more risks yet. We want more miles between us and our enemies and we want to get out of the state and across another one or two before we stop. How about it, Andy, are you tired driving? Want me to take the wheel?"

Andy grinned amusedly.

"Just beginnin' to get my wind, Chan," he drawled. "Haven't got quite ovah being an old woman yet."

A spirit of hilarity seemed to be in the air. The two faithful servitors in the driving seat seemed to be one with them in spirit, and there were no social distinctions. It was as if even Chan was set aside now, and these two men were taking care of Chan and his girl together.

"Might as well make a couple of days of it, and do the thing right," remarked Jim, running his finger along the line of the map to study out a new and quick way to elude any possible pursuers.

"That's all right," said Chan firmly. "But after we've had breakfast somewhere in some nice quiet farmhouse, Miss Rainsford and I are going to take the front seat and I'll drive while you two get a good sleep. There's no sense in all of us getting worn out at once. We are not by any means out of the woods yet, and we've got to save our strength!"

"And what about you taking a sleep, Chan?" asked Andy lightly. "I don't believe you even took one eyelash off the road yet."

"Well, that's different," said Chan placidly. "I've done altogether too much sleeping in my life and I can stand a week or two of waking now before I get a sleep."

They watched the rose of dawn turn into golden day, and still they could not talk much about the night before or the things that they had escaped.

"We'll get a little further away from it all before we dip into it," Chan said, seeing Rachel's cheeks pale at the remembrance. Then he and Andy joked about the old bonnet and shawl.

Andy said he wanted to keep the things to give to his best girl, and Rachel helped fold them all up and stow them away in the pockets of the car. Andy and Jim gave her respectful grins, and were ready to defend her with their lives if need be. In fact, Andy and Jim loved Chan like a brother, and well they understood the look in his eyes, even though Rachel as yet did not.

They were taking one of Jim's shortcuts when they came upon a farmhouse. It was back from the road, but not too far for the aroma of frying ham and bubbling coffee to float out on the breeze. They stopped and Jim got out and arranged for breakfast. As they were getting out of the car, and while Andy was engaged in putting the old lady's bonnet and dress and shawl away more securely in the touring trunk behind, Chan slipped off a gorgeous diamond from his little finger.

"Put it on, Ray," he pleaded. "It needn't mean anything afterward if you don't want it to, but you must wear it now for protection. We don't want anybody saying things about us, not about you anyway. Yes, I insist!" as Rachel lifted a protesting face. "Really, you know—— Please! No, not on that finger, on the third of the left hand. There! Now this old lady won't get a false notion!" and he laughed comfortably as he lifted her down from the running board and helped her over the rough ground around a flowerbed. "It isn't set quite as I would like to have it for a lady, but it will answer for the present purpose, and let us trust that the old lady who is frying our ham does not know the latest styles from Tiffany's."

"Oh, but, Chan——" said Rachel, her cheeks suddenly pink as she caught the twinkling of the wonderful stone.

"Now, don't Chan me! Remember you are to do as I say until I get you—somewhere—home!"

So Rachel wore the ring on the third finger of her left hand, and was almost frightened as she saw its gleam against the thick coffee cups, as she handled the old plated spoons and steel knives and forks. But the breakfast was great, and was ready in almost no time. Plenty of cornmeal flapjacks, puffy with good sour milk and soda, brown as berries, and with golden syrup dripping over them, more ham sizzling in the frying pan, coffee like nectar and great beakers of rich creamy milk. No breakfast could be better for hungry, weary, excited travelers. The danger was that they would linger too long over it. But Jim was back to his road map once more, asking a few canny questions of the farmer by which afterward he would never have known which way the travelers were headed, and soon they were on their way again, doubling on their tracks a few miles to save detection in case anyone was following them.

Chan had taken the precaution to buy all the doughnuts the farmer's wife had, paying a fabulous price therefor, and to fill his thermos bottle with coffee, and purchase two bottles of milk and some apples. There really was no reason at all why they should stop for lunch.

Chan was driving now, with Rachel by his side and the two men, slumped down in the backseat with caps drawn over their faces, were soon asleep.

"Now," said Chan, settling down to his wheel. "You may

tell me in the fewest words you know how, just what happened last night and then I want you to forget it. You look worn to a frazzle, and we've got to take care of you. You know you've been on the continual stretch for two days and two nights, and no knowing how much yet before us. Make it snappy!"

Rachel told her story. There was not so much to tell. It had all happened so quickly. Chan did not tell his. That he was saving till some other time. Perhaps he would never tell it all. When she questioned him how he knew where to find her, he answered briefly:

"God sent me. I guess that's what you would think. I happened to hear the old skunk telephoning to Trevor. If you'd waited fifteen minutes longer I'd have saved you all this. I was onto him only it didn't come soon enough. But now, that's over. We'll talk about it another day, but not now. We've got something much more important to settle. I've been thinking a lot. Where do you want to go?"

"Oh," said Rachel, the tears starting in her eyes, "I don't know! I wish I could go home!"

"Where's that?" asked Chan, blinking to keep his own tears back at the homesick wail. "Beechwood?"

"Yes, Beechwood. It seems that I started out all wrong and ought to go back and begin over again, only I don't see how I possibly can."

"Why not?" asked Chan thoughtfully. "At least for a short time. Is the house sold?"

"No," said Rachel with troubled brow, "not sold yet, but rented. The people are going to buy it if they can sell their other house, and they hope they have a purchaser, but they paid something down which was to go as rent in case they don't buy it, only—I've used that all up—almost, and I've nothing left to live on. I gave a terribly big tip to that maid to give you and Mrs. Southerly the notes, and not to tell you till I was gone."

"Foolish child!" said Chan, smiling down at her, "but what's money?"

"Money is a lot when you haven't got it," said Rachel, her cheeks flushed with her troubled thoughts. "I cannot possibly take your money, you know. My father would think that was wrong. You know I cannot."

"Oh, sure, I know," said Chan easily. "I wouldn't have you compromised in any way, little Ray. Don't worry about that for an instant. Your reputation is dearer to me than my own, and I'm going to try to take care of it as well as your father would have done if he were here. At the worst, I could arrange a loan from a bank with your house as security, you know, but I've a better plan than that even I think, if it pleases you. Only I'm not going to divulge it until you promise me that you'll tell me the truth about it, whether you like it or not. There are lots of other ways to finance this business if you don't like this one. Will you promise?"

"Of course," said Rachel eagerly.

"Well, I was wondering if you remember an old desk your father had? It used to stand in his study. Have you got it yet? Or did you sell your furniture?"

"Oh, yes," said Rachel, puzzled to know what the old desk could have to do with finances, "I have it yet. I didn't want to sell the furniture, not yet, anyway. Besides, it wasn't worth much, and no one in Beechwood wants to buy old furniture. I did think of selling some things but the local dealer wanted me to almost give them away, and then when I got the job I thought I mustn't wait to attend to it. So I had everything stored in the garage."

"That's okay," said Chan eagerly. "Well now, the question is, would you be willing to sell me that desk? It has very special memories for me and I feel that I would be a better man if I had that desk in my room. It has a pinhole in the left-hand front corner that I made while I was making a very important decision, and your father was great! I'd like to have that desk, and I would pay you five hundred dollars for it! It would be worth every cent of that to me."

"Oh!" interrupted Rachel indignantly, "I wouldn't think of taking all that for it. It's only worth twenty dollars at the most. The furniture dealer told me that, and he said he doubted if I could get fifteen out of it."

"It's worth five hundred to me," said Chan stubbornly, "and that's what I pay."

"How could you suppose I would take anything from you for it? I will give it to you. I would love to have you have it, and I know my father would like it, too. I am glad I have something to give you which you care for that will show you just a little bit how grateful I am for all you have done for me."

"I don't want to be shown how grateful you are, little Ray. I want something far bigger than gratitude and some day I hope to ask for it, but not now. I'm not worthy. Only, there's one question I must ask, and I want you to answer me straight. Ray, is there someone else ahead of me, someone else you love? You needn't tell me who it is or anything, only I want to know it if there's no chance at all. And I am going to take care of you just the same anyway if there is, till I can put you in his or someone else's hands to take care of, but I want to know."

For some time a motorcycle had been like a speck in the distance miles behind, while Jim and Andy slept and Chan, absorbed in his theme, talked. Now suddenly Andy unfolded from his sleep and spoke at Chan's right ear:

"That'll be about all just now, Chan. There's a whizzah on our tracks. Been theah five mile back. Just keep calm. If the lady will climb right over the back of the seat heah and take my place I'll take the wheel, and you can get back with the lady. Don't get excited. Just smile. Right ovah heah, Miss. Theah, you all right? Now, Jim, get ovah and take the wheel while we change. Chan, you step back. Hustle, Jimmy. Ain't got time to look at the scenery. Picture ahead. Kodak as you go. Look natural please! You are now Mr. and Mrs. Idle Rich on a pleasure trip. I'm goin' thirty miles an hour, only, Chan, see? Now look bored."

CHAPTER XVI

Things were not going well with Mrs. Southerly's house party, in the luxurious cottage by the lake.

In the first place the charming young woman with the delightful manner and the gorgeous red hair whom Chauncey Prescott had so opportunely produced to fill the place of her niece who had sprained her ankle and could not come, had departed as suddenly and mysteriously as she had arrived, just asked permission to telephone and slipped out in an instant.

True she had left a charming little note behind, excusing herself on the ground of not wishing to disturb Prescott, which was so sweet and thoughtful of her, and promising to explain later. But in the light of all that had followed, her sudden departure seemed mysterious to say the least.

Then, as soon as her absence was made known, Prescott had acted most strangely; just dashed out to his car, without even waiting for his hat, and off out the drive into the night. Not a word heard from him since, either. It certainly was strange. She felt inclined to resent his indifference to her and her guests. What kind of a hold must the girl have over him to make him act like that? It was most discourteous. Of course, she was looking for his return every minute now, with adequate explanations. These explanations she had already formulated for him and stated as possibilities at the breakfast table. Doubtless he had found that the lady had missed the train and had taken her all the way to Chicago. Of course by the time he reached there, it would be too late to telephone as it would have disturbed the whole house. Most thoughtful of him not to have roused them!

Reassured by these smiling explanations she had vaguely invented friends, a close relative, taken suddenly acutely ill, about whom there had been some disquieting word in that telephone message for Miss Rainsford after dinner. Undoubtedly she had felt the necessity was grave, and it was so thoughtful of her to attempt to leave without disturbing Mr. Prescott who would, of course, have felt he must go with her.

But there were other disturbing elements in the case.

There for instance had been the constant ringing of the telephone bell, nearly all night it seemed, an incessant calling for Mr. Shillingsworth. It was inexcusable for a man to let his business tag after him in this way when he had accepted an invitation for a house party.

And there had been an obnoxious man by the name of Trevor, who had fairly haunted the house that morning, and was even now in close conclave with Mr. Shillingsworth in the summer house down by the lake. She could see the two silhouetted against the bright water as she stood in her own room and looked out through the organdy curtains blowing in the breeze. They looked like two bulldogs growling at one another, a little one and a big one.

Moreover, Mrs. Shillingsworth with a timid air of worry had gone furtively down the path toward the lake but a few moments before, as if to reconnoiter, had remained in the little grove near the summer house for a few moments without emerging on the side of the lake, and had but just returned coming up the walk with hurried steps and an agitated countenance, going straight to her room.

Following her a moment later had come Mrs. Southerly's older son, Archibald, with an angry look on his face and his hair awry. He had been down by the water, just below the summer house, tinkering in the motorboat. He burst into his mother's room without much formality, and persisted in speaking in too loud a voice.

"Mother, if you don't get rid of those Shillingsworths, I will. That old man is a rotten skunk and not fit to have around, and the girl hasn't two ideas in her head. If you want to know, I think that's why Prescott and his girl cleared out!"

"Why, Archie, it was you who insisted on inviting them. What do you mean?"

"Well, I know better now. I've learned a few things about him and I'm sick to death of Gladys. She's a pain!"

Mrs. Southerly, much relieved that her son's heart was still intact, decided that now was a good time to make sure of it, for she had never relished the Shillingsworth girl for a possible daughter-in-law.

But when, after brief deliberation, she decided to have a sick relative in Maine who needed her immediate presence, and went over to Mrs. Shillingsworth's room to begin her tactful excuses, she found that agitated woman in the midst of packing! What could it all mean?

Mrs. Shillingsworth was very vague—a letter in the morning mail—they would have to take the noon train. Would Mrs. Southerly mind asking the maid to send her daughter up to her room at once? It was just possible that Papa's business might take them all abroad.

Relieved, Mrs. Southerly made haste to send for the daughter, and after duly offering her aid and having been refused, she retired to her room once more to think it over. The house party was melting away. There remained but the Warrens, good, comfortable, middle-aged, who had driven to the village for another size of knitting needles, and their son and daughter, who were literally daffy on golf. Things were brightening up. When the Shillingsworths were gone she might telegraph the Hamiltons to run up. They were always good company. But how could she tell whether Chauncey Prescott was returning? Strange he didn't call up. It was getting late in the morning. It was really quite rude of him. She must think up some girl to invite for his benefit, for Lorena Warren was no good unless one wanted to play golf every living minute, and she was so unearthly perfect in the game that no one could beat her. It really was unwomanly for a girl always to want to excel.

Mrs. Southerly went and stood at her window again, and watched the two silhouettes. They were standing up now,

gesticulating. One—was that Shillingsworth?—shaking his
fist in the other man's face. And the other man had a taunt-
ing air as if he had the best of things. Mrs. Southerly moved
back away from the window with a worried sigh. They were
coming toward the house now. She wished they were gone.
She wished that Mr. Prescott would come back. When he
did she must have a talk with him and find out all about that
lovely girl. Perhaps he could somehow explain all this mystery that was going on about her house. She had half a mind
to excuse herself from lunch, say she had a sick headache, or
else have an errand in the village that kept her waiting—no,
the country club would be better.

Was that Mr. Shillingsworth coming up the stairs? Then
that other little rat of a man must be gone at last. There was
that to be thankful for, at least. Was that somebody crying?
It must be Mrs. Shillingsworth? How unpleasant! That was
what came of inviting guests that one knew nothing about.
But Cousin John said he was awfully rich and was making
quite a success socially. Or no, perhaps he said politically.
But it was always so interesting to have people who were
prominent politically. It brought one in touch with the great
questions of the day and gave an atmosphere to a house
party. Then of course it was her duty to bring to the house
the girls Archibald was interested in. Gladys Shillingsworth
was said to be very attractive, but she herself couldn't see it
and she was glad that Archie had changed his mind. She
was much relieved that they were going. Perhaps it would be
judicious to slip down the back stairs, now while they were
talking and would not hear her, and have the man drive her
to the village. It really was going to be horribly embarrass-
ing to have to meet them again if they kept on talking so
loud, and one had to be known to have heard them.

"I heard you, Papa," Mrs. Shillingsworth was saying. "I
heard all those terrible things you let that man say to you,
and you didn't deny them. And I think it's time I did something. I've stood a great deal for Gladys' sake, but it doesn't
get us anywhere, and I've come to the end."

Things had reached that stage when Mrs. Southerly slipped out of her door, closing it silently, and stole down the back stairs.

As the lower back stair door closed firmly but silently Shillingsworth was breaking into a loud guffaw at his wife's expense.

"Why, that's nothing!" he exclaimed. "That girl's insane! If you had stayed long enough you would have heard the whole story. She's insane and I'm a trustee for her property! She's causing me no end of trouble from beginning to end. I'm sorry I ever undertook it. Her father was an old friend of mine years ago and I hadn't an idea she was off her bean when I undertook it. She's made me trouble enough before, and now she's beat it from the asylum and is at large. Nothing doing going to Europe, Mrs. Shillingsworth. We're going to camp right here where I can be in touch with my men until that girl's found. So you can hang up your coats and dresses in that closet and go down and tell Mrs. Southerly it was all a mistake, that I haven't got to go to Europe after all and we're pleased to pieces to spend the next two weeks here with her. I haven't found such a convenient spot for a rest in a long time, and I intend to make the most of it. And Mrs. Southerly is a peach of a hostess. Come now, mop up your eyes and call Gladys to get ready for lunch and look her prettiest. The young Southerly is hit hard or I'm no judge. I'm gonta stay here till I get ready to leave. And I'll tell you another thing, Mrs. Shillingsworth, if you get up any more crazy notions about your husband you can go just as soon as you get ready. There are plenty I know would enjoy your income, and the jewels you wear on your fingers, and I don't have to ask any woman what I do. But you were all off this time, sure thing!"

Mrs. Southerly came home at lunchtime to find Mrs. Shillingsworth seated on the front piazza with a well-powdered nose and a large embroidery hoop into which she was fitting the corner of an elaborate table cover in the latest design. By her side sat Mrs. Warren placidly knitting with her new needles.

"We don't have to go after all," she announced radiantly, settling plumply back in the big porch rocker and crossing her cushiony little feet in their tight, high-heeled slippers. "We're so happy! Papa had a message, a telegram I think it was, and he doesn't have to go, so we can stay the full time. Gladys is out playing tennis with Archie. He's such a dear, isn't he? And Papa is going to play golf with Mr. Warren this afternoon. It was charming of them to ask him. Papa loves golf. Only he gets so little time to play it, poor dear!"

Mrs. Southerly went in to see about the lunch salads, feeling that life was growing very difficult indeed, and that perhaps after all she had better look up a sick relative in the mountains or better still take a trip to Europe herself. Now, what would Archie do? She was never sure of Archie. He had very strong likes and dislikes. But was he really playing tennis with Gladys after all he had said? Really Archie ought not to talk that way about respectable men. Calling them by such names. Rotten! And "skunk!" It wasn't decent to speak to his mother about people that way. She must really speak to Archie. But her chief worry now was that perhaps Archie would change again and think as much of Gladys as ever.

She looked about on her well-appointed summer home, on its luxurious furnishings, its wide piazzas facing toward the silver stretch of lake, with just enough trees between to give the feeling of seclusion, on the clear blue sky with little lazy clouds floating like bits of down, on the view down the road where other cottages equally well-appointed could be glimpsed through the trees, and she wondered why all this comfort had to be spoiled by a mistake. It had been a mistake to invite the Shillingsworths. She could see that now. They were common!

When Mrs. Southerly said "common," she had gone just about as low as she cared to stoop.

Meantime in a little inn down in the village the man

Trevor was keeping the wires hot at various points trying to get some clue to the lost girl. The thousand-dollar check in his pocket burned to his very soul. To come so near to that much money and then to lose it! To say nothing of the five hundred extra that had been promised for putting her safe in the asylum. And to think he had gone to all that trouble and placed her safely as arranged, and then it had been for naught! He made the life of the tortured nurse one long torment. He got at the local police and questioned them like a little gimlet, boring into their very souls. He even ferreted out the little robin's-egg blue runabout that Andy had left in the garage, though it was ten miles away from the village. But there his clue stopped. The description of Andy did not fit the young man who had been with Rachel. And who was this third individual? A hired assistant, or a new element to be dealt with? Also, where would one look for the missing girl? Not out in California where she was supposed to be going to wait on a fake old lady, for there was no such place nor such woman as he had described in his decoy advertisement. Neither reasonably would he suppose that she would return to her home, for why should she have left it if there was anything there to attract her? Besides, she had no money. She could not travel far without money. Also, what relation had the strange young man to her? Was he a stranger who had struck up an acquaintance with her on the train, or an old friend? And if so, how powerful? Trevor was cunning but not clever. These matters greatly perplexed him. But both for the matter in hand and for his future reputation in his unholy traffic of souls, he felt that he must see this thing through. Shillingsworth was not a man to be trifled with, nor to be easily dropped if one could possibly keep in his good graces. Therefore Trevor lingered and kept the telephone wires hot, and tried new methods and new clues with every new hour that dawned, for underneath it all he was terribly afraid of Shillingsworth.

That night at dinner Archie Southerly announced his intention of leaving the next day for Bar Harbor, and Gladys

Shillingsworth went into a fit of sulks. The next morning Mrs. Southerly decided that it was time to do something, so she kept to her room and sent down word that she had taken a slight cold and was sorry not to be with them, but she hoped they would amuse themselves and have a fine time. She suggested motoring, and ordered the servants to pack a lunch, so the Warrens and Mrs. Shillingsworth and her daughter went glumly off in the big touring car; but Papa Shillingsworth stayed at home and spent the day telegraphing and telephoning. There was no denying the fact that Papa Shillingsworth was roused and meant to punish someone for the failure of his own plans, for the truth of the matter was that there was far more involved in this matter than just the loss of one pretty girl. His reputation was at stake. There was no knowing how much of this might leak out among the board of trustees of that sanitarium. That nurse was so overwhelmingly conscientious that she would have the whole story in all its details spread all across the continent if he did not look out. Already it had cost him a goodly sum to suppress a newspaper account that told too much without giving the right atmosphere. Trevor was a fool, and all the other people who were in the business were worse than fools. And the very worst of it all was that there seemed to be someone on the girl's side who was uncannily clever. Could it be that young man who had acted like such a fool out there at the side of the railroad, cutting stakes, and measuring out imaginary property? He must have that young man looked into. Strange he had not thought of that before. The young man had been at dinner, too, that first evening of the house party, and had disappeared. Up to this minute Shillingsworth had not thought much about Chan. Now he turned his concentrated attention to him. What had his name been? Prescott? Hm! Couldn't be his old enemy Prescott of New York, could it? His son, of course! Well if it was he'd give him a good fight for interfering!

Now as soon as Mrs. Southerly came downstairs he would

question her about that young man. Who was he? What did she know about him? Where did she pick him up? What was his father's name?

Why didn't Mrs. Southerly come down?

He found her maid. He sent her up with a message. Would Mrs. Southerly come down and talk with him for a little while about a very important matter?

Mrs. Southerly would not. She was indisposed.

Would Mrs. Southerly let him come up for a few minutes and ask some important questions?

She would not. She was not feeling well enough to talk with anybody.

Shillingsworth frowned and betook himself to the telephone again. There were other ways of finding out what he wanted to know. He had a man in New York who knew everybody, could trace all their goings within a few hours after you asked him. He called up New York, and within an hour had in motion the whole diabolical machinery which he had built up through the years for his own private unscrupulous machinations. The matter was no longer purely personal nor trivial, it had become of vast importance bordering on the edge of an old feud.

When he had done all that he could, he retired to the newspaper and a fat, black cigar, assisted by his silver flask for which he had tramped up to his room. He returned to be near the telephone, unaware of the fact that its extension cord reached into Mrs. Southerly's private room.

And presently, when the flask and the cigar were beginning to soothe his troubled spirits, there came a sharp ringing of the telephone at his elbow, and Trevor's voice exultantly:

"Well, I got track of that other bird at last, the one that was with her I mean, the feller that brought her to where you are. I think it won't be long before we have the whole case unraveled now, and believe me I'm glad! I certainly have sweated blood over this thing. I've got my men out all along the line, and when we get him we'll put him through the grill and find out what he's done with her. Oh, yes. He's the bird all right. That nurse described him to a T. He's got more nerve than a brass monkey. Walked right in and put up a story large as life. Said he came from you. Brought her old nurse to help get her to sleep.

"The thing now is to find the nurse. I have't quite figured her out. They say there's a woman out on the pike sells doughnuts and hot dogs and such. They mighta hired her. I'm going to see her now. Got a party waiting to take me. I'll let you know the result. But I gotta clue. And he'll come back before long. Say, do you know if he took his baggage when he left your house so sudden? Well, find out. No, not now. I can't wait. But that's important. I'm most certain he's coming back. He'll come to throw you off the scent. See?"

Shillingsworth hung up the receiver and sat erect, his eyes bright. This was a good time to find out. Nobody around. He heard a bell tinkle in the region of the kitchen and a door open and steps going up the back stairs. They lingered lightly, back and forth for three or four minutes and then went down again.

The maid had answered the ring.

"Go and lock the room where Mr. Prescott's things are and bring the key to me."

"Yes, Mrs. Southerly." The maid brought the key and retired to the kitchen.

Presently Shillingsworth rose with a cautious squeak of his expensive shoes and tiptoed out of the library and upstairs. He tried the door of Chan's room and found it locked. He slipped around to his wife's room which opened on a little balcony, and looked across to a corresponding balcony that opened out of Chan's room, but the distance was too great, for even his long legs. It would be undignified to be found lying below with a broken leg when the servants came out to inquire what had fallen. Shillingsworth retired below to the library once more to soothe his spirits with flask and cigar, and presently he was rewarded by the tinkle of the telephone. After fifteen minutes' conversation he hung up with a satisfied smirk on his countenance. He, too, had a clue now. And he, also, was satisfied that Chan Prescott was going to return.

CHAPTER XVII

The motorcycle rode up alongside Chan's big racing car with a flourish, and the officer held out an imperative hand importantly. Andy slowed up and came to a halt with a puzzled sympathetic expression on his face.

"Was it us you wanted to speak to, brothah?" inquired Andy innocently.

"How fast were you going?" snapped the officer. "Let me see your license."

The licenses were forthcoming promptly.

"Reckon I mighta ben going thirty or thirty-five," drawled Andy. "I wasn't just noticing. Didn't notice no signs to the contrary."

"Where you going?" the officer was eyeing each one in turn sharply.

"Why, I was just taking this man to his own wedding," twinkled Andy appealingly, nodding toward Chan, who grinned appropriately. "Wouldn't be surprised ef I did go a little fast. We're running on short time and mighty 'fraid we're goin' to be late."

"Not going over the border?" snapped the officer incredulously.

"Not today, brothah," assured Andy.

"Well, what you got aboard? I'll have to search you."

Andy got out with a tired alacrity and selected a key which he fitted into the traveling trunk.

"What's this?" The officer grabbed eagerly at the old black bonnet, surprise dawning on his face as he lifted it out.

"That, brothah, is some cloes belongin' to an old servant of the family, who left 'em over in Illinois when she was visitin', an' her friends are sendin' 'em back by us. But you could have that bonnet, I'm sure, brothah, if it would do you any good. It's not important. Think it might be becomin'? Try it on."

The officer turned with a grin, slammed the bonnet back, poking a minute or two under the old shawl, and then into the corners of the trunk, merely out of form, and sheepishly now, and then waved them on with a formal word about watching their speed.

After they had gone a good two miles Andy slowed down and spoke to Chan.

"Reckon we gotta be cautious, Chan. That brothah was a good deal worked up. And he ain't goin' to forget that bonnet. Whaddya think? We better strike across to the Lincoln Highway and skirt around some till we get into Ohio? Jim, getcher map out an' find a new route. This here one is about played out."

They struck through an old back road that led through timberland, bad going, but safe, for they met not a soul, and in about an hour came out on a better road that finally led them to the highway.

There were towns here, but Jim studied out detours and avoided several, and they met with no further interruption.

Rachel had been frightened when the motorcycle stopped them. Chan could tell by the wideness of her eyes and the white rim around her lips, and as soon as they reached smooth quiet going again he insisted that she should take a sleep. Even if it were only for a few minutes, she must rest, for they had yet long miles ahead of them before it would be safe to stop, and she must not overtax herself at the beginning. He reminded her that she had already gone through many hours of weariness and excitement and been up all night. He talked in quiet, matter-of-fact tones, and cheered her immeasurably. He told her that the more states they got between them and Illinois, the less likely they were to be troubled by followers. For even Shillingsworth could hardly follow them all over the continent, and the nearer home they got, the more friends could be called upon to help.

"My dad's up in New York," Chan said comfortably.

"He'd give a good deal to be able to do a good turn to your father's daughter. He feels that your father saved me as a child from going to the dogs. I've heard him say it. And besides, this man Shillingsworth is an old enemy of his or I'm much mistaken. He'd give half his fortune to get something on him!"

"Oh, does your father have to know?" exclaimed Rachel in horror. "Do other people have to know? It seems such a disgrace to have happened to me!"

"No one has to know, kid," said Chan comfortably. "Not if you don't want them to. I figure we are going to make out all right without any help from anyone but Jim and Andy. All the same, it's pleasant to know we're near my dad if anything else unpleasant turns up. But I figure to swing this proposition without any further assistance if possible. Now, snuggle down on this whole seat and take a nap. I'm going to sit in the middle and talk to Andy and Jim. We've got to make plans before night, you know." Chan unfolded one of the middle chairs and slipped into it, turning about to arrange a pillow out of the robe for Rachel, and she was presently sleeping so soundly that a whole army of Trevors and Shillingsworths and motorcycles might have held her up and she would never have known it.

Chan leaned forward and talked in low tones, using covert phrases that would mean nothing to the girl if she heard them. His voice was grave. He was not so sure of the way ahead as he had tried to make out. That matter of the bonnet was bad business. If any sort of word had been sent out among officers to watch for them there was a clue. They ought to get rid of those things at once. Andy owned he had been wrong to keep them. So when they reached a stretch of woods with a sparkling creek coursing its way for a few rods beside the road, Andy got out, bundled the old nurse's costume all into the stream, and drove away like mad. The next day some neighboring boys found them when they went down to swim and dragged the creek for miles in search of a body, and a column came out in the local paper all about the "murder." It even excited mild interest in the nearby city and a couple of reporters took a day off and came out in search of copy.

They did not stop for dinner that night, though the milk and coffee and doughnuts they had bought at breakfast time were long since demolished. They dropped off Jim at a small village to purchase supplies picking him up again after half an hour, and made a merry meal from grocery-made sandwiches, cheese, olives, crackers, celery, and ginger ale.

Andy and Jim were shy with the lady, but Rachel was so pleasant and natural with them, and treated them so entirely like equals, that there came to be a friendly comradery, which made them all feel quite at their ease, although Jim and Andy maintained a tremendous attitude of respect and treated Rachel like a young queen, whose minions they delighted to be.

They carefully selected isolated service stations when they had to stop for gas or oil and, for the most part, took the back roads where there was little traffic. Chan was most insistent about this.

As soon as it grew dark, Chan and Rachel took the front seat and insisted that Jim and Andy sleep for five hours straight. So Jim took the backseat, stretching out with his hat over his eyes, and Andy opened up the two middle seats and contrived to be very comfortable with one of the robes stuffed into the space between the cushions.

At last there was time for Chan and Rachel to talk, and the girl's heart began to flutter as she remembered the last words Chan had said before he was interrupted by that motorcycle officer. Would he ask that question again? She had thought about it a great deal, wondering how she should answer, for she realized that it might lead to other questions which she was not ready to discuss.

But Chan did not mention it. He seemed to have forgotten entirely what they had been talking about. His mind seemed to be wholly occupied with concern for her immediate future. His face was serious and his voice was grave as he talked, and she began to feel a blank disappointment the cause of which she did not in the least realize.

Chan was asking her about her home. Just how was the matter left? Had the people signed a lease, or was there any sort of a contract about their contemplated purchase? He was so grave and businesslike that he seemed like a different person. She could hardly realize that he was the same rollicking friend who had jumped trains and played tricks on insane asylums to save her. He seemed entirely concerned about her property now and whether it was perfectly safe for her.

"Oh," said Rachel, rousing at last to defend her old friends, "they are perfectly lovely people. The man was one of Papa's best friends, they taught together for years, although I guess he came after you left Beechwood. He followed Professor Randall Hopkins. You remember him?"

"Old Hoppy!" exclaimed Chan, a light breaking through his gravity for an instant. "I sure do remember him. We boys made his life miserable for him, hopping to class whenever the notion took us. And I don't believe he ever found out what we meant by it. But about these Thorntons," and Chan was suddenly grave again. "Would they let you stay with them for a few days, and are they the kind of people who would look after you in case anything unpleasant turned up from this experience? I mean in case they tried to get funny again. I don't think they will. I'm taking measures to be sure, but I want you with someone I can trust till everything is straightened out."

"Why yes, I could stay there," said Rachel thoughtfully, "but I don't want to. You see that was what I was going to do until I found this position. But I found out they are having a very hard time financially. Professor Thornton lost all the money he had put away in the failure of a bank not long ago, and they really cannot afford to keep me, or to spare the room for me even if I could afford to pay for my board, because they want to rent out two rooms. I don't know whether they have succeeded or not. They had somebody

almost promised when I left. But anyway, they won't let me
pay them, and they insisted on giving me two months' rent
in advance. But I suspected that Professor Thornton borrowed the money on his watch for it, for he came home that
night without it, and had to go to the neighbor's to get the
correct time to set the alarm clock, the night before he left."

"You don't say!" said Chan startled. He had not realized
that decent respectable people ever got into such straits for
money. "But I don't see how he can afford to buy the house
then, if he is so hard up as that."

"Why, he is going to sell some property he has out west,
if he can. He hopes that will pay for my house. But it doesn't
seem to sell very fast. He has been trying to sell it for two
years. He has been asking six thousand for his western property, but he said the other day they would probably have to
let it go for four. They had one offer for it of four thousand,
three years ago, but the people have moved to California,
now."

"Well, suppose you find out where the house is. I have
several friends interested in western real estate. I might be
able to sell it for him. Meantime, the question is, could you
stay there with the Thorntons for a few days? If I buy that
desk at five hundred you would be able to refund the money
they have already paid you down for rent, and you could tell
them you wouldn't take any rent till you left, see? Of course
I don't want to insist about the desk. I can find some other
way to manage the financial part if you don't like that. The
only thing was, I thought that would be a quick, easy way to
provide you with money enough for the immediate necessi-
ties without your being at all beholden to me, as you seem so
opposed to that."

"Not beholden to you!" exclaimed Rachel, wrinkling up
her face into a smile. "As if I shouldn't be beholden to you
just the same, you buying an old desk that isn't worth twenty
dollars and paying a young fortune for it!"

"Why, you're mistraken," urged Chan earnestly. "An old
desk like that is worth much more than that sometimes. It's

solid walnut and finely made. I remember it perfectly well. And besides I want it, and I shouldn't under any circumstances take it unless I paid a reasonable price for it, much as I want it. You know it has a personal value to me. And of course, if you ever want it back I'll be glad to hand it over."

"Oh, Chan, you are wonderful!" sighed Rachel, the tears suddenly coming into her eyes. "I wish father could know—perhaps he does know what you've done for me. I never can repay you."

"Look here, Ray, we haven't time to talk about nonsense like pay just now. We've got a lot of business to transact before you go to sleep, which is going to be as soon as those two back there have had a good rest. We may not be able to talk again before you get home and we've got to have it all planned out, for I may have to leave right away."

"Leave!" said Rachel with sudden blankness in her voice. "Oh, will you have to *leave?*"

"I'm afraid so," he said hurriedly. "I may not, but I think I will. You see there's some business out there that I've got to attend to. I'm not just sure how long it will take me, but I'll get back as soon as I can, and meantime I want to be sure you are all safe till I can get here and fix things right for you."

"Oh, but, Chan, you don't have to feel responsible for me, you know. You certainly have done all that anybody could be expected to do." Rachel was trying to drag back around her shoulders her garment of independence, but her voice was faltering.

"I know. I'm not responsible and all that!" said Chan shortly. "You're coming to your home where you have lots better friends than I could possibly be. I know all that. But I want to be sure there is someone who understands and will be ready for any emergency. You know this isn't just an everyday occurrence, what has happened to you, and until those men are jailed or walloped or something there is no telling what they might take it into their heads to do."

"Oh!" gasped Rachel. "Not at home! Surely—why Chan,

I've always been perfectly safe there. Everybody knows
me!"

"Yes, but what's everybody's business is nobody's. I intend to leave somebody in charge. Now about this Professor
Thornton, has he got any backbone? Is he anything like
your father? He was all right, but so many of these teachers
are like a rubber sponge, you can't depend on 'em to do anything but suck in. Excuse my plain speech. Your father
wasn't that way, and it isn't of course the fault of the pro-
fession, it only shows what an A number one job it is that so
many poor fishes want to get into it. The wonder of it is they
get there somehow. What I want to get at is, if Trevor should
turn up at your door someday, would Thornton knock him
down or would he run out the back door?"

Rachel laughed with a hysterical little catch in her voice.

"Oh, I'm sure he would knock him down if he was sure it
was he, but, Chan, Professor Thornton is in Europe this
summer, studying new methods of education. He has been
appointed by the board to get together some facts. I don't
know what it is all about. But anyway he isn't here, and I
don't see why any of my friends need to know about it."

"Well, perhaps not," said Chan evasively, watching her
little white, anxious face against the night, "but if they're
gone then how could you stay there? You couldn't stay
alone."

"Oh, Mrs. Thornton and the children are there," said Rachel. "That was the first intention, that I stay with her and
the children until fall and then Professor Thornton thought
he might be able to get me some tutoring to do. There is always a lot of that in the fall. But that was before I found out
how very little money there was left after all the expenses
were paid. Also how hard up the Thorntons were."

"But would you *like* being there with her if she would
take you or would you rather be in a strange place? Andy
here has been telling me that his sister is up in a little camp-
ing cottage in the Adirondacks and would likely have plenty
of room for you. You could board there for a short time for

almost nothing. It might be a bit rough, but it would be safe enough, I should think."

"Oh, I must be at home," said Rachel decidedly. "I can see that I ought not to have left until I knew what kind of a place I was going to. It was all wrong and I'm glad to get a chance to begin over again. I am almost sure Mrs. Thornton will like to have me back. If she doesn't I might get a chance to wait on tables at the Stanton. That's a big apartment hotel in Beechwood. They always want waitresses there."

"Nothing doing!" said Chan, putting his lips in a tight thin line. "I'm not going to let my old professor's daughter do that! Besides that would be the most dangerous place you could go. Trevor might be the first man you had to serve. No, little Ray, you're going to be taken care of even if I have to kidnap you over again myself! And what's more, you're not going to be left alone in any house without a man either. We'll have to get Mrs. Thornton to rent a room to someone."

"Oh, her father is there! He's all right. He's very kind and pleasant, and quite nice. We'd not be alone."

"An old man wouldn't do much good."

"He's not so very old. His hair is gray, but he is quite strong."

"All right! That sounds better. Now about that desk. Is it empty? Could I get it at once? You see I'm anxious to have that bargain concluded. I won't leave until I can hand over the money and be sure you will take it."

"Now you are putting me into a place where I have to say yes again," protested Rachel. "Of course I will not hinder your going to where your duty calls, and I'll have to take the money, at least until you come back. No, it isn't empty. It is full of father's papers, but I can empty it. But I insist that you look the desk over and be sure you want it before I use that money. And anyway that is an awful price. I'll tell you what I'll do. I'll take the money and put it in the bank, and then if I absolutely *have* to use it I will, but I will have the

privilege of buying the desk back again in case you find you
don't want it."

"Well, that's fair enough, only I know I'll want the desk if
there is a stick of it left because it is a sort of memorial of a
very pleasant time in my life that I would like to keep in that
way. I'll tell you, suppose you get that desk cleared out for
me ready to take away while I'm gone, and then when I return I can get it. I won't have time to look after its crating
until I get back. But I'll take it if I have to carry it on my
back, if you don't take the money for it at once."

"You are very fair to everyone but yourself," said Rachel.
"I'll borrow the money of you till your return then. That will
sound better to me, and then if I absolutely need it, why it
will be there."

"But you absolutely will need it," said Chan firmly.
"You've got to pay your board. You can't let that teacher's
little wife wait. She may be in a tight hole herself. Look
here, suppose you clear out that desk and I'll have Jim or
Andy come up and get it, say a couple of days after I leave."

Rachel's heart suddenly felt very heavy. A couple of days
after he left! Then he was expecting to be gone days!

Well, what had she expected? Did she think Chan was
going to spend the rest of his life waiting upon her? She had
declined to marry him when he courteously made that proposition, probably because he saw nothing else to do to help
her out of her predicament. She certainly had wanted him
not to feel burdened by her. And now this ghastly disappointment when he took her at her word. She did not quite
understand herself, and felt very little and old and tired. She
was even glad, when, at the next filling station, Chan roused
Jim and Andy, and tucked her into the backseat with a robe
over her, himself sitting in one of the middle chairs, talking
in low tones now and again with the men.

There was a dull ache in her heart, and when she tried to
analyze it, it was not so much that Chan was going to leave
her soon, for that was silly. Of course he was going to leave

her. But because he had not completed the conversation begun before the motorcycle incident had broken in upon his question.

Rachel was long in going to sleep, but slept heavily even after the sun arose. She did not rouse till Chan touched her gently on the hair and whispered that they were coming into the city and perhaps it would be better for her to sit up.

She came back to life with a sense of heaviness still on her heart but tried to shake it off and smile.

Chan smiled back, a faint, half-abstracted smile.

They ate breakfast at a little restaurant in one of the suburbs and drove on down into the center of New York, Rachel sitting far back in the car, and being very careful to pull her hat down over her face, and to poke her hair under, out of sight. It seemed ridiculous for her to be afraid with all these miles between herself and her persecutors, but Chan had somehow given an atmosphere of caution by his very manner this morning, and she had retired within herself as much as possible. Indeed she could not help noticing that even Jim and Andy were grave and abstracted.

They drew up at the curb in a crowded business street, and Chan got out and walked swiftly across the road and halfway up the block, disappearing into the doorway of a bank. Almost at once Rachel heard Jim say in a low tone:

"Yep. Look there! Just what I said."

"Is that one of 'em?" asked Andy, watching an indifferent looking man in a common gray suit, who ambled slowly across the street, and sauntered along, pausing in front of the bank as if waiting for someone, and casting an occasional idle glance into the doorway.

"It sure is. I've seen him before. He's got the look."

"How would one happen to be right here at this minute," doubted Andy. "They wouldn't know he was comin' here."

"Then they'd be mighty dumb if they didn't," said Jim. "Where would a man go if he had been on a journey, but to his bank? You bet they've got their eyes on the bank, and the old man's office, and the house, and the country club, and the seashore house, and the mountain place, and the farm in Maine. That is if they're doing anything at all at follering."

"Well, I doubt if they are," drawled Andy. "Must be mighty anxious to carry it so far as all this."

"More involved than you and I understand!" said Jim wisely. "There! Watch him. He's gone inside to see what's become of Chan. Say, Andy! I'm uneasy. I'm goin' over to give a warnin'. You drive the car around the next block below here, down there, see? I'll tell Chan where to find us, and I'll give that bird the once-over while I'm about it. If he don't move on pretty soon Chan better go out the back way. We don't want that bird to get sight of the car."

"Better hustle then, Chan'll be coming back."

"Not yet. He has to go back in the room and get some bonds out of his safety deposit box. Got some coupons due today or somethin' he was mighty anxious about."

"All right, Jim, I'll stop on the next block!"

So Rachel found herself driving through the streets of New York with Andy alone, shivering a little as she thought what she would do if some of Trevor's emissaries should appear and claim her.

It was a long five minutes before Jim finally emerged from the crowd and swung into the car.

"S'a'right!" he said, lighting a cigarette with a relieved air. "He had gone into the inner room. I sent him a note, and waited till I got word from him. The bird is still hanging round the door waiting for him to come out. I gave him the once-over and I'm sure it's one of Halloran's men. Anyhow we're on the safe side. Now, it's up to us to be passing that alley as Chan turns out. Let me take the wheel, Andy, I know just where he'll come!"

Five more breathless minutes passed before Chan appeared with a long envelope in his hand and slid into the car, sitting far back beside Rachel, and putting the paper in his inside pocket.

"Drive, Jim!" he said, and they slid away through traffic and finally out into the quieter ways at a pace no foot sleuth would care to follow, but Rachel noticed that both Chan and Andy were keeping sharp watch on every side.

CHAPTER XVIII

It was like Chan to go back to Chicago in an airplane. From the moment they left New York he seemed feverishly anxious to be off. He was kind and gentle, but grave and abstracted. Now and again he would jot down something on a bit of paper and hand it over to Jim.

As they neared Beechwood, Rachel's excitement grew until her throat was dry and parched and her feet and hands cold, and Chan grew more and more silent. She wanted to ask him questions, but when she opened her lips to do so the words were not there wherewith to express her anxiety and dismay. Just what was it that made her feel as if the earth was reeling under her, anyway?

Almost on the threshold of Beechwood after three hours' hard driving, Chan suddenly turned to her and began to explain.

"Jim has to stay in Beechwood for a day or so. The car needs attention. I'm having him stop at the Stanton House, and he will telephone in the morning to see if there is anything he can do. You could call him any time, in the night even, if you got frightened."

"Oh, thank you," said Rachel. "But I shall not need him now. I'm sure I shall not."

There was a catch in her breath. She was trying to realize that she was just Rachel Rainsford, a lonesome girl who had her way to make, and that she had to begin all over again. It did not seem real at all now, what she had been going through. She was back among the old landmarks. In a few minutes they would pass the schoolhouse where her father had taught so many years, pass the corner where she used to come and meet him when she was a little girl; pass the church they had always attended, and from which so recently her beloved father had been buried. They would come to the little vine-clad cottage and it would be just as it had been two, or was it three or four days ago? Really, she could not remember. Those days all seemed now like a dream, full of terror and pain, but also filled with a strange dear sweetness, and she did not want to wake up. She had a feeling that when she did get thoroughly awake and Chan was gone life was going to be intolerable. Those terrible men who had put her in an insane asylum were going to rise in spirit if not in body and torment her the rest of her life, and when there were brief respites from their haunting memories she would be tormented with the aching sweetness that the memory of her rescuer had left. For she would not deceive herself. She felt that Chan was going from her life in a few brief moments now, out into the world that was his own, and that she likely would never see or hear more of him ever again, save perhaps a formal word of inquiry or some chance kindness. Chan was kindness itself, but of course he did not belong in her world.

But just for this little while he had been hers, in a peculiarly dear way. Hers and nobody else's, while he was rescuing her. She might have had him for always of course if she had accepted his impetuous proposition. But that would not have been right, and she thought that even so soon, now that he had come back to his habitual setting in life, he had begun to see that she had been right. Else why did he not go back to that question which he had asked her just before the motorcycle came? Would there come a little moment of farewell when he would do so?

Mrs. Thornton was at home, and pitifully glad to see Rachel. The baby had been sick, and she was all worn out.

Chan lost no time in coming briefly to the point.

He introduced himself as a former pupil of Professor Rainsford's, an old friend of the family, who had met Rachel by accident and found her disappointed in the position she had expected to take and anxious to get home. He was glad that he had been able to bring her a good part of the way in his own car, and he was anxious to know whether she could make this a refuge for a little while till things cleared up. There was some danger that the man whose advertisement Rachel had answered might make some trouble and annoyance for her because she had unfortunately signed a contract. Rachel seemed to discount this possibility, but the man had gone to such lengths, even seeking forcibly to detain her by shutting her up, that he felt it was wise to use extreme care. He wished that he himself might stay in the neighborhood for a few days until he was sure about it, but important business called him away. Would Mrs. Thornton be very watchful of Rachel and not let her go anywhere alone? He also told Mrs. Thornton of the presence of his chauffeur in the village, and asked her to feel free to call upon him at any time.

Rachel felt almost tongue-tied. She tried to smile and thank Mrs. Thornton for letting her come home again. She tried to say good-bye to Chan in a sprightly way so that he would not hear the tears in her voice, and to thank him so that he would know how grateful she was for all he had done, but when he had gone, as he did all too swiftly, she realized that she had said nothing. Just stood there letting him crush her hand for farewell and smiled that hurt, tired, frightened smile that was full of tears.

Chan had almost taken her in his arms and kissed her before Mrs. Thornton and Jim, and realizing this, he was fairly gruff in his farewell. Almost he rushed back when he reached the car but knew he must not, and so rode away with scarcely a look back. And Rachel stood in the doorway and did not realize that the reason she could not see the car was because her eyes were full of tears.

Mrs. Thornton, thinking she understood, took the girl by the hand and led her gently into the house, speaking kind words of comfort:

"There, dear child! Don't feel so disappointed. I know how it is. I went and answered an advertisement. It was to paint Christmas cards and said it paid real well. I had had

years of instruction in the art school then and knew I could
paint flowers on Christmas cards. But when I got the cards
they were little three-folder cardboards with a stereotyped
flower on each folder, a daisy, a sunflower and a rose, one on
each panel. I was instructed to paint all the white petals first,
on five hundred cards. Then all the centers, then all the
green leaves, and so on. They said that only so could I make
it pay by doing a great many in a short time. I was to be paid
seven cents a hundred! Think of that! My heart sank and I
came home and worked night and day for three days at my
five hundred, and they were really pretty, too, far ahead of
the copy I had brought home. And when I took them back,
don't you think the man told me that I hadn't done them the
way he wanted them and he couldn't pay me a cent for
them. I might take another five hundred and try again; people usually had to try several thousand before they got to be
experts, but he couldn't pay me for these; they were not like
the rest."

But Rachel was not listening to Mrs. Thornton as she
talked on, she was just sitting there, trying to smile and control those silly tears that would roll down her cheeks one
after the other and drop in large splotches on the pretty
green dress that Chan had bought her!

After a time she rallied and was able to tell Mrs. Thornton
something of what she had been through. Quite sketchily it
is true. She said nothing of Shillingsworth, nor the house
party, nor the insane asylum and her kidnapping. Somehow
she shrank from it all inexpressibly. Kind Mrs. Thornton
would scarcely have been able to believe it all if she had told
her, and she had her hands full with the sick baby. So Rachel stopped after a few words, saying:

"Oh, please, let's forget it. I don't like to think about it
now. Another day I'll tell you perhaps. I feel so sorry and
ashamed, and you had such trouble to pay me that money in
a hurry, too, for my journey, but Mr. Prescott wants to buy
Father's desk, says it has pleasant memories for him and
perhaps some of his books, too, when he comes back, so I

shall have money enough to let you have it back till the rent comes due, at least, and I also shall have money to pay my board till I can get something."

"Dear child! Don't speak of it! We shall be quite all right I'm sure. Father had a letter from his lawyer saying that some stock he owns is coming up. We'll be able to pay you more perhaps soon. I'm so glad you've come. And don't bother about telling anybody else in Beechwood. Just say you discovered that the situation wasn't what it was represented to be. Now come upstairs and take a hot bath and get to bed. I'm sure you must be all worn out."

"No indeed!" said Rachel, lifting her firm little chin. "I'm going to help you. What can I do first? Stay with the baby or get dinner? You look as if you need some sleep. Why don't you go and lie down by the baby now, if he's asleep, and rest while I get dinner? No, I'm not tired a bit. I'd love to. I feel as if I *wanted* to work. Have you got an apron? My baggage hasn't come yet. Indeed I'm not sure if it ever will come."

"Well, what's the difference if you've got back safe. There's an apron, if you really think you're not too tired. I am just dropping over on my feet. I'll rest just a few winks and then I'll come down."

"Don't dare come down till I ring the bell!" ordered Rachel, and went into the kitchen where she had got so many meals for years and began to get dinner.

Lighting the gas oven to bake potatoes, it occurred to Rachel that it was exactly seven days since she had lighted it last, the day before the Thorntons moved in and she moved her goods into the garage. What an eventful seven days they had been. It was all like a dream. Only dreams did not leave things behind that pricked and hurt. Dreams might leave a haunting memory of fear sometimes, this one did, but not enough to trouble her because it seemed so utterly intangible. But dreams did not leave an aching longing in one's heart which was like a heavy weight to carry around. A face, a voice, little turns of sentences, a smile, a touch of the hand, how they haunted! Would she ever, ever, get over it? She must of course, but what a fight she was going to have with herself! She was ashamed that it should be so. The daughter of such a mother and such a father should not entertain vain regrets! And how vain! Chan belonged to another world. She had vaguely felt it before, but she knew it as soon as she arrived at that house party. The atmosphere of luxury, of caste, of wealth. The cocktails, the constant cigarettes of both men and women! They were utterly foreign to her life, and she hated them with a healthy vigor. She could never be happy in such an atmosphere, even if she ever could fit into it otherwise. They were things against which she held a principle. Chan didn't of course, else he wouldn't have been there. She could see he was at home, although he seemed scarcely to touch his glass, and when he saw she had refused, he went and put his back on the tray. Chan was a perfect gentleman anyway. But one couldn't make a soul life just on the basis of gentlemanliness, although without it life would be a sordid thing.

But why think about it? She slammed the refrigerator door shut vigorously after exploring its empty shelves, as if to shut in the uneasy thoughts that would keep filling her mind. She tried to hum a little tune while she prepared a pan of apples for baking, but a sudden huskiness came in her throat and her eyes blurred over as she remembered the red apple out of which Chan had taken a big bite to test its flavor and then handed it over to her to sample. Oh, would she ever forget the beautiful things about that wild, sweet ride they had taken together? But she must forget it or her life would be utterly unsettled. Oh, if she had only remained here quietly and waited for a chance to teach, getting along some way, this would never have come to her life to unsettle her peace.

Yet even while she faced that thought she knew she was glad she had had it all, yes, even the terror and dismay, so it brought her that merry companionship. It was something to remember all her life, that thoughtfulness, gentleness, courtesy.

Rachel had decided in her lonely little heart that she would probably always be lonely and that life did not hold for her the romance and beauty that storybooks told about. She was not a rich girl, neither was she in society. There would likely be small chance of her being thrown in the company of young men whom she could enjoy. Oh, perhaps in the way of work her life might touch others sometimes whose companionship she might like, but young men did not choose their companions usually, she thought, from among the ranks of those they worked with.

She had been brought up in a peculiar way, perhaps, and did not look on life as a thing to be enjoyed. She had been taught that self was not first. There were other things to be considered before what one wanted. And so now she could not understand the sudden sinking that came over her as she looked forward into a blank future. It was the same future she had faced last week with a reasonably cheerful countenance. What had made the difference? Certainly the heavenly Father had shown His care of her in a most marked manner. Certainly she had not only been rescued and kept in time of trouble, but she had been exceedingly happy. What right had she to feel depressed here in the dear home where she felt so safe? Two nights ago she would have given everything in life just to be back here. She must not be sad. She must get back her sense of values. She had put Chan too much in the forefront, that was all. Tomorrow perhaps, or at most the next day, she would be able to see things in their right relations. Tonight she was tired; too tired to think. She would go right to bed the minute the dishes were washed and sleep and sleep and sleep! Tomorrow was Sunday, and back in the dear old church where she had sat Sunday after Sunday with her father and mother, she would get the sense of nearness to God again, and be comforted. Life would not seem so lonely then. She had something yet to do for God or she would not have been left alone on the earth. That was sure.

Strange, how excited she had been last Saturday night at

this hour, getting the last things laid in her trunk prepara-
tory to the Monday morning's journey! That trunk that she
would probably now never see! All that she had accom-
plished by that trip had been the losing of everything she
possessed on earth, except those few pieces of furniture out
in the garage. Also, she had learned a very terrible lesson,
the horror of which would perhaps never be erased from her
mind. Well, it was over. She was here at home again, a sad-
der and wiser girl. The quicker she got back into life and
forgot that she had ever been west at all, the more tolerable
things would be.

So, she reasoned with herself, as she cut bread, got butter,
made coffee, set the table, and did a thousand little things
that go toward the preparation of a dainty evening meal.

Mrs. Thornton came down to the table refreshed and
brightened. The baby was sleeping. His little hands and
forehead were moist and natural. There was a great deal for
which to be thankful.

Rachel tried to echo her thought, and smiled wearily, but
somehow her thoughts would follow Chan. Where had he
gone and what was he so interested in that he could hardly
take time to say good-bye? Perhaps there was some girl that
had a claim upon him! Some beautiful girl who belonged in
his life. Perhaps he had found a letter or something in that
bank that had called him to her! The thought seethed in her
mind and slithered across her quivering soul like a sharp,
bright knife edge on raw flesh. And then she realized what
she was doing and laughed, trying to make the laugh fit into
what Mrs. Thornton was saying, but the laugh was at her
poor, silly self. Here she was being a fool like the girls she
had always despised, who fell in love at first sight and pined
away with sorrow. No, she would never be a girl like that.
And hadn't she declined to keep him for herself? She had
not the slightest doubt but that he would have stood by his
proposal if she had gone halfway. This really was getting beyond bounds. She positively must not think more about it.

She was growing daffy. She would be all right in the morning.

The nice old grandfather helped to clear off the table, and they all washed the dishes together. It took but a few minutes, and then Rachel was free.

She went back to her own old room, the bed, which belonged to Mrs. Thornton, still made up as Rachel had slept in it the last night before she left.

"I haven't had time to change it," explained Mrs. Thornton, "and nobody has been in there since you left."

Rachel took a warm bath and donned the borrowed nightgown that Mrs.Thornton laid out for her, too weary to think what she was going to do for clothes during the days that were to follow; too weary even to pray when she knelt beside her bed in the moonlight, tears on her face:

"Dear, Father, forgive me, I just can't seem to help feeling this way about Chan. But it's all right, I want to be what You want me to be! And I thank You that I am safely home!"

She cast one wistful glance out into the clear moonlight through which but last night she had been riding along, and then got into bed, and from sheer weariness fell asleep.

High above the clouds in that same moonlight, Chan Prescott was skimming along in an airplane, on his way back to Chicago.

CHAPTER XIX

Chan took Andy with him.

He arranged for the air trip and a few other important details by telephone as soon as he landed at the Pennsylvania Station. It was not the first time he had gone in that way. He had a friend who owned an airplane and made trips like that just for a pastime. He did not in the least object when Chan requested that the trip be made at night, dangerous though it was.

Chan had time before he started for a brief talk with his father. It was at a crisis like this that they came nearer to understanding one another than under any other circumstances of life. He discovered that Shillingsworth was as he had suspected, his father's bitter enemy, and revealed enough of the story of the last few days to cause his father to be a strong ally in the enterprise in which he was about to engage. Chan went out from that interview, with his father's blessing upon his head, so to speak. Not that the elder Prescott would have expressed it in just those words, but there was a grim smile of satisfaction on his face as he watched his son dash out to the taxi that was waiting at the door for him.

"He's all right!" said the father half aloud as he turned back to his chair and his paper. "He's all right! I thought he'd quit fooling someday and *do* something!" But perhaps he would have been astonished if he could have known some of the ideas that were floating around in his son's brain.

The father sat thoughtfully awhile and then he went to the telephone and began to pull some wires. There were things that he could do also, and he would. He hunted down two or three powerful friends and made them allies also, and he worked out a neat bit of diplomacy that would have made

Shillingsworth writhe if he could have known it. But by the time Shillingsworth did know it he was so engrossed with several other matters that it scarcely made any difference to him.

Chan was going back to Chicago to right wrong, he told himself. All the way as they skimmed the clouds and shot through the silver of the evening he was telling himself that he was going to right wrong.

It had always been a weakness of Chan's even as a very young boy, to think that he was divinely appointed to mete out justice for all that were oppressed. He was impatient with that old poem:

> Truth crushed to earth shall rise again,
> The eternal years of God are hers.

Truth might have plenty of eternal years, but he hadn't and what was the use of waiting for eternal years to set things right? That had been his great trouble in school. He was always righting some wrong and letting everything else go hang so to speak till it was righted or he had a black eye from the attempt.

It was a fact that usually the wrongs were real wrongs and needed righting. The trouble was Chan never could realize that he must wait for justice to take its orderly way.

In this case notably, out of his whole life, Chan felt that never could adequate justice be dealt through the machinery of the law. He felt that it was his divinely ordered mission to see that it was administered. He had the same reason in kind that the boys of the great World War had when they went overseas. He had to make the world safe for Rachel, and never would it be safe until those two men were either wiped off the earth or made to understand where they were to stop.

As he sailed along through the night, Chan looked off into the silver atmosphere, and up at the kindly stars, and began to think about God. He had never thought about God before when he was riding in an airplane. Strangest thing, but somehow it seemed as if God were all round him, looking at him, as if he had come right up near where God lived and had, by his very being here on this errand, brought himself more than usually into heavenly attention. It embarrassed him to think these thoughts, as it used to embarrass him to meet one of the professors on the schoolhouse campus when he was on his way to thrash some miscreant who had been fighting some of the smaller boys. It was the first time Chan had questioned whether what he was going to do might or might not be ordained of heaven. He tried to turn his thoughts in other directions. He felt he had too much to plan to be distracted with thoughts like these. But persistently through the silver-blue of the air about him there seemed to come the soft foldings of angel wings, something drawing and tender.

"When I have done this," he promised within himself, "I will start to find out about the other part. Follow the King! I must know about the King! For her sake I must know!"

But somehow, nevertheless, through the silver distances there seemed to be the flash of angels' wings, and sometimes when far down in a dark valley he sighted little lights of human dwellings twinkling, or a blur of larger light that meant a whole city of lights, he could not help thinking that this was how the world looked to God. Only God could see right down below those lights into the houses, where the people sat reading or talking or working or playing; nay, could see farther still into the very soul of each one as he sat, could see his thoughts and just how he was going to react to what he was to meet on the morrow. And again Chan would turn away quickly from such a thought.

Two or three times he thought of Rachel, with her head against his shoulder as they had ridden while she slept, and his heart would yearn strangely and thrill, yet he drew back from this as if it were something holy that he must not approach at once. He had to make good before he might claim those memories as his own. And the first thing he had to do was make the world safe for Rachel.

Andy was not troubled with any such thoughts. Andy was filled with exhilaration. Had he not been chosen for this flight? Was he not close to Chan once more? Were they not to go over the top tomorrow? It was France all over again. Andy loved it. But he was not troubled with silver thoughts about angels' wings and azure peace enfolding him. He was thrilling for the fray.

They landed in an aviation field not so many miles away from the country club where Mrs. Southerly was a member and where she frequently took her guests.

Silently as an air bird can be made to drop, they floated to the ground, early in the morning when the dawn was in the sky and country club members were not abroad. As silently and almost mysteriously they melted away from the great plane, and became a part of the morning mists. When the sun rose there was no plane in sight to tell the tale, and no path left in the sky where it had disappeared. Chan knew how to pick his friends. He could depend on them.

About nine o'clock as Trevor sat in the hotel dining room eating a dainty breakfast of honeydew melon, and cereal, sausage, fried potatoes, and hotcakes with syrup and many cups of coffee, a waiter brought him word that there was a gentleman in the lobby waiting to see him.

Trevor hastily gulped the last succulent fragment of hotcake reeking with maple syrup, washed it down with the last of the third cup of coffee, and hurried into the lobby, looking sharply around. He had a walk like a wary fox, lifting his feet furtively, poising, and moving sinuously. He looked about with his keen little eyes alert. At first he paid no attention to the lazy, good-looking slim fellow, lolling on the big plush davenport smoking a cigarette as if he had nothing in the world to do.

Andy slowly unfolded his slim length, as if he were inches taller than he really was, and came lazily around to his notice, removing a wide-brimmed soft felt hat with a pleasant sweep that reminded one of a cross between a western ranchman and a southern gentleman of the olden time.

"Mistah Trevor?" he questioned with a slight lifting of his eyebrows. "Why, I was lookin' foh a lahgeah man. Got that impression!"

Trevor glared.

"Come ovah int' th' writin' room," suggested Andy. "I got somethin' confidential to talk ovah."

Trevor, still lifting his feet warily, followed.

"I understand you're lookin' fer a man named Prescott," said Andy as he settled into an easy position, hunched into a big chair with one leg thrown over the arm, and lighted another cigarette.

Trevor glared again:

"Who are you?"

"One minute, Mistah Trevor," said Andy. "You're acquainted with the New York people that do a little wohk foh Mistah Shillingswuth, now and then? You understand, Mistah Trevor? I don't care to mention names in a public place like this. Well, I saw one of his men yesterday, one of his regulars, you understand. And I found out through him that you was looking foh Mr. Prescott. I thought I might be able to help you, if you would make it worth my while."

Andy smiled nonchalantly and lolled back as if it were a matter of indifference to him whether the gentleman accepted his suggestion or not.

Trevor relaxed into a chair with a kind of relief of tension. "That's different!" said he. "How much do ya want?"

Five minutes later Andy was bidding him good-bye, still in that same lazy manner:

"Well, so long, Trevor. Glad t'have met yoh! I'll be round then, 'bout two o'clock. Got a little cyarh in a garage round here I c'n bring. It's a good piece from here, but we can easy make it and back before night with that little cyarh. She's got plenty a pep, that cyarh. Yes, shore. I was intentioning from the staht to bring yoh'all back. Yes, shore, bring Mistah Prescott back, too. Plenty a room! Well, or revoir! See you at two!"

In the interval Trevor had a long telephone conversation

with Shillingsworth. He told him gleefully that he would absolutely produce his man that evening, and he might make arrangements to put him in a place of safety.

In the interval Andy was busy with maps. He had not come to this point in the game without understanding the lay of the land. He was punctual to the minute, and Trevor, who had been nervously standing in the door of the inn awaiting him, registered relief, and climbed into the little blue runabout with alacrity.

"We better stop at the station house and get a man to come along with us, don't you think?" asked Trevor anxiously. "I don't want this thing to fall through."

"It won't fall through, brothah!" drawled Andy. "Just yoh trust me, an' we'll come back tonight with yoh man all right. Yoh take an officer along an' nothin' doin', see?"

"Well, I've got a pair of handcuffs," said Trevor.

"Oh, that's all right, drawled Andy good-naturedly. "So've I. But I hope yoh all ain't got any gun. It's against the rules, yoh know."

"Yes, I have a little gun. I usually take one with me."

"Bettah give her to me foh safe keepin', brothah! We don't want enny accidents, yoh know. We ain't out t'kill. I'm wohkin' undah ordahs, yoh know. Hand her ovah. I gotta be boss here or tha' ain't nothin' doin'!"

Trevor reluctantly handed out his gun, and Andy examined it, unloaded it, and put it in an inside pocket. Then he suddenly threw in his clutch with such fervor that Trevor was almost thrown out of his seat.

"Excuse me, brothah," yelled Andy. "We gotta make up foh lost time."

For two hours they fairly flew, through towns, over hills, around curves, shooting by all cars within sight, never halting, never hesitating, now dashing into a wood or turning suddenly with a lurch to take an almost obliterated wood road for a mile or two, like mad they tore over the ground. Trevor had much ado to keep his seat steadily, and his face looked pinched and anxious.

"You're a pretty fast driver," he ventured to remark breathlessly when they just grazed a curbstone, and barely escaped a great truck that had been thundering ahead of them.

"I aim not to lose much time," assented Andy.

"You sure you know where you're going?" questioned Trevor again half an hour later. The silence and the speed were getting on his nerves.

"I shore do."

And at last they dashed into a deep wood road, which wound around and suddenly came out to a stretch of open field with a railroad winding across in the distance. Here Andy brought the car to a standstill.

"This'll be about it," announced Andy, getting slowly out of the car. "Bettah get out, Mistah Trevah."

Trevor got uncertainly from the car, and took a step or two forward. There was a haunting memory in the scene, but he had not time to identify it, for Chan stepped suddenly out from behind a tree and came to meet him.

"I understand you want to see me, Mr. Trevor," he said, and there was a look in his eye that suddenly made Trevor feel sick. He gave a quick glance at Andy, who stood just behind him leisurely chewing a twig which he had plucked from a tree, and then began stepping warily off to the side, like the fox he was.

But Chan gave him no time to carry out any of his own intentions. He stepped quickly forward.

"I've been wanting to meet you, too," he said, "and I'm right glad to see you. I'm going to give you such a walloping as you never had before in your life and never will again. Take off your coat!"

There came a sick look of fright in Trevor's eye and he cast a baleful glance at Andy.

"Here. You! Get those handcuffs on this man!" he shouted, fumbling in his side pocket.

"No, sah, I'm not interferin' between gentlemen," drawled Andy. "I'm here to see faih play."

But Trevor had no time to hear what Andy said. A smashing blow hit him fair in his foxlike nose, and a grip like steel seized him. Held as in a vise he took what was probably the calmest and most thorough corporal punishment he had ever had in his life, certainly since his little-boy days.

Weak and trembling and thoroughly licked, one eye swollen shut where it had come in contact with Chan's fist as he tried to resist the steady advance of justice, his nose bleeding, a gash on his left cheek, Trevor was finally set upon his shaking feet, too unsteady to stand, and click! Andy's arms encircled him, and snapped on the handcuffs.

"Thought we might have need of these, membah brothah?" he said affably. "Now, you jus' step ovah to the cyarh an' I'll keep my othah promise to yoh! We'll be back in plenty of time foh dinnah! All set, Chan?"

"All set!" Chan's face was stern, his eyes hard and bright. There was a look of righteousness and judgment about him.

Trevor slumped into the seat with Andy's ungentle assistance and cowered between Andy and Chan. He was too undone even to glare. For some time he did not even attempt to wipe his bloody face. As the car sped steadily back over the road the three sat silent, two of them grim and stern, the third plain scared, white and trembling.

But after an hour had passed and they began to get back into familiar highways, where cars were flying back and forth and houses were closer together Trevor gathered courage. He wasn't dead yet, and he began to discover that he was still alive and unbroken in bone even though he was bruised and sore from head to foot. Every muscle ached and every nerve cried out with pain, and Trevor's temper began to get the better of his fear.

"I-I-I'd l-l-like to kn-n-now, what this is all ab-b-bout!" he managed to stammer out at last. Then gathering courage in a tone that was almost a swagger:

"Y-y-you'll both have to s-s-suffer f-for this!" It was almost a threat in its final whine.

"If yoh all don't know, brothah, yoh all is dumber than yoh look, an' that's sayin' a great deal," drawled Andy.

Then spoke Chan:

"He knows well enough what he's done. Probably a good deal more than we do, but since he asks it's only fair to tell him. Mr. Trevor, we have four indictments against you. One in New York State for misrepresentation through the columns of the public press. One in the state of Illinois for a deal you made with a man named Shillingsworth promising to hand over to him a young woman who was under your protection, and to connive with him if there was any trouble with the young woman, telling the conductor of the train that she was insane——"

"That's a lie!" said Trevor, suddenly flaming into fury.

"——for which you received the sum of one thousand dollars in a check," finished Chan calmly.

"I say that's a lie!" screamed Trevor furiously. "I'll make you eat those words in court. You'll suffer for this. I swear you'll suffer for this. I'll appeal to the passersby!" and he raised his manacled arms and began to call to a passing automobile.

"That'll be about all of that!" said Chan sternly, and Trevor looked up to see the gleam of a revolver held capably in Chan's hand.

"Andy, I think this is where we turn off, and when we get to that piece of woods yonder we stop and find that check. It will be safer in our possession."

"I haven't got any check!" sneered Trevor. "And besides if I had you don't suppose I'd carry it around with me, do you? I'm not an entire fool."

"I think you would," said Chan calmly. "You wouldn't have any other place to leave it. And besides, I happen to know Shillingsworth has stopped payment on it, anyway."

"That's a lie!" said Trevor with a frightened look. "He promised!"

"You cur!" said Chan. "I thought you'd hang yourself if I gave you rope enough. We'll stop right here, Andy. Now,

Trevor, you may hand me out that check, and while you're doing it we'll take the contract you made Miss Rainsford sign. Come, be quick about it, unless you prefer to have us search you. Ah! I thought that would bring you around. Yes, that's the check!"

Chan smoothed it out and put it in his pocket.

"Now, the contract!"

"She never signed any contract," parried Trevor, glaring. "I'll have you jailed for this. This is a regular holdup game, you know; handcuff a man and take his money away."

"That's all right, Trevor, we'll take our chances with you when we get back to town. The contract, please."

"I tell you I haven't got it. There never was any!"

"Andy, search him!" Chan stood with the revolver leveled at Trevor and he shivered nervously.

"All right, I'll give it to you!" agreed Trevor hastily.

He produced the paper in a shaky hand, and Chan, studying it briefly, found enough to make him even angrier than he was. And Rachel had signed it without having read it carefully, perhaps even before some paragraphs had been added, for the whole thing was written with a typewriter, and by it Rachel had bound herself to go anywhere or take any job that Trevor desired for the year, in case the one she had taken failed, or she failed to please the customer. It was cunningly worded, and perhaps Rachel would not have realized her danger even if she had read it all. But Chan understood.

"You hound you!" he said, looking sternly at Trevor. "This ought to give you a life sentence without anything else. You're not fit to live in the world with decent people. This is the proof for the third indictment in the state of New York. The fourth is for kidnapping Miss Rainsford and confining her in a private asylum in the state of Illinois. Drive on, Andy. To the station house now as fast as you can!"

And Andy did drive!

Trevor sat like a wild thing caged, fairly gnashing his

teeth with rage and fear, but whenever he turned his eyes toward Chan he caught the gleam of a pistol held in his right hand.

"But you can't do a thing like this, you know, and get free!" he gasped at last as they began to draw near to the town from which he and Andy had started out early that afternoon. "The law won't allow it. You got to have a warrant!" He almost swaggered weakly as he brought out that word. He had just remembered that this was so.

"We have the warrants all right!" said Chan crisply. "Don't you worry about that."

The little man cringed at his tone.

"You'll suffer for this!" chirped Trevor. "You'll suffer for this! You attempted my life, you did! I'll get witnesses to prove it. There was a man cutting grass across the railroad track. I saw him. He'll testify that you tried to kill me! And Shillingsworth will bail me out! I'll see that you suffer!"

"Bunk!" said Andy cheerily and hit a higher pace.

They whirled into town in great shape and up to the station house, and Trevor clambered down eagerly, appealing in a broken whine for justice to be done to him, and demanding that they send for Shillingsworth.

"I'm going after Shillingsworth now myself," said Chan coldly. "But it won't do you any good! Officer, see that this man has some medical attention at once. He's pretty well bruised up. Better give him a rubdown!"

Trevor was shaking a manacled fist at them as they drove away, and the smiling officers were hustling him inside the station house. They had just held a long telephone conversation with Chan's father in New York. They understood the situation even better than Chan did. Chan's father had influence when he chose to use it that could reach even out to Illinois.

Chan stopped at the village inn and made himself tidy. Then after making an appointment to meet Andy, he drove straight out to Mrs. Southerly's house by the lake, arriving just a few minutes before dinner and announcing himself quietly to his hostess.

So it was that when the Warrens and the Shillingsworths walked out to dinner at the call of the butler, they found their hostess standing in the dining room talking brightly with Chan, and there was no escaping from that dining room no matter how much anyone might have wished to do so.

CHAPTER XX

Monday morning, bright and early, Rachel went out to the garage to get that desk ready for shipping.

The Thornton baby was better, and its mother was resting late in bed as Rachel had besought her to do, while the baby slept. The breakfast was over, and the dishes washed. Rachel was beginning to feel as if she had never started at all to go west and work for a rich old lady who didn't exist. With the morning light and the possibility of working hard, she was better able to control her thoughts, and life did not look quite so long and dreary ahead of her as it had the evening when she bade Chan good-bye.

But still she could not get him out of her thoughts, and so she planned to get that desk ready to go, for she felt that then she would have done all in her power to repay him for his great kindness, and would perhaps be the better able to put him in his right relation in her thoughts.

She unlocked the garage and stole up the ladderlike stairs to the gloom of the storage room. Already it seemed years since those familiar articles of household use had been carefully stored away. The dust was even gathered on the top of the desk though it was but a week and a day since it was put there.

Rachel found herself going to it almost excitedly to see if that pinhole was really there, about which Chan had told her. It came to her as she ran her fingers lightly over the top that perhaps he had made up that story in his kindness just so that she would feel free to let him have the desk at that enormous price. It was ridiculous of course, and she did not mean to keep it, but if it made him feel happier why she would take it till she could honestly tell him she was financially comfortable, which she would be as soon as she got any kind of a job. It took very little to keep her, and now she had learned her lesson she would stay at home where she was known and find something to do. Oh, if she had only done so without having to go through that awful, humiliating experience. She shuddered at the thought of Trevor and Shillingsworth, while her fingers traced lovingly the smooth old desk top, and lingered like a caress on the little indentation that was Chan's old pinhole. How dear of him to remember that all these years, and to say such beautiful things of her precious father! Almost she was willing to have gone through all this experience just to know that the boy he had loved and excused and been anxious about had loved him back.

It was dusky here in the loft of the garage, with only a window at either end in the peak of the roof, much too gloomy to sort out the papers with which the desk was filled. Rachel had brought out a large pasteboard suit box to put them in and she meant to take them to her room and do the work at her leisure. It would occupy her thoughts and bring back her common sense and her sense of belonging again to the life that used to be before she went away.

She unlocked the drawers and emptied them carefully, lovingly, one by one, into the box, packing them closely. Her father had been very orderly and everything in his desk had been carefully filed and done up in rubber bands. She had gone over them only hurriedly to hunt out the necessary business papers, his bankbook and checkbook and a few bills and receipts, at the time of his death. Professor Thornton had been with her, and they had taken out of the desk everything that had seemed necessary to a full settlement of the estate, which to tell the truth had been so small that it was not worth calling an estate. Professor Thornton had been distressed and had secretly blamed his old friend and colleague for not having been more careful to provide for his only child. Still, he had not done much better himself. Look at the way his investments had turned out. Scholarly men as a rule were poor businessmen, and teachers were notoriously ill paid. Thornton had resolved to take a lesson from his friend and try to get up in the world by the time he was called away so that his children would not be left destitute. Of course Rainsford, though, had bought and paid for the house, and it was well built and would eventually be worth more, for the community was growing and the location was good. He must not blame his friend too much. So Thornton had locked the desk for Rachel, whose heart was too heavy with sorrow and whose eyes were too filled with tears to care to look over the papers then, and they had come away and left the old desk much as its owner had left it the night he was taken so suddenly sick, never to come back to his study again.

Rachel thought of all this as she transferred the bundles of neatly folded papers to the box, and the tears sprang to her eyes again and flowed down her cheeks till even her hands were wet with them, and some great blistering drops fell on the papers and boxes she was removing.

At last the desk was empty.

She turned on a little flashlight she had brought out, and examined every drawer, and the little cubbyholes inside the door at the side, but all were clean and empty. She locked the empty drawers, ran her fingers once more lovingly over the surface of the old top, lingering again at the place where Chan had dug his pin, and then with a sigh picked up her big box full and returned to the house.

Rachel was a long time going over the contents of that box. Some were only business letters of little account and having no further bearing on life. These she carefully burned after having read each one. Some were letters from parents of his pupils, and these she laid aside for further tender perusal, for they were filled with praise of the teacher and gratitude for his generous kindness that had made him go out of his way to pull some lazy scholars back into line. They made her heart throb with pride to see that others knew and appreciated the painstaking labor which had never saved itself from weary tasks, if only some poor stupid boy could be made to "pass" his examinations.

There were bundles of receipts which must be kept, items of expenditures, and a precious diary, which, when she glanced into it, gave promise of many days' delight in her father's companionship again, as she would read over the everyday happenings of his placid earnest life. Once she caught Chan's name and stopped with cheeks suddenly aflame to read the entry through:

"Chauncey Prescott conquered himself again today. He stayed away from the football game in the city to finish the theme I asked him to write. Bless that boy! I believe he is coming to himself. I somehow have faith in that boy. If he only knew the Lord, what a difference it would make in his life!"

Rachel closed the book then and slipped down upon her knees to pray for Chan. It had come over her that her father must have prayed for him, too, and now she would take up the work and never lay it down until she knew he was the Lord's. It brought her nearer to her father and nearer to Chan to read that. She felt as if somehow her father's blessing had been put upon their friendship, and she was glad it had been this particular pupil of her father's that had been sent to rescue her and not any other, glad, glad, glad!

She went on for two hours examining the papers. It was almost time to go down and begin to get lunch. Mrs. Thornton was having a good long sleep and so was the baby, but when they awakened they would be hungry and the other children would be coming from school very soon. Rachel hesitated with her hand on a box, the last article left unexamined. It could very well wait till another day perhaps, if she did not get time in the afternoon to go through it. Then some inner sense prompted her to open it and see what it contained. It might be something that could be disposed of in a moment and then the whole task would be done. Better get it over, for there was no denying it was a heart strain and she felt as if she could not stand it soon again—not very soon. It brought back those first sad days after her precious father's death so keenly.

The box was one that had contained typewriter paper, and it was fastened neatly, as all the other bundles, with broad rubber bands, one each way. As Rachel slipped the first one off she noticed what she had not seen before, in small neat letters the words "The Book," and below it, still smaller letters, "Notes for the Second Book."

Feeling almost as if she had heard her father's voice calling her she opened the box. There lay manuscript, neat pages in her father's careful handwriting, a whole box full of it, three or four hundred pages, and on the top there lay a letter, addressed to her father with the name of a well-known New York publisher in the upper left-hand corner of the envelope. It had been torn open, and something written across the envelope in pencil in her father's handwriting. Rachel took it out and read it curiously:

"This came this morning in answer to my prayer. It will tide us over until my salary comes due next fall and perhaps leave a little over for a nest egg for Rachel. I must deposit it in the morning."

The date on the envelope was the day before her father was taken so suddenly ill and never returned to his desk again. Could he have had a premonition when he made that note? Not necessarily, for Rachel knew his habit was to make memoranda on all his school papers. He was most methodical. With a feeling almost of awe she drew the letter forth and found within it a check. The check dropped unheeded to the bed while she read the amazing letter:

My dear Professor Rainsford:

The manuscript of your book came as promised and we are forwarding herewith our check for twenty-five hundred ($2500) dollars advance royalty, as per our contract. We are much pleased with your final chapter. It seems to us that it meets all the requirements suggested and that the book will be a great success.

We are much interested in what you have told us of your other manuscript, and are hoping to have it for a reading in the near future. We like to keep our work well ahead for the sake of publicity, and would suggest that you forward it to us at your earliest convenience.

We hope that the results of your book will fully justify your highest expectations.

Sincerely,

Rachel stooped and picked up the check and stared at it. Twenty-five hundred dollars. She had never held so much money in her hand before. Twenty-five *hundred!* It seemed a fortune. And the letter spoke as if there might be more. Her father had written a book! And it had been accepted and payment made partly in advance! How wonderful! So that was what her father had been doing those long evenings when he had told her he was busy and must not be interrupted unless some very important call came. While she sat in the other room and practiced or studied and she had thought he was correcting high-school themes he had been writing a book!

And this had been here all the time for her need and she had lightly passed the desk over and locked it away out of sight, going her own way to find help in another part of the country! Why! That was just what the children of Israel did, wasn't it? when they went down into Egypt, the land of sin, to buy corn in time of famine, and did not ask the Lord their God who had promised to help them in time of need. Here her father had provided for her, and she had not even looked to see! And just like the children of Israel she had got into all sorts of trouble by going away, even got into bondage and made a prisoner. Rachel sat down with the letter in one hand, the check in the other, and the box with the unfinished manuscript in her lap, while she let the old, old story from the Bible sift its way through her heart and stir up her conscience to accuse her. Suddenly she found herself repeating softly the verse: "And all these things happened to them for ensamples . . . upon whom the ends of the world are come."

"I always knew what that meant," she meditated. "I've taught it many a time to the little kids in the Sunday school, that all the stories of the Old Testament were kind of pictures of the things we do today, but I never really thought it might come to me, and that I would walk into those very mistakes. What a fool I have been!"

With the check and the letter still in her hand, pressed to her heart, Rachel knelt down beside her bed, her head resting on the box of manuscript, and began to pray:

"Dear, Father, I see what You mean. I have been so foolish. Will You please forgive me and help me not to wander like that again. And I thank You. Oh, I thank You for having saved me this time in such a wonderful way! Please help me not to be foolish and not to feel so lonely, and please take care of Chan wherever he may be and show him the way to know the Lord as my dear father prayed. Please hear my prayer for him too."

Mrs. Thornton was awake. Rachel could hear her moving about. And the baby was whimpering. There were the children coming in from school, too. It was late and she must hurry down and get lunch!

She rose hastily from her knees, dashed cold water over her eyes, brushed her hair away from her face and hurried down. The next hour and a half was full of hurry. There was no time to think, but all the time there was a singing in her heart. Her heavenly Father had not forgotten her, and her earthly father had planned a way to provide for her! And now, now she could *give* Chan that desk and pay him back his five hundred dollars. How wonderful that things had come out that way! And there was that other manuscript! Perhaps it was far enough advanced so that she could get her father's notes together and copy the rest of it out. It seemed to be a sort of nature study book, with photographs that he himself had taken of birds and flowers and little beasts. Perhaps—oh, how wonderful if she could finish it up! She

would write and ask those publishers by-and-by after she
had read it over carefully.

After lunch she took the check and the letter down to her
father's bank, to the friend who had helped her settle the little matters belonging to her father's estate, and he promised
to see that everything was fixed up for her within a few days
so that she could deposit the check in her own name. Then
she went home and began to read her father's second manuscript and to plan the letter she would write to the publishers.

In this way for several days her mind was turned from the
sorrowful thoughts that had been hers when Chan first left
her. But at night, when the lights were out and she was trying to go to sleep they would all troop back, and she would
go over and over again each step of the way through that
wild, sweet journey they had taken together, from the first
minute he had entered the car, and the first note he had
dropped in her lap, to the moment he waved his hand so
cheerily and rode away from her door.

Every day Jim called up to ask if there was anything he
could do for her, and to know if she had been troubled in
any way by her enemies, and every day he said that the car
was keeping him a little longer, something that had to be
sent to the city for, some intricate part she gathered, without
which he could not run so far, and so the days went by and
Chan seemed farther and farther away, and Rachel still
wondered why he had asked her that question, just before
the motorcycle interrupted their conversation, and why he
had never recurred to it again.

As the days grew more and more in number and still no
word from Chan, she was aggrieved in spite of her common
sense. He might at least have sent her a postcard or a bit of a
greeting. After he had been so kind it seemed strange for
him to drop it there with never a word. Oh, of course he had
said he was coming back, but it was so long now, it was not
likely he would come. Or perhaps he might drop in for a few
moments' call some morning unexpectedly; just come to in-

quire, and that would be the end, likely. She must get used to expecting that and not be disappointed when he would not even stay for lunch perhaps. Well, it was right of course. He was not her kind. But yet, she would like him to come and give her a chance to tell him about finding the money and the letter. It would give her a more self-respecting feeling. She would hate to have to write it all out.

And then one morning when Jim called up, he asked her if she had heard from Mister Chan. Quite casually he asked it, yet Rachel seemed to feel that underneath it there had been uneasiness. And suddenly it came to her for the first time that perhaps some evil thing had happened to Chan. Perhaps he was somehow suffering for what he had done to save her? And now that she had thought about it, it seemed altogether possible. The people who would do what those two men had tried to do to her would be quite capable of doing even worse to her protector if they thought they could get away with it. What could she do about it? If she didn't hear from Chan pretty soon she would have to do something. She had money now and she could. And of course she must. He had saved her and she must save him if he were in danger.

But how could she find out whether he was in danger? Dared she talk to Jim about it? Well, if he spoke of it the next time he called up she would—she must. Perhaps Jim could find out from Mr. Prescott, call him on the telephone, or telegraph to make sure all was well. At least she would suggest it to Jim. She could not forget that uneasiness that had been in his voice. Oh, why had she not asked him to do something at the time? Would the next morning never come?

But though she hovered around the telephone all the next morning Jim did not call up, and when she finally mustered courage after another day of anxiety, to call up the inn where Jim had been staying, they told her he had checked out the morning before.

And that was that!

CHAPTER XXI

That was a very trying dinner table.

Mrs. Southerly was most vivacious, and Chan was charming, never more so. He told incidents of travel, described an experience flying in an airship at night in a storm, related racy bits from his war experiences, not too gruesome and full of humor, and dashed into serious moments that made them all think he was a most brilliant young man. The spirits of the company were lifted by his presence and the foreboding atmosphere of the past few days seemed to have vanished. Even the younger Warrens were moved to merriment.

Only old Shillingsworth glared, though he tried to conceal it by a sort of death's head smile, and under cover of the merriment motioned to the butler and whispered to him to call up Trevor at the inn and get him on the wire.

But the butler presently returned to say that Trevor had not been at the hotel since lunchtime and no one knew where to find him. They had paged him but with no result. Shillingsworth finished his dessert in deep gloom, drank a good deal of champagne, and was about to retire to the library for a smoke without even looking toward Chan who had so far ignored him. And then Chan suddenly turned toward him.

"By the way, Shillingsworth, may I have a word with you in the library? I have something important to show you." He said it in the tone of an older man who had important business on his mind, and now that the moment for recreation was over, was back to more important things again. Shillingsworth glared at him, growled, and glared again. There had come a quick silence in the room as if something tense had clutched at each one present, and every eye was turned toward Chan and then toward Shillingsworth. There was intense curiosity and interest, and the hostess, whose soul had been deeply tried during the last few days, and whose telephone had made her wiser than she cared to be, yet without enlightening her much, cast anxious glances toward her guests.

"You must not be long," she said in a high unnatural trill. "You know we want Chauncey to sing for us in the living room. You mustn't let him stay with you too long, Mr. Shillingsworth."

Shillingsworth turned without a word, giving a shrug of his ugly, loose-hung shoulders, and walked away toward the library. Chan followed alertly, and the door was closed behind them.

Shillingsworth sauntered on over to his favorite huge chair, lounged down into it indifferently, and lighted his long, black cigar, glowering under his heavy brows with an inscrutable gaze.

Chan stood easily beside the door, the air of a young commanding officer upon him:

"Mr. Shillingsworth," he said, and his voice was clear and decisive. "You are leaving this house tonight. At once, do you understand?"

Shillingsworth continued to glare, with his chin stuck out, and his lower lip protruding, the smoke from his last inhalation rising in blue circles about his head, his wicked old eyes heavy with hate.

"So-o!" sneered Shillingsworth, and put the cigar in his mouth again. "So-o-o! You better run home to your papa now, or you'll get into trouble!"

"Mr. Shillingsworth," said Chan, holding his self-control, and taking his watch from his pocket, "I'll give you just one hour to get out of this house and *stay*. If you're not out by ten o'clock I shall put the evidence of what you have done into the hands of all the Chicago and New York papers within ten minutes after ten."

"Evidence!" sneered Shillingsworth, his bushy eyebrows

elevated ominously. "What evidence could a kid like you collect?"

"Among other things, I have the check which you gave to Trevor in return for introducing you to the daughter of my old friend, a distinguished teacher and scholar. I also have the first draft of the agreement you and Trevor made out on the parlor car, and tore up and threw at my feet. If you are not out of this house within the time I stated I shall be obliged to inform this household, and the press of your doings. And that is not all. You are going to leave this country or be put where you cannot do any more harm. For the sake of your family, I will give you one week from tonight to leave the country. If you are not gone by that time I will see that your character is known from east to west of the whole country!"

Shillingsworth sprang to his feet, his apoplectic face crimson with rage:

"What have you done with Trevor?" he shouted, springing at Chan like a great cat.

But Chan had disappeared from the doorway, and he found himself clutching at empty air. Too furious to realize who might be listening he roared out the doorway:

"Bring Trevor, and I'll talk with you. If you don't bring Trevor you'll have something to answer for, which won't be child's play, I'll tell you!"

But the only answer he got was the sound of his wife's hurried step hustling away through the corridor and up the stairs. He knew that frightened step. Amelia had been listening again! It sobered him. No one else seemed to be about.

He turned around and rushed to the telephone, and Mrs. Southerly, who had taken refuge in her own room at the first hint of loud voices, heard him frantically calling the inn and demanding Trevor at the phone, demanding information about when he had last been seen, and finally demanding another man who had been working with Trevor. The clerk did not know the new name. It would seem from what Shil-

lingsworth said that he was a stranger who had recently
come on from New York. What was it all about anyway?
What right had they to make a battleground of her summer
cottage, guests in her home? She was almost on the point of
calling for police protection, and sending off a telegram to
her son Archie to come home at once. It was only the
thought of Chan that restrained her. Chan's behavior had
been beyond reproach. Of course he had brought that girl
there, but the girl seemed to be a sweet, well-behaved little
thing also, and had been most polite about it all, trying to
keep Chan from knowing she had to leave. Mrs. Southerly
had that very morning received a dear little note from her
thanking her for her charming hospitality, and saying that
she would not have left if it had not been imperative that she
go in another direction immediately. She had been afraid to
come for that very reason, and she had only accepted the
gracious hospitality in the first place because her friend, Mr.
Prescott, seemed to think it necessary to stay away from his
engagement at her cottage and see her through what had
been a very trying bit of experience. Rachel had closed by
saying she hoped that sometime she might again meet Mrs.
Southerly, and tell her how much she a stranger had appreciated being invited, and made to feel so much at home.
Mrs. Southerly was charmed with the beautifully expressed
letter, and resolved to look the girl up and invite her again
on some more auspicious occasion.

But it did look odd, all this fuss being stirred up as soon
as Chauncey Prescott returned. Still, putting together the
bits of conversation she had gleaned from her extension wire
during the last few days, there was evidently something rad-
ically wrong with the Shillingsworths, at least with the head
of the house, and she would be glad when they left. If they
did not suggest it in the morning she would have to fall back
on her original plan of a summons to the city, or even Europe if necessary. She could not have a state of things like
this going on. She was a nervous wreck, and the whole summer was being spoiled.

A maid tapped at the door and said that Mr. Prescott was asking for her. Mrs. Southerly went down to meet him in the deserted sun parlor, the Warrens also having fled at Shillingsworth's roar. What a state of things in a respectable house! Then she came face-to-face with Chan, his frank eyes meeting hers clearly, and her annoyance fled.

"I'm so glad you have come back," she said impulsively, and Chan gracefully thanked her and handed her a comfortable chair. Mrs. Southerly was an old schoolmate of Chan's father and there had been always a warm feeling of friendship between the families.

"I want a chance to explain and apologize," said Chan, drawing up a chair confidentially. "I left you in a most abrupt manner last week."

"Oh, my dear boy, I understood perfectly," said Mrs. Southerly warmly. "Of course you couldn't let that little girl go flying around alone in taxis at that time of night. It was dear of you to go. Did you reach her in time? I suppose you did, as you did not return. I've had the most charming letter from her this morning."

Chan's face flamed into eagerness, and she watched the light in his eyes with a half-suppressed sigh. Now if Archie would only find some girl like that, pretty and cultured and sweet, and feel that way about her, instead of flying around with all kinds of girls, like this Gladys Shillingsworth, and insisting on her family being invited. Of course Archie had got disgusted with her and her family in the most inexplicable way. Archie must have known something or he never would have run away to the mountains that way, after having demanded to have the Shillingsworths invited. If Archie were only here, perhaps Chan would tell him all about it, for Chan evidently knew something, and it would do Archie no end of good to find out the truth. She would telegraph Archie this very night to come home at once, and she would keep Chan if she possibly could until he came.

But Chan at that moment began to tell her that he was

sorry but he would have to leave again, very soon, possibly that night. There might come a message!

Chan had got so far when the maid appeared in the doorway and said that Mr. Shillingsworth had sent her to say that he was leaving almost at once. He had been called away—he probably would have to go to Europe after all.

Mrs. Southerly arose nervously.

"I must go and see if I can help Mrs. Shillingsworth," she said anxiously. "Oh, Chan, I wish you would stay till tomorrow at least. I want Archie to see you. I am wiring him to come home. Can't you possibly stay?"

"I'll try to stay tonight at least, Mrs. Southerly. I'll see if I can arrange it, and then we shall have a little more time to talk. Now go. Don't let me detain you. In any case I shall see you again before I leave."

The Shillingsworths left in an hour. All the servants in the house were kept busy helping them. Mrs. Shillingsworth was weeping and Gladys was obviously angry. The Warren young people were pressed into service to hunt up golf clubs and tennis rackets and bathing suits that had been left in various places about the grounds. Mrs. Southerly was most solicitous for Mrs. Shillingsworth's comfort, offering aspirin tablets for the headache she professed to have, and throwing her own silk scarf about her shoulders as she was bidding her good-bye. "You will need it before you get to Chicago," she said, "and don't bother about returning it. It isn't important in the least."

The Shillingsworths were off. They were going in Mrs. Southerly's car to the junction, ten miles away, where the Chicago trains stopped. Mrs. Southerly drew a deep breath of relief as she saw them drive off into the darkness, their trunks strapped on the back of the car. She fervently hoped that that was the last of the Shillingsworths.

Chan was not in evidence until the car had turned the curve in the drive and disappeared out of sight. Then he was suddenly among them as they all stood on the piazza, and no one except Mrs. Southerly seemed to realize that he had not been there all the time. But Chan did not have the same assurance that he had seen the last of the Shillingsworths, even after the chauffeur returned and reported that they had caught the train easily and had five minutes to spare. Chan was mindful of the baleful light in Shillingsworth's eyes as he asked about Trevor, and after the rest of the household had gone upstairs Chan sought out the chauffeur, who was still moving about in the lighted garage, and asked quite casually if Mr. Shillingsworth had time to stop at the inn and see Mr. Trevor as he had been wanting to do, and the chauffeur said with not a little disgust that he had.

"He made a regular scene there, Mr. Prescott," said the chauffeur, "shouting around and as much as saying they had hid him somewhere. I felt ashamed for my car having such folks in it. Why, they're common folks, they are. I don't see what Mrs. Southerly asked 'em for. They ain't her kind. But I guess she don't know it. She's such a lady herself she expects everybody else to be."

Chan went to his room after that and lay in his bed a long time thinking about Rachel, and glowing over Mrs. Southerly's words about her. Somehow when Mrs. Southerly said those nice things about Rachel it made him feel as if she was giving him a priceless gift.

Quite early in the morning Andy telephoned that he had seen two men from New York whom he recognized as belonging to the crew that they had learned were usually employed by Shillingsworth. This was no more than Chan had expected, but he felt sure it was an indication that Shillingsworth was not yet conquered. He told Andy to dispose of the little car in any way he thought fit, either by selling at a low price to someone, or by leaving it with some garage for sale. He also arranged that Andy should give the signal, which had been agreed upon with Chan's friend of the airplane, that they would be ready early that evening to return to New York. Chan preferred travel by night as it left no clue for

Shillingsworth to follow, and gave him that much chance to get in some good work in New York before Shillingsworth realized that he was there.

Chan put in the morning playing golf at the country club with Mrs. Southerly and the two Warren young people. They lunched at the club and took a long drive in the afternoon, Chan making himself so charming that his hostess entirely forgave him for his brief stay, and began to picture what it would be to have this delightful guest for the whole long summer to companion with her son and keep him from doing wild things or falling in love with the wrong girls.

But when they returned they found a message from Andy that all was well and the plane would be ready to start at ten o'clock from a field down near Chicago. For some reason the aviator did not wish to start from the country club where they had landed before.

Chan found he had just time to catch the evening express into Chicago, and bidding his hostess a hurried good-bye, promising to return sometime as soon as possible and perhaps coax Miss Rainsford to come also, he was driven quickly away in the Southerly car. As they turned from the driveway into the road Chan noticed a man move quickly away from the gateway and climb into an old Ford that seemed to have been parked by the side of the road, but when he looked back a few minutes later the Ford had disappeared. He saw it again, however, standing across the square from the little railroad station, as he stood there waiting for the train. The man who had driven it was coming out of a drugstore telephone booth which was built in the alcove beside a big window and therefore quite clearly visible from a distance. It occurred to him that this might be one of the men of whom Andy had warned him, and he might be shadowing him, in which case it would be better to get off a little before he reached Chicago and walk to the aviation field, than to go all the way into the city and run the risk of being seen by someone to whom this sleuth had telephoned, and who would surely be awaiting him at the Chicago station.

He watched the man as he stood in the doorway of the drugstore looking up and down the street as if awaiting someone. Finally the man walked off into the darkness, turned a corner, and was gone. The train came in two minutes more, and Chan forgot all about his supposed enemy as he swung onto the train with a feeling of exhilaration that now at last he was off for home, and in a few hours more would be free to go and see Rachel.

He did not see a man with a soft felt hat drawn down over his face, who approached the station from the way of the freight office just as the train was slowing down, and swung himself onto the platform of the last car, with an eye out furtively to see which car Chan was taking.

Andy was to meet Chan at the aviation field, and Chan decided to get off at the station before the last, which would give him a walk of about a mile. It was nonsense of course, for it was practically impossible that Shillingsworth would have been able to get anybody at that short notice to follow him, but the idea of a walk appealed to him after his long afternoon of riding. Also, it seemed an economic loss, to go all the way into Chicago and then to pay a man to bring him out again.

So Chan got off at the station nearest the aviation field and started off at a brisk pace, after inquiring of the station agent the most direct route.

The moon was up and the night was clear. His spirits rose as he stepped off down the street. It struck him that this was a pleasant place where he was walking, bordered with trees and hedges, and paved with silver moonlight.

It was quiet here, also, and he had time for thought. No noise or dust or clamor. An old taxi ambled past, its back tire wobbling as it went. He could see the outline of a man crouched within, and was glad it was not himself. He seemed to know just how an old taxi like that would smell on a pleasant summer evening like this one.

Presently as he neared the outskirts of the suburb, and the road turned a corner into more open ways with larger grounds about the houses, and occasional unoccupied fields, he met the old taxi rumbling back empty, with a vacant, don't-care look about it, old and worn and indifferent as if every day was just the same to it, even a moonlight night.

He laughed aloud to himself as he swung into the open moonlight and looked at the wide sky. Presently he would be up there sailing again with that feeling of God all about him. God—he was going to learn about God now. He had righted wrong, and now he must follow the King.

He thought about this as he came to another turn of the road, where a group of thorn trees made the way dark. The agent had said this corner was about a mile from the aviation field.

As he stepped into the patch of shadow something inexpressibly dull and heavy hit him on the head, and the silver air was quenched into velvet blackness about him. Chan lay at the roadside alone in the shadow, and out at the aviation field his friend and Andy paced back and forth, watch in hand, and waited for him to come, hour after hour.

CHAPTER XXII

An hour later Andy went to the nearest telephone which was in a country club half a mile away and telephoned Mrs. Southerly. He asked to speak to Chan and upon being told that he had left some hours before he asked if he might speak to the chauffeur.

The chauffeur assured him that Mr. Prescott had left on the eight o'clock train for Chicago. He had taken him down himself. Andy hung up and cast about in dismay. Something said to him in his inner consciousness, "An enemy hath done this!"

Andy went back to the field, hoping Chan had turned up, but no Chan had appeared. By this time Andy was thoroughly alarmed. Leaving the aviator to stay by the plane, and arranging a place where he could telephone in case Chan arrived after he left, Andy went back to Chicago and began an all-night search, which was not half begun when morning dawned. Eventually the big plane lifted its wings and flew away to another place, to await further signals from Andy, and the aviator came back to Chicago and joined in the search. They made the round of the hotels and hospitals in the city and the aviator even visited the morgue. They went to the station house and got the police busy. Andy even took two policemen and went to the private asylum from which he had helped to rescue Rachel so short a time before.

The nurse was thoroughly frightened by the appearance of the officers, and led them through the different rooms without demur. It happened that she was on duty again and that the doctor was out.

But Chan was not there. Of course Andy was careful not to give her any reason to suspect that this affair was in any

239

way connected with the young girl who had been so mysteriously spirited away. And Andy was in full chauffeur's uniform now, standing upright like a man. There was no reason why she should have connected the two affairs, save that she had been nervous and frightened ever since Shillingsworth had called her up blaming her bitterly and saying he would hold her personally responsible.

But Chan was not in the asylum.

Toward evening, having been in frequent communication with Mrs. Southerly's house, and all other places that he thought Chan had visited, Andy in a panic called up Mr. Prescott in New York to confide his fears to Chan's father. But Chan's father was not at home, and the message Andy left did not get to him until late the next day. Sometime about midnight Andy called up Jim, but Jim too had gone out, and there seemed no help anywhere. Almost he came to the point of calling up Rachel, only he felt sure that Chan would hate that. No, not yet. He could not call her. What would she know about it anyway?

A wild idea crossed his mind of calling up Shillingsworth. But Shillingsworth would never tell if he did know where Chan was, and it would only give him information if he did not. Andy was at the end of his wits. Toward morning he lay down to rest for a little while, trying to think what else he could do, and what could possibly have become of Chan, and then arose to begin all over again his round of telephoning to all of the places where Chan might have been.

He was in despair, for in his heart was beginning to grow a deadly fear that Chan was no longer living, or else was carried away and hidden in some safe place where they would never be able to find him! Andy shut his teeth and resolved that never would he give up until he had found him, not if it took the best years of his life. Andy felt that somehow this thing was his fault. He should not have left Chan; knowing the danger he should have stuck by him. Having seen that detective from New York get off the train in Chicago, he should have gone at once to Chan and stayed there! No matter what Chan's orders were he should have insisted on sticking by. Chan never did think of himself anyway. That was just the way he was in France, always thinking of others, but no care about himself.

Late in the afternoon there came a telegram from Chan's father:

> Am starting at once, train number 247. Meet me in Chicago station. Wire train if necessary. Consult my man Fergus in office of Dearborn Company. Spare no expense. Do all you think necessary. Don't worry! Chan will come out all right! He always does, but I'm coming.
>
> B. C. Prescott

Andy spent hours trying to locate the man Fergus who was out on a trail after Shillingsworth that evening. He finally found him and took comfort in the fact that there was someone else on the job. The aviator, too, had come back to town and was working along a line of his own. He had a theory that Chan was perhaps in hiding for a purpose, trying to catch the enemy red-handed.

And so the hours turned into anxious days and still Chan did not turn up.

Those were the days in which Rachel was praying, and Jim was anxious and finally took a flying trip up to New York only to find Prescott senior gone to Chicago. So Jim hurried back again to Beechwood to hold the fort as he had been told to do, and the days continued to go by, without any word from Chan.

Chan had lain by the roadside a long time before a couple of laborers, going home from a holiday in town to their little plain cottages out beyond the country club, stumbled across his feet and almost fell.

They turned their flashlight full into his face and thought that he was dead, so still he lay. So one stood guard and the other went to the nearest house to telephone for the police, and by-and-by the ambulance came with some officers and picked up Chan.

"I guess he's croaked all right," said one of them regretfully. "Looks like a fine chap. Wonder who done that? It's time we got to work. Better get him to the hospital first. And, buddy, you call up the office and give the word. This here has been a holdup."

They took Chan to a hospital about two miles from where they found him and hurried away to get on the track of his assailant, waiting only to discover that he had been robbed of everything that his pockets contained. There was not so much as a penny in his pockets, or a cuff link or watch or scrap of paper wherewith to identify him. Then they were off hotfoot to get track of the robber. They could see by his garments that he was not poverty-stricken but there was nothing to do but put him into the ward, and for a long time they worked over him before they could bring any sign of life.

For several days Chan lay in a kind of coma, and the nurses whispered among themselves that he might never rally to tell what had happened to him. But by-and-by he began to moan, and to turn his head from side to side slightly, and once in the night as the nurse leaned over him, he opened his eyes and looking into hers said quite steadily, "You know I must get up now and follow the King."

"He's as crazy as a bedbug!" she declared when she came out in the hall a half hour later. "If he does get well I don't believe he'll be right in his mind. He's not a foreigner, you can see that by looking at him. What would he mean by following a King?"

Chan lay for several days more half in stupor, but gradually began to show signs of getting better. One morning while the nurses were busy with the breakfast trays and no one paying any attention to him, he opened his eyes and looked about him.

There was a screen half around his bed, and only one man lay on the other side of him, with the window beyond.

Chan blinked at him, and up at the ceiling and back again to the other patient. The man smiled.

"Been a long journey, buddy," he said pleasantly. "Glad to see you back."

"Thanks!" said Chan bewildered. "Guess, you're right, but where is this, Cap? We aren't in France again? The war's over!"

"Yes, the war is over. This is a hospital. Pretty nice place to be when you're not up to scratch."

"Yes," said Chan, "but how'd I get here? Where—? Oh, say! I've got an engagement. I've got to beat it quick. How long've I been here? It's morning isn't it? I wonder what they did with my clothes? Say, Cap, do you know how to get hold of a nurse?"

"Sure," said the man, "ring your bell. But don't get excited. They won't let you up yet. You've had a bad case. Just lie still and take it easy. It'll all come out right in the end."

"But I've got to go!" said Chan, trying to raise his head from the pillow. "Someone is waiting for me! Good night! How long have I been here, do you know?"

A nurse appeared in the offing looking curiously, apathetically at the eager patient. She disliked to be interrupted when she was fixing the trays.

"Oh, I say, sister," welcomed Chan with one of his ingratiating smiles. "Get me my trousers if you please, and anything else you have handy. I've got to get out of here right away. I've kept some people waiting all night. Why don't you hurry?"

"Why you can't get up," said the nurse in the tone one uses to a naughty, unreasonable child. "You've been dangerously sick. The doctors didn't even know if you'd live. You've got to lie quite still. If you keep quiet now I'll bring you some breakfast. Perhaps they'll let you have something good this morning seeing you're so much better."

"But I can't, I tell you," insisted Chan, trying to lift his heavy head again. "What's this on my head? Take it off. I

can't go out in the street with this! How did I get here anyway? What happened? I can't seem to remember."

"Nobody knows what happened. They brought you here
about a week ago. That's all I know about it."

"A week ago? Good night! Say, that's tough luck. What
on earth——? Say, did they send my dad word? Has Andy
been here?"

"Nobody's been here. They didn't know your name. How
could they send your father word?"

"Didn't know my name? Why, I'm Chauncey Prescott of
New York. Couldn't they find out that from my pass in my
pocket? Didn't they find a lot of express checks and cards
and letters in my wallet? My name and address are engraved
on the back of my watch. How stupid of them!"

"Why, they said there wasn't a scrap of anything in any of
your pockets. You'd been robbed."

"Robbed?" said Chan wide-eyed. "Wasn't there even that
thousand-dollar check?"

"Oh, don't mind about it," said the nurse soothingly. "Be
thankful you've pulled through. A thousand dollars is a lot,
I know, but your life is worth more."

"All that work gone for nothing!" moaned Chan. "Well, I
suppose it'll have to be done over again. Get me my clothes,
please, quick! There's more to be done than I thought!"

"I can't do a thing like that without the doctor's orders!"
said the nurse crossly. "Here comes your tray. You'll have to
wait for anything else till the doctor comes!"

But Chan was not to be deterred from his purpose. He
demanded the head nurse, and presently was granted the
privilege of dictating a couple of telegrams, one to Andy at
the old rendezvous and one to his father. After that he reluctantly consented to be fed a few spoonfuls of broth, and
much to his own surprise fell asleep while planning how to
get that check back, for he had no doubt that this was Shillingsworth's work.

The doctor came presently and soothed his impatience:
"Why, man alive! You can't get up!" he said to Chan

firmly. "You've just been over the top and you've got to re-
cuperate awhile before you're even fit to talk to anybody.
We'll send any messages you want, but you can't stir from
this bed till you're able. Don't matter what you say. We'll
have to strap you down if you haven't sense enough to lie
there. The quickest way to get out of here is to mind what
you're told. Haven't you got sense enough to see that?"

Chan studied his face awhile and then broke into one of
his sunny smiles:

"All right, Doc. I'm with you, only make it snappy. I'll
obey orders but you've got to get me well quick."

All that morning he lay restlessly, sighing now and then.

The nurse came to fix the bedclothes straight, and spoke
in a low tone:

"You're not half as bad off as that man next to you. He's
had a major operation, and they don't know yet if it's going
to be successful. He's got a wife and four little children, and
nobody to earn for them but himself, and he's had it hard,
but he's just as cheerful and patient. Watch him and you'll
see. He's a poor country preacher and he has to lie there and
think how his sick wife has to go out working, and leave her
little children, and how they may all have to go to a home or
something. Do you think that's very easy?"

"Gosh!" said Chan. "We mustn't let that go on! I'll see
what I can do as soon as I get up from here!"

After she was gone Chan turned his head toward his
neighbor with a worried look in his eyes. It couldn't be that
all that was true and yet that man could lie there so placidly.

The man smiled:

"I've been awfully interested in what you said a few days
ago, brother, when you were out of your head. I wondered
if by any possibility you might be a sort of relation of
mine?"

"What did I say?" asked Chan, alarmed at once lest he
had revealed some secret about Shillingsworth.

"You said, 'I must follow the King.' I wonder if by any
chance your King is my King?"

"Who is your King?" asked Chan in wonder.

"The Lord Jesus Christ," answered the man simply. "Was that whom you meant?"

"I suppose it must be," said Chan thoughtfully. "Can you show me how to follow Him? Because that's what I've got to do next."

"I sure can," said the man. "I've been in His service now for twenty years, and there is nothing like it in the world!"

The man's eyes were sparkling and his face kindled till it seemed to Chan that it grew suddenly beautiful above the lines of care and suffering.

"So it's like that!" mused Chan. "Well, how do you begin?"

If a man who had all that in his life that the nurse told about could look so heavenly happy when he spoke about his service it must be worthwhile.

"You have to be one of the born-again ones, you know," said the man with a light in his eyes. "How much do you know about the Lord Jesus Christ?"

"Practically nothing," said Chan. "Oh, I studied a Bible course in college for a few months, but it didn't make much impression on me. What was that you said I had to be?"

"One of the born-again ones," repeated the teacher.

"What's that? How can a man be born again?"

"A man long ago asked that same question of Jesus. Do you remember?"

"No. How did He answer?"

"Told him it was a spiritual birth, and made him understand that a man had to die to his fleshly life before that could happen."

"You mean if I want to follow the King I must give up wanting everything in life that I like?"

"Not at all. I mean that you must give up yourself, your life, stop living it as yourself and let Him live in you. See? Why, when you went to France to fight you didn't stop loving your home, nor liking the pleasures you had left behind, but you simply gave it all up for the cause. You went away and left it. You practically died to your old life, and went away knowing that you might never come back. It wasn't any case of giving up individual things. You didn't pick up your old baseball bat, or your tennis racket and say, 'Now, am I willing to give this up for my country.' You simply laid it all aside, as if you were dead to it. And many a dear fellow really did die—never came back. You see my point. A soldier gives up himself to be a soldier, to be a representative of the government. You have to love a country a whole lot to do that. You have to love a King a whole lot to follow Him that way, and that's the only way it pays to follow my King. Better not attempt it if you're not ready to go the whole length, die to self. That's it. You couldn't possibly expect to be with Him and be one of His honored ones unless you were *all* His. He died for us, and we've got to die with Him if we expect to be born again into the spiritual kingdom, which is the only way to be a real follower of this King. You know, He's coming again, and it *might* happen to be soon. We don't know the exact time, but things begin to look as if the world was shaping up for His coming."

"Coming again?" asked Chan puzzled. "Coming where?"

"Coming here. To earth."

Chan looked at the man keenly as if he suspected he were not quite right.

"Where do you get all that?" Chan's tone had changed.

"In the Bible. A great many of the happenings that have been foretold to come before His appearance have already been fulfilled. Look at the Jews. Look at the map of Europe how it is shaping up. He might come almost any time now. We are not told just when, but we were told the signs, and the signs are appearing rapidly."

"You don't mean to tell me that anybody really takes the Bible seriously, today!" exclaimed Chan. "Of course it's a great book, wonderful literature, and all that. I studied all about that in college. I'm not exactly ignorant. But I never heard anybody take it for serious fact."

"You'll have to take it for serious fact if you want to follow the Lord Jesus Christ. He took it for that. He quoted it as fact over and over again, and some of the very prophecies I have been speaking of were His own words, or His own repeating of Old Testament words. But all you have to do is read it under the right conditions, and you will see for yourself. It proves itself, and it is proving itself day by day now in a most marvelous way. You can read its fulfilling almost every day in some item in the newspapers. Things are shaping up, the map of the world is taking form just as the Bible describes. Only the world doesn't understand because they won't believe. Belief is an act of the will, you know. It is something you will to do. It is a spiritual thing. Afterward, you have faith because you have seen, but faith is a gift from God, an opening of one's eyes to see that what one has willed to accept is as clear and true as crystal."

"Well, but everybody doesn't see it the same way. They didn't talk like that in college. They explained it all as sort of poetic fancies to teach great truths and morals. How do you know when you have got hold of the right teacher, or how do you know but one man's idea of it is as good as another?"

"It isn't a matter of explanation, my friend, nor interpretation, nor any man's idea of it. It is a matter of accepting the plain words of the Bible and taking them at their face value. There is no teacher but the Teacher sent from God, the Holy Spirit, and it was promised that when we were ready to die to the fleshly life, to sin and to self, that then we should be born again, and be raised up with Christ; and the Holy Spirit would then interpret to us the meaning of God's Word. Year by year the Holy Spirit has been unfolding the meaning of one mystery after another in the Bible until now we are beginning to see great hidden meanings that were meant to be hidden until this time. I said you could not understand the Bible unless you are willing to believe it, and that is the great key to unlock the whole book but there are other keys which unlock precious meanings and make plain obscure passages, and now in this age of the world we can use the scholarship that has been developed, not in a critical sense, but with a believing mind bent on knowing what the Lord would have us to understand, and we are able to see how the whole sixty-six books of which the Bible is made up are one perfect volume, completely fitting together, with not an inharmonious jot or tittle in the whole book. I do not mean that we have learned to know the hidden meanings of every passage fully, because I do not suppose that we shall ever get to the end of it in this life. But there are things like this that help us to understand, like keys to open doors. For instance, there are three classes of people with which the Bible deals, the Jews, the Gentiles, and the Church. It makes a good deal of difference in understanding a passage if we thoroughly understand to whom it was written. Wouldn't that make a difference with any writing, if you knew what class of people it was addressed to?"

"I suppose it would," said Chan thoughtfully. He had never heard talk like this.

"Then there are symbols and types and imagery. Certain things always stand for one idea all the way through the Bible. Find where it is first mentioned and you can trace it through to the end, it always stands for the same thing. For instance, leaven always stands for sin. The fig tree is a symbol of the Jews. There are hundreds of other symbols and types. And then God uses numbers with a special significance. There is a whole study of just numbers that is very interesting and deep. But the most marvelous thing of all is the way the Bible, hundreds and thousands of years ago, worked out and made clear in mystical language, but perfectly clear in the light of the fulfillment, times and events of all the great historical and religious happenings of the world. But I am tiring you. You had better rest. Another time we may talk more."

"You are amazing me, not tiring me. I never heard a man talk this way before, not even a minister. Excuse me, I think the nurse said you were one of those, but you are different from any I ever met before."

"There are many others who believe as I do," smiled the other man.

"And you can smile when you are lying there suffering," mused Chan. "How do you account for the fact that your King allows you to suffer when you are so faithful to Him?"

"I don't account for it," smiled the minister, "I know that He knows why He put me here, and that is enough. Sometime I'm going to understand, when I see Him face-to-face, but for the present I can trust my life to Him. It isn't my life anymore, you know. I died. There might be a hundred reasons why He needed someone to lie in this bed and suffer for awhile. He might even have sent me here to tell you this that you did not know!"

A sudden startled look of awe came into Chan's face.

"You think—He—knows?" he asked hesitatingly.

"Of course. He knew you would be inquiring for the King, and He wants you in His service. You have heard the call. I can tell the signs. You will follow, and you will find out for yourself. I have seen it happen before. You will be one of the born-again ones. You are going to surrender to Him and let Him show the world what Jesus Christ can do in a human soul. I may not be left down here much longer. He may be calling me away. But perhaps He is going to let you be a witness in my place. That's what we are, witnesses, for the truth, for what He has done in us."

Chan was still a long time. He even shut his eyes, and the man beside him thought he was asleep, but again he opened them and asked:

"Did you—find all this out for yourself, or did you learn it somewhere?"

"You mean did I go to school to learn it? Yes, I did, although I found out a great deal before that by letting the Holy Spirit lead me into the truth, just by asking Him to teach me every time I opened the Bible. But afterward I heard of the Moody Bible Institute in Chicago, and I went there and studied. It helped me to know quickly what I might have been years in studying out by myself. It is a wonderful school. And there are others now all over the country. They are springing up everywhere, because men who have surrendered themselves to the King have found out these things and given the key of them to others, and we want to tell it to the world. There is a big school over in New York, called the National Bible Institute and others in Philadelphia and Washington, and in almost every city there are at least a group of people now who are studying the Bible in this way. I am not alone in my belief. God has many wiser greater men than I am who know all this, and you can find it out for yourself if you will give yourself to it. It is strange, but the insight only comes to those who are willing to give themselves to it. And after all, my friend, this life is only a college to prepare for the next. And now, my friend, I'm sure you ought to go to sleep and I am going to talk to the King about you while you are resting."

The nurse came round then, taking temperatures, and Chan lay still with his eyes shut and thought about all he had heard. It was marvelous. It was as if he had been transferred to another universe. He had been thinking so long about Rachel, and how to protect her, about Trevor and Shillingsworth and how to punish them and put them where they could do no more harm, and now to be suddenly brought to see a world where different motives and ideas ruled, was almost upsetting. If that was all true, what he had just been hearing, it made everything different. Did Rachel believe all this? Was that what made her so different? Was that why she had seemed as if she belonged to another world? Well, if she did he would die to the world he had always known and find out how to be born into the world where she was. No, perhaps that wasn't a right motive either. Perhaps he had to even die to Rachel if he followed the King in earnest. Well, was he willing?

And so pondering he fell asleep.

CHAPTER XXIII

For three long days Chan held sweet converse with this new friend. He learned that his name was Montgomery, and that his wife was named Rose.

Rose came one day and brought a few late pansies from the parsonage yard, but she had to hurry away soon because there were only two trains a day to the little town where they lived, one each way, and she must be at home at night to stay with the children. Chan studied her sweet, tired face, and wished he had some money to slip into her little handbag as it lay on the table between their two beds. It was a humbling feeling for Chan, this having no money, nothing; this being attired in an unbleached muslin hospital shirt and having to ask for everything he got, and pay only with a smile. Chan was learning a great deal. He was learning that Chan Prescott was not such a great being after all as he had always, though unconsciously perhaps, felt himself to be.

And he was learning great things about the new kingdom to which he was more than half committed.

It was the second day after he had come to himself that Andy arrived. Andy had been off on a tangent following up some new clue and had not received the message right away. Andy looked worn and tired and old. Chan studied his face in the first glow of their meeting, and found that he loved Andy! Good old Andy! How good it was to see him! Why, he felt as if he had been away from Andy for something like three years!

Andy had much to tell and was too full of joy to tell it. He choked and broke down a dozen times when he began to tell Chan how he had hunted for him that night and all the things he had done, and Chan lay there holding his hand as if he had been a girl, and saying over and over again:

"Good old Andy! You've been great to me!"

And when they finally got to talking there was so much to tell.

"Yoh're dad went back to New York day befoah yesterday," said Andy, rousing to the necessity at last. "I reckon he's on his way back about now. I tried to get him on the phone befoah I came, but they said he was out of town. And Jim. Old Jim'll be glad! I wiahed him. I couldn't take the time to phone before I came heah. Jim, he's ben keepin' the wiahs hot since a week ago Wednesday. He wanted to come on, but he'd promised you he wouldn't leave Beechwood, an' the guryl. Yes, Miss Rainsfoahd's awright. He said they ain't had any sorta trouble. I don' reckon Trevor told the old man wheah she lived, or else he's got an idea she's still out west. Yoh see, meetin' yoh back west again has kinda throwed him off the track. By the way, yoh know the old skunk left the lady's house that night?"

"I sure did, Andy. I gave him an hour to leave!"

"Yoh did, son? Good wuk! I found out he left, from the station agent at the junction. There arn't many officials of any rank I haven't made the acquaintance of these last few days, not around these diggins."

"But, Andy, whoever cleaned me out got the check, and we've lost our evidence now when Trevor's case comes up."

"Don't you worry, Chan, we got evidence enough. Didn't you show that check to me? Didn't you show it to the flyin' friend the othah night when he come to make arrangements? We all is witnesses! We shan't miss a little thing like that thousand-dollah check. Just you rest easy and get well, Chan, an' we'll wipe the earth up with those two birds yet!"

Chan was silent a long time after Andy had left. Somehow a new idea had crept into his head. After a few minutes he looked over toward his new friend who was reading his Bible with a lovely expression on his strong, fine face.

"Say, Montgomery," he had come to speak to him familiarly now, "whaddya do about hates?"

"What?"

"What do you do about hates? You are supposed to give up everything, even if it's all you like, when you go into that service. What do you do about hates? What about somebody that's done you a wrong, or done somebody else you love a wrong?"

"Well," said the minister smiling, "He said 'Vengeance is mine, I will repay, saith the Lord. Therefore if thine enemy hunger feed him; if he thirst give him drink.' "

"That's pretty steep, Montgomery."

"Yes? Well, full surrender always is steep. It means dying to the sinful life of course, to every thought and word and deed and desire that is not in accordance with His will."

"But say, Montgomery, there's a couple of fellows— there's one fellow I really oughtta lick before I begin. He's a skunk! He really oughtta be licked! That is, I've gotta be sure he is licked! I licked the other one. Really walloped him, you know, and stuck him in jail."

Montgomery laughed this time aloud.

"Well, buddy, how do you know that's your job?"

"Well, I thought it was," said Chan seriously. "I really think I ought to get this other bird safe, too. I think it's my duty."

"Well, perhaps it is, but if it is the Lord will make you good and sure. Meantime, why don't you wait a little and trust him to the Lord. I wouldn't worry about it right now. You can't tell what your King intends to do."

"I'd rather like the honor of doing it," confessed Chan.

Montgomery laughed again.

"There it is, Chan, the old self cropping out. I've found it in myself a hundred times a day. But just you trust yourself to Him, and He'll make you good and sure when He wants you to go out and lick a man."

That day Chan began the study of the Bible.

The doctor said Chan might read a little while and Montgomery handed over his worn little Bible from under his pillow. Chan handled it with awe and read with new eyes where his new friend directed, and found it as exciting as any novel he had ever sat up all night to read. He had never read the Bible much, always under compulsion for a class, but it had never entered his head before to read it as if it were all true. And now he found an interest that he had never dreamed could be. It was like stepping into a new world.

He was propped up with pillows the third day, reading thus when three visitors stepped into the ward and asked for Chan.

His father saw the book in his son's hand and a gray shadow of fear came over his face. Was Chan as bad as that that he had taken to reading the Bible? Had the doctors deceived him then when they wired he was on the mend?

But Chan was so engrossed he did not see them coming till they were standing close around his bed.

Chan looked up and a smile like sunshine rippled over his face:

"Hullo, Dad, old man! You've come at last!" he greeted his father hilariously dispelling all his fears at a dash. His father stooped and had him in his arms, the first time since he was a little boy just going to school, and there were tears on Chan's cheek when his father stood back trying to keep from looking sheepish.

Jim stood just behind the senior Prescott, his face a broad smile. It wasn't the first time he had seen a boy with a Bible. Over in France they all took a turn at a pocket Testament now and then when they were going over the top and times were strenuous. It was something like an amulet worn to keep one safe. And anyway there likely wasn't much literature in a hospital ward, and Chan was always one to take up with what there was about and make no trouble. Jim wasn't at all troubled about the Bible. Chan looked like his handsome old self and that was enough. Besides, wasn't he standing high and wide as he could to hide the third member of the party for a minute till some of the excitement was over and Chan could give his attention to her?

Then Jim stepped aside and Rachel came shyly up to the bed.

But when Chan saw her he dropped the book, put out both hands, and drew her down to him, enfolding her and bringing her face to his, her lips on his. He kissed her, right before them all, without even asking her permission. It was enough that she had come. All his questions were answered. She was his!

Yes, and she kissed him back, and let him hold her there in his arms, her warm face close to his, her lips on his for a full minute.

"You came!" he breathed in her ear. "You came to me!"

Rachel's cheeks were rosy when he finally released her to stand beside him, her hands held close in both of his.

"Isn't she great, Dad?" Chan's eyes were shiningly challenging his father.

"She is!" responded the father vigorously. "She certainly is. I've never seen her like. It's the best thing you ever did, Chan! It makes up for all your other scrapes."

Chan's face was radiant.

"But I don't see how you knew anything about her," he said, a puzzled look growing between his eyes. "I don't see how you found her."

"I'm not so dumb as I look, son," said Prescott senior. "You don't realize how much you said between the lines in that short talk we had about old Shillingsworth. Then naturally when we got worked up about you we tried everything we knew. And Jim, here, helped us out. He had the little girl in safekeeping and led us to her. But the fact was she was about to come to me, the day I went down to see her to find out what she knew about your movements."

Chan's eyes sought Rachel's and the color flamed sweetly into her face, but her eyes met his gladly, joyously with whole surrender.

"You went after me, Ray?"

"Of course," spoke up Rachel with a ring in her voice. "Did you suppose I would let you stay lost and not do any-

thing? You've almost given your life for me, I guess, Chan!"
She laid her free hand gently on a lock of his dark hair that
stuck out from the white bandage which he was still wearing.

"Nothing doing!" said Chan. "I'm fine as a fiddle. I was
only lying here till you came to bring me some money. That
poor stew that hit me in the dark took all my change, and I
didn't have a cent to tip the nurses. I couldn't leave that way,
could I?"

It seemed there was a joyous foolishness upon them. They
could not talk sensibly, till Chan suddenly remembered and
turned to his father.

"I walloped him, Dad. I walloped him good! The thin
one, Trevor, I told you about, and he's in jail all rightie, but
I guess you've got to help me out with his trial. I seem to
have been unfortunate about the evidence. That blooming
bandit stole the check and contract I got from him. Reckon I
may have to do it all over again."

"Not much you will, son. I've seen to that. Trevor's safe
for a long time. He's wanted for a long term in New York
State, for a grave offense, and it just happened I was able
to tip them off as to his present whereabouts. Andy kept
me posted, of course. You'll have no further trouble with
Trevor."

Chan made a wry face:

"Yes, but it's Shillingsworth I'm most worried about. He
thinks I've got that check and contract. I ordered him out of
the country and gave him a week to go if he didn't want me
to make the whole thing public. And now I've no evidence
to back me up. I wonder if he's gone? I must get up and attend to him. He still thinks I have the check, unless it was his
man who bagged me. I can't afford to let him get funny
again. He's got to be punished for what he did to Ray, even
if I can't get him on the other lines."

Nobody had seen Andy come softly in and stand with the
group, keeping in the background, his big eyes full of con-
tent. But now he took a step forward and spoke:

"Yoh all don't need to worry about that ole raccoon any longah, Chan, he's done fine foh hisself. He's put hisself out of the runnin' once foh all, an' saved us fuhthuh trouble. I just came in to give you the news. He done stepped into an elevator shaft whah the doah had been left open by mistake, an' he went down foh stories an' broke both laigs an' an arm or two, an' did somethin' to his poah back that he'll be 'bliged to lay on it the rest of his days. It's all in this papah." And Andy laid an evening paper down on Chan's bed.

Chan's face was a study. Not triumph, not joy, not exultation, but a kind of awe and wonder. He picked up the paper and read the headlines, "SHILLINGSWORTH, MILLIONAIRE, walks into elevator shaft and is shattered for life."

Rachel read it with terrified eyes, and drew a sobbing breath, but Chan leaned forward and looked suddenly toward his neighbor in the next bed:

"Montgomery!" he shouted in a tone that could be heard all over the room. "God's done it! I don't have to do it! It's just as you said!"

The man in the next bed answered with a look of solemn trust:

"I knew He would, Chan, if you let Him take care of it."

"But, Montgomery," said Chan, the solemnity still in his face, "vengeance is a terrible thing. I'm glad I didn't have to do it. I wanted to, but now I'm glad I didn't."

"Exactly," said Montgomery. "God knows how, better than we do. He maybe has some work yet for you to do for Shillingsworth. Who knows but you have to witness yet before him for a higher Court?"

Chan looked in awe at his friend for a moment, and then, his face grown radiant again, he turned to them all:

"Rachel, Dad, all of you, meet the grandest minister God ever made. It was all right my being knocked cold the other night. I had to come here to meet this man. He's made me over. I'm not the same man I was." He said it slowly and earnestly. "I died that night out there on the road, and this is a new Chan. I've been born again! And I've got a new work to do in the world! I don't know what you'll think about it, Dad, but I guess Ray here will like it. Anyhow, I've got to do it. And I'm going to build a church over near New York and put this man in it to preach, and show the way to other lost men like I was."

"Go to it, Chan. I always knew you'd amount to something someday. If there's anything you can do with money I'm with you."

"Yes, we want money," said Chan eagerly. "But we want you, too. We need witnesses, don't we, Mont? Dad here would make a great one, and so would Andy and Jim. You've all got to get in line and help out. The world doesn't know about these things, and we've got to pass the word along. But, say, where's that nurse? I want my clothes! I've got to go out and get this girl a ring. I can't have her running around without one. I'm not taking any chances with her anymore."

"Oh, that's all right, Chan, we can telephone and have a case of stones sent over here for you to choose from. You're not to get up till the doctor says it's safe. We're not taking any chances with you, either."

"I don't need a ring," said Rachel softly, her cheeks very pink, "I've got you!"

"Do you mean that, Ray? Are you ready to take me over? No kidding? You're sure we belong?"

"I am!" said Rachel softly.

"How soon?" asked Chan sitting up very straight against his pillow.

"Whenever you say, Chan." Her voice was only loud enough for him to hear.

"All right!" rang out Chan's voice. "Why not make it right now? Here's the minister, and here are the witnesses. We can order ice cream for the whole ward."

"Better wait till the ring comes, Chan, and give the nurse time to doll you up a bit. Perhaps you better consult the doctor, too."

"Oh, well," said Chan, "I don't mind waiting a few minutes if Ray will stay right here."

"How about giving the child a chance to doll up a bit as well, if you're going to have a public wedding," laughed the father.

It was finally settled that the wedding should take place that afternoon, if the doctor thought Chan was equal to the excitement.

"Although," said Chan, "that's all poppycock. What could be more exciting than to have to wait, when everything is here ready?"

Rachel sat with him after the others had gone, and they talked in low tones, with shining eyes, and clasped hands. The other patients in the room cast furtive, pleased glances toward them now and then, and some were thoughtful enough to turn their heads away and pretend to be asleep, but Chan and Rachel were oblivious of all about them.

"Are you sure, now, little Ray?" Chan asked hungrily, holding her hand with a yearning pressure.

"Sure," said Rachel with a true ring to her voice. "I love you, Chan. I don't see how I could ever live without you again. I knew I loved you before I came here, but I wasn't all sure you ought to marry me because I didn't belong to your kind of life. But now, you have learned to love the things that I am pledged to, and I'm *sure* we belong. We shall not be unequally yoked if we follow the same King."

They talked a long time about Chan's new experiences, and then she told him about the desk and her finding of the story and the check, and they had a beautiful time, till suddenly the doctor stood beside them watching them intently:

"Ah ha! And so that's how the land lies, is it?" he said eyeing their clasped hands. "How is my patient feeling this morning?"

"Doc, will you come to my wedding this afternoon?" asked Chan, rallying to the occasion like his old self. "I'm giving a party to the whole ward."

So it was all arranged.

Prescott senior ordered flowers, and a wedding supper for every patient in the hospital who was able to eat it. The ward was a perfect bower of roses and palms and ferns. Some of the patients declared they were getting well from the sight of it.

The case of rings came up from the jewelers, and Rachel wore her sparkling diamond, while Chan hid the little platinum circlet of a wedding ring, which his father went out and bought for him, in the breast of his coat till the time should come to place it with the other on her finger.

Rose Montgomery, coming in at two o'clock to visit her husband, was pressed into service as matron of honor. At half past two the simple little service was performed, the minister being allowed to sit up against pillows a little way while he spoke the solemn words of the simple ceremony.

The bride wore a simple white dress she had found in the suitcase which Andy had brought from Mrs. Southerly's house. It might have been originally intended for a sports costume, but its simplicity of line, and its soft lustrous silken material made it utterly fitting for the occasion. She carried a marvelous bouquet of valley lilies and rosebuds which Prescott senior had been careful to order.

Out in the hall one of the best string quartets in the city of Chicago played the wedding march softly, and so carried a hint of the ceremony to all the other wards that could not be present. Andy and Jim were proud ushers and stood up with the wedding party. Chan's father gave away the bride, though he declared it was all wrong, for he was receiving her instead of giving her away.

Chan was allowed to take off his bandage for the ceremony and sat up straight and handsome against the pillow.

It was Chan's father who handed the envelope containing the wedding fee to the minister's wife, a check for five thousand dollars. And when the overwhelmed couple tried to protest and refuse to take it, Chan waved a joyous hand and said:

"Oh, that's all right. That's just a beginning. I'm going to build that church for you, you know, and this is a retaining fee. See?"

When the wedding supper was eaten by all who were well enough to partake, the guests had departed, the bride sent away to take a nap, and Chan laid flat for a good sleep, he turned toward the minister's bed and said in a low tone that would just reach across to his friend's ears:

"You were right, Monty. He's a great King! To think He let me have *all that! Me!* But Gosh! I'm glad I got bagged that night! What would it have been if I hadn't met you and found out the way?"

Two days later Chan was dismissed and allowed to go home.

They helped him into the backseat of his own big car, with Rachel in her little green hat and dress that he had bought her, sitting beside him, and there at her feet lay her own little worn suitcase!

"Oh, how did you get it?" she cried with joy. "I felt so badly about Mother's Bible being lost, and my photographs of Mother and Father I thought they were gone forever!"

"Sent a kid after it that night," said Chan smilingly. "Andy received it yesterday, but I guess we better drive around that way and thank him a little more substantially. How about that, Jim? Can you work it that way?"

"Sure thing," said Jim grinning happily.

Dad and Andy were following in the other car; and now they started off together, Chan and Rachel going home, on their wedding journey.

"I thought we'd be doing this someday," said Chan leaning back happily, "but I didn't think it would come so soon. There's nothing like trouble to make joy taste great! Ray, do you love me now?"

Said Rachel:

"I do."